THE
VILLAGE

STORIES
1637–2097

Karl H. Schumacher

DORRANCE
PUBLISHING CO
EST. 1920
PITTSBURGH, PENNSYLVANIA 15238

Dorrance Publishing Co
585 Alpha Drive
Suite 103
Pittsburgh, PA 15238
Visit our website at *www.dorrancebookstore.com*

ISBN: 978-1-6470-2291-4
eISBN: 978-1-6470-2857-2

AUTHOR'S NOTE

The Village is a set of historical stories that reflect a slice of life in a place that, in fact, exists. Everything is fiction, but not maybe, totally. The stories do borrow richly on lore and places but do not reveal individuals or facts as they were. I took three real clippings from the Barnstable Patriot of old and manufactured tales for the purpose of story-telling.

The narratives do capture much of what the Village was, and remains, in spirit. The book is short on continuous eras. I researched them but did not know the periods well enough for confident writing. You should think of them all as historical fiction. There are many more stories that could have been told. The stories are of good people of passion living in their humanity and inanity in a small little paradise.

It is an adult book. There is teenage and adult passion. One story tells of old-age romance; another tells of two star-crossed teenage lovers with compassionate, sensual longing. Many are of people coming of age—any age, including a final walk to destiny.

They are true to the heart. More importantly, they bookend the Village history in dramatic fashion. Who knows? I was young and lived all the content in imagination and sometimes fact and survived. It made my life exciting and vital. It was great fun.

The stories were written for the denizens of my Village and the Beach where people often returned for decades. I have for six decades. It is the real Cape Cod of yore. Things were different and fun then, exactly like today. I know a little. These "people" were in my heart. The stories are for everyone who might imagine a summertime enclave of great natural beauty, spiritual intent and characters where a mystical vibe survives.

Karl H. Schumacher

DEDICATION

To Karl and Doris.
You discovered the Village for many
outsiders and brought amazing people to
it with your vision. Now, they advance its
legacy with impact. You live.

FROM THE HOPI ELDERS

To my fellow swimmers:

Here is a river now flowing very fast.

It is so great and swift that there are those who will be afraid,

Who will try to hold on to the shore. They are being torn apart and will suffer greatly.

Know that the river has a destination.

The Elders say we must let go of the shore.

Push off into the middle of the river and keep our heads above water.

And I say see who is there with you and celebrate.

At this time in history, we are to take nothing personally, least of all ourselves, for the moment we do our spiritual growth and journey come to a halt.

The time of the lone wolf is over.

Gather yourselves. Banish the word struggle from your attitude and vocabulary.

All that we do now must be done in a sacred manner and in celebration. For we are ones we have been waiting for.

CONTENTS

1637 – THE BONES

In the early 1930s, the town newspaper carried a four-inch square article stating workers digging a foundation for an estate home in the nearby summer Village uncovered the bones of what were presumed to be a male Indian. The remains were transferred to a nearby grave.

*   *   *

Caleb Farker was a walker. There were a few such men at the time in Plimouth Colony. They were drawn to roam, fulfilling the awe they carried for the beauty of natural things new to them. They roamed without fear of dark forests where Satan lurked, withering weather, cunning wolves, or savages. They were walkers determined to wander more free of the rigid new society recently established. Caleb was of them.

Caleb came to the Plimouth Colony in 1635, fifteen years after the "Compact" and the "Treaty." By then it was smaller and less desirable in terms of opportunity than the Massachusetts Bay Colony to the north begun in 1628 by the Puritans. He knew little of the land patents, religious differences, and financiers of either settlement. Pilgrim separatists rejecting the English church were in Plimouth. Puritans in Salem were seeking reform of it. Each believed in the superiority of their views. The differences were beyond his ken. He knew he was neither. "Saints" and "Strangers" were the language separating those who came with cause and those who came for opportunity. He was a Stranger. He knew not much of what he had entered and cared little for it. It was beyond his figuring.

Plimouth started as a weakened entity by celestial providence, geography, and charter. The maiden voyage of the Mayflower was off track in a bad crossing. The group was set by charter to settle the Virginia territory that included the mouth of the Hudson River, the goal of Mayflower's intention. The journey was thwarted by Ile Nauset shoals off Cape Cod to go farther south. The ship was under duress in a bad season with no passage possible. The Plimouth colony settlement eventually came after the northern tip of Cape Cod landing was seen as unsustainable.

The Mayflower lot moored in safe harbor off the tip. They reconnoitered and pilfered sacred Indian corn stores at a burial site. The act created distrust and near mortal contact with Natives at what became the Encounter beaches on the Cape's forearm. That, kidnapping of Natives by earlier explorers and poor resources had soured the landing ground. The Pilgrims sought safer haven. Miles Standish set out in a shallop with a crew sailing along the inner bay coast searching for more suitable settlement. By a turn of nature, with heavy snowfall blinding at a precise moment, they passed a harbor at the end of the Sandy Neck spit, continued and founded Plimouth farther up the bay arc. But for the snowfall, Barnstable, not known as such then, would have been home to where Caleb began his new lot.

The Plimouth site was an abandoned Pawtuxet encampment lost to decimating disease visited upon the Wampanoag people from pestilent contact with Europeans decades earlier on fishing, trading, and exploratory ventures. The losses were catastrophic—exponentially more than any cannon, musket or blunderbuss of the time could deliver. The majority of indigenous people passed to spirit before Pilgrim boots stood on Cape Cod sand. Still, lacking true land charter, choosing ghost ground, having failed to arrive south to the Hudson, it made the Pilgrims, or Separatists, a committed, reverent, but insecure lot. The inferiority would last for years. The Pilgrims quickly signed a peace treaty in 1621 with the Wampanoags of the immediate area. Despite some conflict for settlers of the region in outlying areas north, south and west with other tribes, the Wampanoag treaty lasted for decades. Though Caleb was, at the time, a toddler in England and divorced from colonial intrigue, the "Treaty" was to define his life.

In the 1630s, the founders of the Plimouth colony and Massachusetts Bay were disturbed by the choice of some settlers to leave and habit the nascent, "future promised" proprietorship towns on Cape Cod—Sandwich, Yarmouth, Barnstable, and Nauset. They were not yet legal, the "rights" were unknown, but settlers were betting on the future. Others went into the Connecticut River Valley. A few ventured to new colonies south and north to establish more comfortable congregations. Much was in flux, a roiling mix. They all were passion-driven zealots with purpose and differences. Unrecorded to history, a small few Strangers went "native."

Caleb had never chosen Plimouth. He had no grand plan. He wanted a new life.

He skipped out on the town of Brighton on England's south coast where his reputation was suspect more from his family than his own deeds. He was both a respectful but "rambunctious" lad in a den of thieves. His parents and brother were a petty, scheming kind of poor. They were often on the edge of respectable, but suspect always. They were a loose-bound family, adept at pilfery and scams and familiar with the local gaol. Caleb was a more thoughtful sort. He wanted no part of it, especially gaol.

At eighteen, deeply suspicious and wary of any satisfactory future in his disapproving community, he chose to run from the shame and random subsistence of his family. He knew of the colonies. Brighton was a sailing town with taverns full of sailors with passing knowledge and bloated stories of the east coast of America. Fisherman and traders had been plying the coast for at least a century or more. The Gutenberg press was a century old. Print news of settlements was noted going back to the late 1500s. Raleigh's Roanoke colony of 1585 was lost. Jamestown of 1607 was established, struggled to near death, and then resurrected. Plimouth existed, later the Bay Colony and New Amsterdam, there since 1625, all growing. *Think boldly,* he thought. *Go.*

Escape to the colonies was no simple exercise. Ne'er-do-wells, by action or association, were not desirable souls for acceptance in the fledgling settlements. The investors wanted warranted, able men and women certified by church belief and basic means who could help repay those willing to fund voyages with profitable settlement. In late 1635, the time of his departure, the rules were more lenient. More skills were needed. Even the Mayflower group in 1620 held space among the 101 souls, demanded by the investors, for a laboring class of tradesmen and military leadership.

Caleb stole hearty pieces of recently, ill-gotten gold—booty from privateers from what actions or where they occurred he knew not—from the bed stand of his besotted parents as they snored as rasps on barrelhead staves. He was taken by a pang of guilt, but he was not religious and figured he was stealing the stolen. It was his only chance for a life hopefully better than the one before him. He travelled north and booked passage on a ship just days before it was sailing to the colonies. He was taken aboard upon recommendation of an investor on the Southampton docks to whom he paid gold for his assent. Caleb carried naught but a large duffle, an oil-slicked leather sack stuffed with meager clothes and three full kits of awls, knives, shears, stitching tools, skeins of sinew, and hefty a bag of adornment trinkets from his four-year apprenticeship in a leather shop. He had stolen them, too, justifying in his sensibility his Master was stingy and late—very much true by many months—with his pay. The tool bag sealed his passage.

It was a bad crossing, roiling, wet, and fetid. He reeked and festered with juicing sores. Amidst the travelers, there was little succor toward him. He was a pariah, having no history or recommendation of minister or master. He knew the contempt but did not care. At the mercy of the Atlantic, he owed no person anything. Little was worse than living a life as the suspect, crime underclass in England. He sensed freedom from something.

Caleb was savvy but not brilliant—street smart. He knew ciphers, practical numbers, and measurement of small things. He was a gangly, solidly built youth with brawling, sloping shoulders, penniless and not "with God." He could carry himself. Caleb also held a higher power ill-defined, a wisp of strong morality imbued by a beloved, failing aunt who spoke of righteousness. They had loved each other. His ilk, not religious believers, simply spiritual, were known and not highly regarded. They were often "warned off" from settling. It happened often. He had an uphill climb ahead for meager existence.

Upon his landing, Caleb would not have passed muster to settle eventually as a freeman and been driven off. His good fortune was that Plimouth was experiencing the leakage of the youngest and sturdiest to the promised Cape Cod proprietorships soon to come and interior settlements. Much happened before legal record. For those early Cape settlement origins, it was done more by disgruntled Bay Colony émigré's from Saugus, Lynn, Scituate, and the surrounds who believed their charter allowed expansion. It was not true. Those Puritans chafed at their self-righteous Pilgrim brethren who had well-considered claims. History would show it was Plimouth who had the charters-to-come on the Cape.

There was no mystery about it. The Cape was festooned with abundant forests of hardwoods and softwood pine swarming the peninsula essential for homes, ships, and infrastructure. Salt hay was beyond plenty—a marsh grass in inexhaustible abundance that eliminated the need for clearing fields for hay fodder, roof thatching, insulation and bedding stuffing. It was multi-purpose and infinite. The shoals were abundant for fishing and shellfish gathering. It was a Garden of Eden.

The Plimouth colony was not gentle on the young man initially nor he on it. He was not a fit. Non-Pilgrims, Strangers, were their own sub-class—small in number and eyed suspiciously. At his arrival, the colony totaled only 547 souls and needed servile labor. He was given, as his own as the laws decreed, a plot to raise his bounty from a Bradford experiment in 1623 to increase productivity. The largesse came from the fact that communal property was less productive while individuals prospered. Caleb's efforts on his allotment were agriculture failure—lack of skill, bad timing, and little interest. His welcome was threadbare.

His failure was compounded by his indifference to dead-day Sabbaths with naught else but two services, reflection, and prayer to be had. He walked afar on service days much to community disapprobation. Money? It did not exist. He had little currency in his early days. Bushel corn, wampum, furs, crops and barter were the currency and he was wanting. He had no steady place, having not the means or authorization to raise a structure.

Caleb's trump card was his skill from apprenticeship working hides and leather which proved a Godsend. Though his plot was sorrowfully unproductive, his leather goods were considered masterful in the Village, and, despite anemic harvest, he made progress, paid rent, attracted customers, and insinuated himself into the colony. His Brighton skills were rewarded. He showed himself hardworking on furs and skins, reliable and creative—a tradesman.

In any spare moment, he walked the farthest boundaries of the colony—forests, shorelines, and wading deep across marshes. The freedom he experienced was sacred to him.

He wanted to walk farther, explore more and find his comfort. He fancied he could barter his talents for fixing breeches, sewing waistcoats, crafting top-grade footwear, and conjoining hides to fashionable jackets and shoulder sacks for carry. He was an early entrepreneur in an environment that cherished farmers to survive, timbermen for English trade, and fur trappers to pay off debt to investors, but also valued needed skills. He became a solid citizen. Something else called him. It was not the God of Scriptures drilled into him from the everyday talk of village life. He was consumed with more discovery.

Goodwife Collins was his benefactress. He treasured her kindness and regretted her disappointment at him as a "black sheep." Her husband had died. She took in his bedraggled soul upon landing and gave him temporary shelter. She was an early, second-wave settler and had a small living enclosure, a "booth" as known, where Caleb lived in a side hovel and plied his trade.

"Gooodwife Collins, I shall go walking for a while. Will thou abideth?"

"Art thou a troubled soul, goodman? Why, pray thee?"

"'Tis a big and glorious land. Unknown. I came from naught. I must see it."

"Master Farker, I will abideth your journey and wish ye Godspeed, but worry your ignorance of the Lord and worry the wagging tongues in the colony."

"Goodwife, your faith will sustain me. The choice is my preference. Pray remember me."

Caleb packed a fox-hide shoulder sack of his making for his tools and adornments, tightly woven and smeared with polished tallow for the rain. He stuck in a waxed linen shawl for bad weather. In a second sack, he provisioned salt cod, vinegar venison, and dried squash patties. He rued he had so much to carry, knowing the local bounty would suffice. As a last thought, he stuffed a neatly crafted, deer hide shoulder sack of his design and a small, leather pocket sack filled with tobacco as gifts he may need for the savages.

He made a short stop at the roadhouse tavern in outskirt Plimouth for a pour. In law, liquor was not sanctioned, yet there were few days for anyone he knew that the "pour" did not start early and end late. Everyday. There was more faith in the fermented draught as the water of the common well. Fermented beverages—the Rattle-Skull, Whistle Belly, Sling and Toddy—were as much a part of life as praying. Most of whom he was familiar with imbibed with gusto.

"Prithee a toddy and not so lacking as to make it English tea."

"Where fetch ye?"

"Knoweth not. A walker."

"Fool, I say, brother."

He was strikingly warned by wags that the Natives would just as soon kill him as let him live through a walk-about. He heard from others it was most definitely not so. The word of original settlers and the praise of abundant and profitable traders in Bourne told little worry with savages. The Natives were not a warring sort. The Cape Wampanoags, decimated by three-quarters through pestilence introduced by European explorers, traders, and privateers before the Pilgrims landed, were forever weakened with no shot fired. Still, fear of Natives abounded.

"Caleb, art ye going walkin' true?" the bar man asked.

"Yea."

"Dangerous, lad. The savages, if ye get the wrong ones, will slit your throat."

"Tis not the way as toldeth me. Never has happened. I could get my throat slit in your inn as likely."

"Not likely, but cheeky, yeoman."

"No offense. Pleasure to you."

The settler and Indian interaction was amicable in its way. The prescient "Treaty" held. The current condition was peaceful, helpful, but sometimes tense. The loose confederation of Cape tribes under the Cape Wampanoags––the Pamets, the Nausets, the Monomoyicks, the Manomets, Cummaquids, the Scussinosetts, and the Aquinnah on the Vineyard—were wary, tired, and resigned. The Pilgrims were near helpless. The tribes decimated. Why fight?

The savages could have wiped out the Plimouth venture from the Provincetown landing with its initial, poorly equipped reconnoiters on the Cape and first winter suffering on Pawtuxcet grounds. Instead, there was helpful corn, teaching of agricultural techniques, and a buffer from Indian unrest elsewhere. The appearance of Squanto, a clever slave from the Hunt raid a decade before Pilgrim arrival, now from Europe returned with translation skills, was a huge boon. His introduction of Massasoit, principal *sachem* of local tribes, led to a treaty of decades of peace in the Cape region.

★ ★ ★

Caleb set afoot out of Plimouth. His wanderings thus far had apprised him. He knew well of Aptucxet, the trading post in Bourne that stoked his passion for trade and made him wampum.

It arose from the Plimouth settlement in earliest form. The Plimouth founders bemoaned the Cape, with its crooked finger and long, dangerous passage around the north tip and down the forearm as an impenetrable barrier to trade with the colonies below. All wanted commerce with the new Bay Colony extensions on the Connecticut River and the Dutch colonization in New Amsterdam. Absent a free waterway cutting across the base of the Cape finger,

Aptucxet was established in 1627. It was brilliant. It was a transfer point situated to use the Cape marshes and rivulets through the shallows of the Cape peninsula now known as Bourne, to transcend the barrier to markets north and south. Shallops and small, coastal windjammers of whatever persuasion would tender on either side - the Cape Bay or Buzzard's Bay. Paddling craft from Aptucxet would stroke over the rivulets and transfer goods from the post to fill cargo on both sides. Savages abounded there, trading furs, corn, produce, and wampum with good spirit.

Caleb had his education at Aptucxet. He had keenly observed a basic, constricted language of words, hand signals, and intermixed phrases for trade with Natives. The lingua franca was a mish-mosh to make a deal. The savages knew far more English than the Europeans knew of Native tongue. They had been at it longer. He felt fit enough in the way things worked in this energetic, complex, fearful, optimistic world. He understood barter.

He knew the path of his intended wanderings had been forged. Although Cape Cod looked, from the sea as a wilderness forest, centuries of Native travel had carved defined pathways sufficient to move people and small sleds. He was not distracted. He knew of a new community named Sandwich where discontented emigrants from the Bay Colony and Plimouth people gathered. No rebellion, differences for sure, it was a hopeful emigration. Caleb's paths were not of the bushwhacking sort at all—they were ancient by-ways.

He took little trails on the paths eastward toward the Sandwich enclave. He encountered two Nauset Indians far afield of their eastern Cape habitat, probably couriers. He had weak weapons, only a belt knife and a short sword. He had no knowledge of their intentions. It was his first encounter with Indians outside the colony stockade and Aptucxet. They came upon each other abruptly around a sharp curve of a water-carved trail. He raised his hands up from the elbow, palms raised facing them in a sign he had seen at Aptucxet. The two glared solemnly and he stepped off the path for their passage. They ignored him but with a palpable and mystical shunning. It was not indifference, more fear and bravado.

Caleb lamented the Nausets had intentionally disregarded him. He was free and would accept all. No rancor. Something was different and he had no reference. Something bad had happened. He felt hated. He had no precise knowledge of the early European ventures years before Plimouth, like Gosnold, making landfall, bringing horrible disease, and others of his ilk enslaving small numbers from tribes. The pestilence had devastated three quarters of the small

Nauset tribe. Cause and effect were not a science of the times, but intuition was. Stay away from the pale-skin, bringers of death. The pale-skin germs were a death plague well beyond that in percentage of the devastation in Europe centuries earlier.

Caleb kept walking with a continuing fascination of a benign territory so rarely travelled by people of his sort. The land was sand and scrub, sea marsh, and small pine forest. The elements did not daunt him. He was soothed.

He came upon Sandwich, a tiny clutch of offended Pilgrims and wayward Puritans. The Village was naught but a few huts and an inn barely greater.

"Where might ye from, Master?" the inn keeper asked.

"Plimouth in home, Goodman."

"A right set of bastards fit for nothing," the keeper shrugged. "What'll keep you, pilgrim?"

"Anything ye keepeth from adulteration and bugs that do not fester."

"Impudent lad, but spoketh with age. Why fer ye wanderin' afoot?"

"To be free. Tis all."

"Free tis a burden."

"Not to me, Goodman."

"What can ye find in forest and sand?"

"I have no need for answer, Keep. Freedom will tell. Prithee, well."

"I warn ye, Master, the Injuns are barbarians. Some love our Yaweh. Others would take ye scalp."

"Same as whither I came in England with no Injuns," Caleb laughed.

Caleb drank a fermented brew from local corn, more strong than palatable. He was mindful but impaired. The Keep offered lodging, but Caleb had no trust. Tales about recent emigrants to the peninsula being robbed without recourse called for a sleep in the woods. Sandwich was raw and small. There were ten men of Saugus who chose without land patent to settle three score families there in the 1630's. Only the first few had arrived—a score and a little No huge transgression would go unnoticed, but theft of his personals—hardly. His Brighton days served him with knowledge of being nothing but sensing a lot. Here he was King of doing what felt right. He slept in a moss hollow near to a tumbling creek.

*   *   *

Caleb had the faintest sense of the geography he was travelling. He knew he trod a hooked peninsula extending out into the ocean. No metric—miles, kilometers—existed. A day's walk. Eighty surveyor chains to today's mile. An oxen plowing slowly for an hour. No measure, but he could feel it. The peninsula was small, narrow. He knew he was on the bay the early Pilgrims reconnoitered by shallop to Plimouth. He estimated a day's walk south, southeast, if the trails permitted, would bring him to the south coast, a little east on the midpoint of the crooked, lower finger.

The trails were not well-travelled and not always easily decipherable. A dry water sluice looked as promising as baked, naked path. He was not on the bay coast any longer, heading south. It was, to him, a paradise. Never had he seen a progression of ponds and lakes so pristine that when he swam in them, a rock seeming within reach was several body lengths below. He sat naked in sunshine on a sand beach beside a blue-water pond, rippling with a gentle wind, the small water curves turning sunlight to diamonds.

What he was doing, Caleb could not say. He felt both powerful and small. As he took stock, there was little sense. With so little experience, his leather goods and tailoring made him a craftsman, whereas in Brighton, he would have been insignificant. Now he could survive. The colonies, Plimouth and Bay, struggled with disease, governance, and sustenance, yet, in total they grew. Change was at hand. The foothold of arriving people was established. The weakened Natives were a question few had pondered forward except in fear. The sentiments about it bode badly.

He came upon a switch decidedly wider than others and took it to be the rumored trail south. It was clear the switch was not trampled to conveyance with Pilgrim's progress, few had been there. It was a well-worn route among regional tribes. To go forward guaranteed encounters with settlements of savages of which he knew little. Caleb did not hesitate. He knew ways of communication from trading at Aptucxet. He knew the Wampanoags were, at heart, peaceful. He pushed on for several miles on the trail, his pace rapid with excitement.

It was mid-afternoon when the forest brightened looking ahead. Caleb figured it was the thinning of forest to the coast south. The bay side looking north was the preferred route of travel. Still, he figured, keep walking toward the southern sea. He did and arrived upon on a small bluff overlooking the southern ocean and a nearby sea marsh. The beauty was different, and to him, greater than Plimouth, Bourne, or Sandwich. To his simultaneous apprehension and delight, he scanned down and right. He saw his first Native village. It was nestled on the crook of an inland, tidal river hummock. It boasted huts, cooking fires, drying racks and the sound of children laughing.

Caleb did not hesitate. He wanted to engage these people. Besides, there was no farther south to travel. He questioned his sensibility: Too brazen? Too intrusive. He quieted the thoughts. In his heart, he felt them all the same on this abundant continent in an abundant land.

There was no easy "there" to the encampment from where he was except to forge the tidal marsh river. He heard cries he thought were warnings from the far bank but realized a dugout canoe, a boat he would come to know as a mishoon, was dispatched. They had seen him. Anxiety draped him. Did the savages feel attacked? Was he in danger? On instinct alone, or foolish hope, he reasoned not.

The mishoon crossed the marsh river quickly, and Caleb stood on the sandy shore below the bluff, mesmerized as the boat, with two savages paddling front and rear and a powerful man seated in the middle, landed. They deftly put the canoe on sand and motioned him forward.

Caleb raised his hands upward, palms outward in the signal he had witnessed at Aptucxet of greeting.

"*Cowaúnckamish,*" he said. *I pray your favor.* He heard it said many times.

The men in the boat looked upon him with surprise and began laughing, but in no harsh way. It was probably at his pronunciation, which Caleb knew was none too good. Actually, it was the first time he uttered the words out loud.

"*Túnna Cowâum Tuckôteshana?*" the middle man said, obviously the leader. *Whence come you?* The intonation was a question to his ear.

Caleb labored hard to remember the fragments of the question from Aptucxet, though he knew not the words. He decided it should be followed by a declaration of place.

"Plimouth," he offered, not knowing if he was close to saying anything of merit. "*Tocketussawêitch?*" Caleb said, exhausting his Wampanoag vocabulary except for a few pidgin phrases he knew from trading. *How are you called?*

Show respect, his instincts commanded. His welcome, maybe his life, depended on such amiability. He suspected the leader knew more English than he let on. The Wampanoags generally did.

"*Habbamock,*" the leader answered.

"Hab-ba-mock?" Caleb tried to repeat as accurately as his hearing of the name allowed.

The men laughed good-naturedly as if saying, *Good enough.*

Without awaiting the question, Caleb pointed to himself.

"Caleb," he said as clearly as he could pronounce it.

"K-lib," Habbamock repeated.

Caleb nodded and thought, *Close enough.*

He had exhausted any further dialogue. It went no deeper. He signed with forefingers pointed at each ear and twirling them, and shrugged he knew no more. They shifted in the mishoon, made room in the middle, and waved him on board, sitting ahead of Habbamock.

There was only a single exchange crossing the marsh.

"Why K-lib here?" Habbamock asked from behind him in the mishoon.

Caleb did not answer at first. The natural tapestry of the tidal river and marsh-scape struck him so intensely. The low-country flatness. The vivid greens of salt reeds. The fine, subtle tan of shore sand linings against the low scrub bushes. Sparkles on the sunlit caps of blue water everywhere. The circling of marine birds above—gulls, osprey, an eagle. There was unity to something. He felt it.

Caleb's response came intuitively.

He halfway turned back to look at Habbamock. He raised both his palms upward with a shrug, then pointed to his heart and walked his fingers along the mishoon gunnel. *I am walking,* he signed.

In an unexpected response, the savage grunted with satisfaction and went silent.

*   *   *

His arrival on the encampment shore was unnerving to the anxiety of a little educated wanderer. Every single one of the inhabitants gathered as the mishoon ran ashore. Caleb recognized immediately he was a circus freak show among people most of whom had never experienced proximity to a settler. In this thought, he took pause. He, personally, had no direct contact with these people but for the few who traded at Aptuxnet. Still, they knew. They knew something different as from a collective conscious of a changing world, not as yet defined, and he was the manifestation.

He tried to show amiability—loose, nodding, smiling. The children ran about him, some daring to poke him and run. The boat welcome across the marsh, the entry to the encampment, were signs of open hope. He knew that much for the moment. Fear drained from him as with the ebbing tide of the

marsh river sucking before them. The chief had recognized him as safe and silently passed a blessing of sorts in his demeanor to his minions.

With deep-felt gratitude and relief, Caleb felt he was a guest, not an enemy.
He had a need to respond to murmurs and suspicion. He reached into his sack
and pulled a masterful deer hide carry bag and presented it to the chief with
a slight bow and body language of loose friendship.

Habbamock took the bag, fingered its stitching, smiled, and held it aloft.

The encampment murmured with a collective sigh of peace and, from
the manner of the women who fingered the bag as the *sachem* passed it on, a
clear respect for the craftsmanship. Caleb exhaled relief. Along this salt marsh
river, below a beautiful bluff, a place scarcely known to settlers, he had gained
entry, however small, to the real essence of why he came: freedom to be—
with everyone.

Every sense was alive and vibrating in Caleb. It was so far from Brighton
and Plimouth disapproval. The experience thus far was beyond the understanding of anyone to whom he had spoken in Plimouth. It had no precedent.
He was a lad of near twenty-one in an Indian village in the middle of nowhere—a walker. He felt he was where he belonged for the moment. Caleb's
mind was both keen and disoriented. He was in a new reality among people
with a totally different way of existing.

He set about to understand the encampment on tour. A small cluster of
wetu huts surrounded a gathering place on this marsh sluice. He knew the
word "*wetu*" but had never seen one. They varied in size but looked formidably
sturdy. They were formed from strong cedar branches grounded and bent in a
dome structure, some circular, some more oblong for more people. They were
covered with large panels of tree bark, tightly bound to the limbs with roped
sea grass twine. Others were draped with woven salt grass, some both. The inside perimeters that he ducked his head into on a tour were set with benches
for sitting and sleeping. There was a central smoke hole. The insides were
draped with tapestries of tightly woven grasses and neatly cut hides for insulation. The word "cozy" came to mind.

To the east by a 150 steps from the encampment was a huge pile of oyster,
clam, scallop, lobster, and mussel shells—a midden of shells. It was placed so
the encampment was upwind mostly, but a bad wind probably brought a mild
odor to camp. The pile was a telling sign of easy marine bounty. The midden
was long in the making to Caleb's eye—decades at least, maybe a century.

The encampment was safely high enough from what he could determine would be the highest of possible tidelines. Ancient wisdom, he supposed. Looking up a farther footpath to the north, rising a hundred steps to a bluff, was a sizeable crop field. Though he stood lower, he, who failed at agriculture, could discern the leafing of corn, the broadleaf squash plants, and climbing poles of beans. It was the "Three Sisters" the Pilgrims were taught. He knew more bounty grew below his line of vision—tubers and ground bounty. Judging by the size of the plot and the population he encountered, he surmised excess bounty from the field was traded. He counted twenty mishoons of various sizes. The marsh waterways, harbored from the open sea by the barrier island, were a gentle path for barter and visiting

Upon landing, after the tribal meet-up accompanied by a large clam shell of fish stew offered him, Caleb was led to a small, unoccupied *wetu* that was empty due to an untimely death. Caleb's wonder was piqued.

Common wisdom had it the savages were dirty, unwashed, and foul. Instead he entered a dwelling that offered pine and sage scents. It was a smell so different and heavenly from the close, dirty closets of Plimouth. The woman who lived in this place was clearly a healer and had gone to spirit. An entire section of a curving wall was hung with dried herbs. He had no sense he was being conveyed an honor. It was inconceivable his appearance was perceived as a sign. He was seen as good, a hope for things. It felt as an undeserved burden unknown to him.

He napped in dreams in the *wetu*. They came upon him in fitful flashbacks. The splash of unwelcome storm waves in one instance on the crossing, spilling below deck, sloshing icy Atlantic waters over him. It was lost in his stirring. A wolf in the forest, fangs bared, staring him down and departing in silence. Savages around him with purpose unknown. He caught the fragment, and then it was lost to him. He shuddered from a deep sleep that was grasping to keep him.

They came for him to join the shared meal. During his sleep, much had been going on. Spits were twirling duck, venison, and beaver slabs and a few quail, all dripping fat into the fire. Unhusked corn ears were lying barely visible in a rock fire pit with shellfish covered with seaweed along with squash and beans lain atop. The smells were overwhelmingly, deliciously powerful. He sensed the aura of an uncommon feast, but thought too, *No, this is living from bounty—near effortless bounty.*

The main pull on his nostrils was a venison *sobaheg* bubbling in a large clay cauldron lying on the coals. His mouth watered. It was a stew of venison chunks, corn grit, beans, and squash chunks, Jerusalem artichokes, and nuts spiced with small onions and herbs. He had never smelled something so delicious. He thought to Plimouth fare and laughed to himself. Nothing there was ever exciting.

Those in the encampment gathered, and the bounty was gathered and placed on long, wide, flat boards in the midst. Everyone had places encircling the feast.

Caleb was led to a place next to Habbamock. It took little for him to realize he was, unfathomable as it was, the guest of honor. Again he faltered in disbelief. A few hours before, he was a walker trying to find his soul, and now he was an honored guest at an encampment. He clung to two hopes: show heart and show gratitude. *Anyone, anywhere would know that,* he thought.

Hell, he was barely tolerated in Brighton with suspicion and pall around him, given only limited access to the privy bucket on the voyage while his bowels roiled. He was looked at askance in Plimouth until it suited their wants to bear tolerance for his skills. Always the outsider. For a ridiculous moment, he was guest of honor. He would not lose this moment but had no idea how not to. He was no Pilgrim in any way, yet he was as a stranger in another place where he was not understood.

Habbamock was first to approach the feeding boards filled with the most luscious spread Caleb had ever seen—fowl, venison, beaver, corn, venison *sobaheg*, vegetables, lobster, oysters, mussels. Habbamock motioned him behind him. He followed. Habbamock ate off the boards, choosing and selecting for his fill, and was given a clay bowl of *sobaheg*. Caleb followed religiously, selecting the same and in choice. It was penance for a bad life. He could have stayed stuffing away his hunger in the clean, natural food. Instead, he followed the lead and followed Habbamock in his discipline. The others followed in what seemed to Caleb a pecking order. There was ample for a second pass in which he greedily indulged.

In a moment, as if on cue, hide drums and gourd rattles started; leg rattles attached to calves clattered. The similarity in dress to the Morris Dance of England stunned him. The savages arose, circled, and began a simple right to left footstep. They smiled toward him, motioned him and each other. It was a dance of welcoming—subtle, easy, and fun. A maiden came for him.

"K-lib," she said, reaching out both hands to encourage him off his haunches.

She laughed as he stumbled while uncurling from the ground. His stumble was from his inattention to balance while looking into her face. He had missed something in life. She was to him a handsome mix of strength, balanced features, and playfulness with a lithe body borne of a natural life.

He pointed to himself. "K-lib!", then to her.

"Wetamu."

"Wetamu?" he asked, wanting the pronunciation to be correct.

She nodded, shyly. He only was to find out later if any translation of her name were possible, it was "sweetheart."

Caleb had danced more than a step or two in Brighton. True, he was large but highly deft afoot. He joined her hand in the circle and picked up the rhythm of steps. He had nothing to do or say, a relief beyond meaning. Flow. Just join and sway to easy steps, to drums, rattles, and a wafting tune of flute. Wetamu smiled with and at him. He realized he had never been close to a relationship before. A pang of confusion struck him about how sad and lonely that was. It was too crazy, too much, insensible and insulting to any sane person. This was a welcome dance for him before a fire pit in a place he was little more than a deaf mute. It filled him with surreal astonishment. He was confused that he, a Brighton lad wanted Wetamu in a pure way beyond his knowing or experience.

Caleb joined other dances with enthusiasm of which he knew not their meaning. As he bollixed up the steps and stepped on toes or twirled right instead of left, the laughter was not derisive. He absorbed the goodwill of people who had suffered and still gave respect to a person trying, with mistakes, to be among them.

The encampment damped fires and retired. Caleb and Habbamock were left.

"Good, K-lib?" Habbamock asked.

"Good," Caleb signed with both hands thrusted outward, originating from his heart.

"Friends?" Habbamock asked.

"Forever," Caleb signed, pounding his heart and raising a palm to the universe.

He retired to his *wetu* and tried to figure the unlikelihood of whatever seemed to be going on. The only recurrent theme was Plimouth was not his home, and, if not, where did it reside? He belonged nowhere yet felt he was somewhere. The somewhere could not understand his tongue, felt him strange far more than the colony, but it all felt more peaceable. He was not a savage but, this night, wished to be one. He saw a maiden who had awakened a rainbow of feelings that were too unfathomable and ridiculous in his mind.

Though he fought it and struggled against it in the *wetu,* his awareness awakened. He feared dearly for these natural people. They knew nothing of Brighton and how richer classes grew then dominated and humiliated the underclass with tools of power. Ships and ships were coming. The tribe may, through stories and guidance, have perceived a relentless tide of newcomers who lived to conquer the land but not live in harmony with it. They could know little of planned settlements on Cape Cod that were coming like a nor-'easter. They had suffered near extinction already from European plagues, yet celebrated life. The grim imperative to always have more among the Pilgrims and northern, omnivorous Puritans growing by legion would be relentless. Caleb, young, a little educated, now an international soul, knew that much. Back home, and in continental countries, he knew little save for this: They wanted all of this beauty and freedom. Right here. It was too beautiful. They would be ugly about it.

Caleb arose early. His unease as an honored guest without purpose or portfolio gnawed at him. The only sensibility in his head was the knowing he carried to Plimouth: Earn your keep. He went to the center of the encampment. The women were long up cooking and gathering. A squaw offered him a *nasaump* porridge in a clay bowl. He marveled how simple and delicious a stewed cornmeal, berries, and nuts bowl could be.

Wetamu was about, puttering, and he longed to greet her. A simple nod and smile was the best he could afford.

Near the cooking fire on a pelt he audaciously took, he laid out two sets of his leatherworking tools: deft hammers to soften pelts, several awl sizes to punch holes, reels of gut twine, grommets to protect punch holes with a plier to fasten, sewing needles of all sizes to stitch, two scissors—large and small—with acute accuracy to shear hides and cruel, hooked knives for dirty, carving work. The women oohed and aahed. Tools! He also had a valuable, small bag of gem beads and a scroll of basic design templates from Plimouth. The tools of this community were shale and shell-based along with some bartered steel tools, but not European quality. Leatherwork. Caleb had seen the creativity in the dress of the natives. He approved of the flowing drape in concept but thought it crude in execution, too loosely stitched.

He asked for a hide by pointing to drying racks. A deer pelt was brought to him. He took a template from Plimouth for moccasins for a man and took a charcoal stick from the fire and traced. He economically cut, no waste, the figure with scissors and began punching sew-holes and lightly tapped in the grommets he brought.

The gut twine was not right for the job. A squaw went quickly to get double-braided deer sinew—coarser, but right. Caleb smiled and shook his head low, humbly. They all laughed. His cutting, grommeting, stitching and lining produced a pair of beautiful moccasins in an hour. He left the tools on a blanket, knowing no etiquette, and curled his arms inward saying "mine," then thrust them out saying "yours." No one understood, so he put tools in the hands of the nearest, not knowing if he had given them away.

Habbamock watched all and tried to understand. Women's work. K-lib was doing women's work. He sensed him brave and fearless, but women's work was not good for the encampment. All was always the "ways." It was a rhythm. It was constant. Everyone understood the harmony of the "ways."

Habbamock approached Caleb and used his signing of the day before—fingers walking—to indicate a walk. Caleb joined him, honored for the attention.

Along the marsh shore, Habbamock stopped and sat on a tidal sand bank and motioned Caleb to sit. He pinched his leather tunic up and laid it out.

"Women work."

Caleb was not stupid, nor was he aware. Attentive that something was being said, he nodded in assent to the solemnity, if not the message.

Habbamock pointed at him.

"Plimouth." Caleb nodded.

Habbamock pointed to himself. "Mashpee."

Caleb nodded.

Habbamock pointed again to himself and gave the walking sign. "Plimouth," he said.

Caleb nodded.

Habbamock pointed to himself again. He gave sign of *sit,* raising his rump and settling.

Caleb nodded.

Habbamock signed *with women*, signaling hair, breasts, and swinging arms for babies.

Caleb understood. What if Habbamock entered Plimouth and sat with the goodwives? He was horrified. If Habbamock had gathered and sat with good-wives, he may have been slain. He realized a good purpose could be an egregious assault. He felt stupid and alone. His effort was insulting and divisive.

He nodded and pounded his heart and lowered his head. *Sorry.*

Habbamock sat impassively.

Caleb understood his reaction might be salvation. Hoping to avoid something ill-formed and defensive, he looked at Habbamock and said, "Trade."

Nothing was lost on that word to either. Commerce. Barter. Corn. Wampum. Plenty.

Caleb signed to Habbamock, *you,* pointing to him, *tell,* signing words coming from mouth, *say trade,* fingers pointing both ways.

Caleb had no idea Habbamock was a *sachem,* a regarded chief, of the Mashpee region. He was responsible for the well-being of a proud but diminished nation. Caleb was amidst royalty in a different universe. Still, he felt the calm majesty and equanimity of his friend. Was friend a right or a possible word?

The *sachem* pointed at him. "Trade?" he asked.

Caleb nodded.

Whatever tension existed evaporated. K–lib saw his acceptance as a trade intermediary. It could work.

The settlement men came to understand he was a brother to create goods— —moccasins, leggings, tunics, sacks—for trading. The women were already skilled and adept, some braves as well, but for the most part, they only created for need. With Caleb's instruction and tools, the women became more purposeful to produce excess for trade. In a quiet, soft way, he demanded quality. He would walk among the women and girls, and sometimes shook his head "no" as discreetly as possible. The "no" meant tear the stitching out or toss the piece and be more careful.

The nights now came with a cooling that hinted at the coming change of seasons. The green vibrancy of surrounding vegetation began to dull to olive as if tired of preening. The first color changes to the leaves of less healthy trees and those highest on the bluff appeared. The composition of fish caught began to change with migrations. Autumn loomed, slowly, but with relentless intent.

Caleb had been at the encampment for six weeks, though he had paid little attention to passing time. For much of it, he conjured no thoughts of Plimouth.

When thoughts of Plimouth arose, none were celebratory. His recollections were of a bullying place, rigid in piety, and little better in acceptance from what the citizens had emigrated. The strictures and punishments, the commands and control, offended him. It was Brighton reborn but with equally dedicated suppression. The Pilgrims, however, were all exhausted, and it had spawned a definite renegade factor of which he was now one.

★   ★   ★

Wetamu came to him, to his *wetu*, silently, without shame, without many words. He could not understand his white, pasty skin on her soft, mocha beauty. He would forever wonder. It made no sense and never did. She said only in limited language it was his heart and pressed it. His heart. His love, their love, was a beautiful and strange marking for a new society.

The weeks brought a new language to his tongue. It was Wopanaak. His tongue and brain were weak in it, he felt, but he prided himself on listening and learning. He chastised his glacial progress. He could talk with the children as if he lived in their world—birds, food, games, very simple. Complex discussions were not possible.

He was no hunter, but the men had him tag along. A Brighton furrier hunting brought a nervous chuckle to him and fear of disgrace. No skills. No bow. No tracking, but he learned. Clumsy and noisy. He watched as the hunters interpreted game paths, set blinds, and waited. He understood and marveled––people living in a certain harmony, taking as needed but no more from the land. They did not want to conquer but to reap as needed with respect. True, it was a willful exercise with cunning and intent, but a kill was honored with spiritual gratitude.

It was a sunny, breezy day on the ocean that the soul of the hunt took him. An animated cry arose from a watch point. The words escaped him except "quickly," "now." A pod of the smaller pilot whales was spotted a quarter mile offshore. Caleb knew of them—far bigger than any land animal, but not leviathan. The pod of about eight lolled, breached, and undulated off the beach with insouciant disregard. Hurried, excited calls for actions sounded across the sand bar.

Caleb had taken to the mishoons, the only boat he had ever entered to water, and he did it often, alone. Not just paddling the tidal inlet, he took them often to sea for adventure in the swells. He was seaworthy and powerful. Habbamock signaled to the two largest mishoons and pointed Caleb to one of the two boats—eight men each. A brave ran to a storage *wetu* and emerged with two glinting, viciously sharpened harpoons—probably traded for—with skein coils of rope of attached and placed one in each canoe. On order, the men dug oars with an exhausting frenzy to the inlet break then to open sea. The pace was furious.

With little time for thought, Caleb realized he was going whaling. *Whaling?* The thought astounded him. *Why? Do we not have plenty? Why beasts on the open sea? Game? Crops? Trade?* He was not with Wampanoag ways entirely yet. The understanding crept into his brain. It would be the big kill for insurance against a tough winter. These people put it on the line with no question when it came to survival. Panting, he dug harder to paddle equal to the others. The sea was medium chop. The afternoon wind rose to onshore. It was not an easy dig with paddles, but they entered the small pod.

There was a hunting strategy afoot and he could see it evolving. The last in the pod was the target. The mishoons flanked each side of the lagging pilot whale, and a harpooner in each bow steadied for thrust. Big as he was, Caleb was one, crouching wide-legged for balance, and he thrust, as told, behind the head to vital organs. The strength behind the harpoons was all that could be given in rocking seas and the frenzied, white, frothy churn of the desperate whale. Still, they thrust deep to half-shaft.

Then all hell broke loose. The pilot spasmed with a ton and a half and fifteen feet length of life. The thrashing was an animal reaction to insult, a declaration of being. The tail whip capsized Caleb's mishoon, knocking all into an indifferent sea. Grasping the canoe gunnel, he watched the rope uncoil away unattended, the whale running, but barely. From his vocal chords and heart, he whooped like a warrior loud and with force.

"Get back aboard, lads. Work to do," he yelled above the waves. His words were not understood, but his passion was.

Righting a round-bottom mishoon was easy with teamwork.

There was balance, the men equal to each side, one per side hoisting in at a time. All were in and accounted for with adrenalized chatter and smiles. The harpoon digs were fatal to the pilot whale. No one was lost, no desperate pull from the beast in a "sleigh-ride" run for life. The boats synched, recovered the drifting rope of the capsized mishoon, and tied the carcass aft of the two boats. They pulled to shore with a small pilot in tow. It was a huge bounty for the upcoming winter. Caleb swaggered onshore and knew he had acquitted himself as a warrior.

Processing the kill, and it was a community effort, was amazing to him. The pilot was dragged on to the beach.

Both women and men flayed the beast with care to protect the skin for rain gear once cured, peeling it off in broad strip layers.

Caleb was offered blubber slabs from the skinned carcass that would later be rendered to oil. He ran to the bushes and puked on the tasting to laughs. The viscosity, fishy flavor, and squishy oil were disgusting. Whale blubber was foul to eat. Caleb took note of the wood-frame racks—a quickly built, a very large array of bent willow constructed while the men were at sea. They draped the racks with thin-sliced whale muscle, salted and herbed, drying to fill reed baskets of sustenance for winter. A successful hunt.

*　*　*

Far more than the changes in landscape and season, Caleb was absorbing a culture that made little sense to him. No sense. Clear, Habbamock was *sachem,* but women ruled in a way. They owned, he learned. They passed parcel rights and property to their lineage. They had voice and power. The word was beyond him, but the Wampanoags were matrilineal. The rights of heredity and property were female. In Caleb's world, females were breeders with no rights, subject to male domination at every turn. Not here. He tried to figure Habbamock's role with women ruling. There was no precedent or understanding in his mind.

He only knew Wetamu had no reticence or shame coming to his *wetu.* On first light, she had no shame leaving the *wetu* and joining the rhythms of a day's preparation. The freedom was unimaginable and difficult for him to process. Their soft, fun, and passionate congress was allowed, actually encouraged with nods and teasing. Once again, the Plimouth strictures brought a choking sense to his entire mind and body. He was ridiculously in sin, but why and how did it feel so wonderful? Not just their passionate sex, but it was the acceptance of natural ways by the community.

*　*　*

Caleb was nervous. He and Annawan walked, a brother with whom he had sloshed in the waters of the capsized kill and befriended, with four others. They carried six very large, heavy sacks as big as large boulders with four young braves to the Aptucxet trading post in mid-fall. They panted and stopped often. It was stupid to have taken on so much. Three huge sacks held pelts of beaver, fox, and deer hides, fine-tuned to how Caleb knew a furrier wanted to buy them. They were meticulously cured and trimmed to easy, dimensional cuts as Caleb himself would have liked, and separated by a thin layer of fresh-water rinsed, dried salt grass to keep them sanitary, clean, and ready. The other three equally heavy bags were fashioned leather goods. Mashpee mishoons followed a sea course with abundant produce to the post.

It was the high trade season before winter at Aptucxet; the time to strike. Caleb had suggested to Habbamock they not trade piecemeal with streaming visitors from other Wampanoag and Narragansett camps and wait to sell for a higher price at the post. It was a heretical thought and, truth be said, "capitalist." The highest price for the village would be at Aptucxet. The *sachem* nodded with an arched eyebrow and instructed them to barter for camp provisions and wampum.

The post was as crowded as he had ever seen. It was different as Caleb had known it, more amplified. New traders from new areas said emigrants were arriving up and down the coast. They were joining new communities with names he knew not, born of disagreements and a flight to or from greater purity. Everyone wanted goods. Shoal boats sat bobbing in marsh waters awaiting cargo to steer through the swamps to either direction and transfer the goods to coastal schooners going north to Boston or south to Connecticut and New Amsterdam, perhaps Jamestown.

He and Annawan grabbed space on the lawn and spread their wares. Everything, everywhere was selling in a frenzy.

The pelts always sold. Cut well, treated well, preserved well. The Mashpee Wampanoags did that. Quality goods were high value. It was the palpable care of pelt goods that drove bidding beyond normal response. They sold out in under an hour. High quality fur pelts at premium.

The beauty and subsequent demand for the village craftsmanship in finished leather goods left Caleb and Annawan in a panic. They looked at each other in uneasy horror at the aggressive, near violent buying. Buyers were swearing and fighting with fists over Mashpee leather goods.

No sooner laid out than gone, there was no equal competition for the style and quality of Mashpee. None. The village was a factory of beauty. Caleb felt sorrow he and Annawan often settled too low in trade from lacking confidence and experience. They could have gotten more. The crop produce arriving late day from the mishoons sold out before it was taken to the selling point. True, gone at the landing point. The proceeds far exceeded what was expected by leagues. The leather work of the encampment women was an amazing gift—artisanal, focused, and productive—augmented by quality crops of abundance.

The yield sustained by the barter of pelts, leather goods and crops was outrageous bounty. Wampum for trade. Corn and bean bushels for sustenance. Iron implements for agriculture. Cloth for blankets and clothing. War weapons for defense. More leather good tools.

They had to hire two carriers plus themselves and the mishoons to return the bounty of the barter to the tidal river.

★   ★   ★

A note turned sour.

Upon leaving Aptucxet, just short of the woods, a Plimouth resident, Goodman Cobb, with whom Caleb was not friendly, accosted him.

It was an intrusion given the wonder of success that Caleb felt.

He was not prepared.

"Goodman Farker. When return ye to the righteousness of our settlement? Goodwife Collins fears ye fate and wonders your fortunes. Her wonders beset us all. Have ye lost the path?"

"Goodman Cobb, my path has been righteous. I was not beloved in my crossing and not accepted for a deficit of piety. I walked. My spirit now is full, and I wish to all good. My forward choice is unknown."

"I fear ye gone wild and away from the path. You were made townsman on your benefit, a vote for the future. You have disregard of destiny for the wonder we create."

"To all, I abide great sentiment. The world is larger, though we deny it. I harbor nothing ill. I find these Natives peaceful and soothing."

"I fear your destiny."

"Tell Goodwife Collins I remember her well and pray for her best, and tell the colony we would be frozen corpses without the skills and industry of these people."

Every statement of Cobb was a wounding reminder of all he loathed of Plimouth. The piousness. The certainty of righteous resolve. The cowardice of communal progress to no known end except domination of thought. He knew he was gone to a greater thing—gone to his people, and the people were not in Plimouth.

★   ★   ★

Caleb and Annawan, along with their carriers of great goods, left the bordering woods and knew joy on the last leg to the Village. The large bags they bulled in and the promise of trade canoes soon arriving came to a scene of thanksgiving. The homecoming on the village hummock overlooking the tidal river was raucous and playful. A feast. Drumming. Dances. A pile of wampum mounding like a small snowdrift was spread on a large deer skin for all to see. It was beyond thanks for one year, at the very least—with the harvest, the pilot whale kill, and outstanding trade—all was at ease. A good life with no suffering was promised for a long while. Grain beyond winter need. Iron tools for spring planting. Root vegetables for stout sustenance. Weapons for defense. Cloth for conversion to clothing. Wampum for any trade ongoing. It was strong in the moment.

Yet Caleb was withdrawn.

In the *wetu,* with his beloved Wetamu nestled on his shoulder, Caleb shuddered with a fear.

He felt himself more at one with these new, natural people than anywhere else. Each day unfurled in a real welcome of being and calm. His eyes darted to find the anxiety and fear of recrimination that beset his Plimouth experience. He could not find it. People and families here had occasional flare-ups, sometimes from drinking fermentations of pumpkin or fruits, but did not constantly quarrel, resent, or conspire to disrupt. Every action seemed to call for harmony even from the most offended. Petty pilfering. Adultery. Inheritance squabbles. The few Caleb saw, barely understanding the issues, were solved in a seemingly ancient way all accepted.

It came to him. There was no question in his mind. He had "gone native." There was no going back to Plimouth as it is and would likely always be.

Everything was complex in Caleb's turbulent, young mind. What was to come? He had heard plenty.

✳   ✳   ✳

Plimouth and the Bay Colony may have wished dominance of the history of colonization for their pride. Caleb knew it not true. He suspected differently. From Aptucxet scoundrels, coastal traders, wayfaring settlers cut loose of colonies they hated, they told stories of colonies far more fantastic that were eerily believable. Plimouth was a blip born to be myth. It was not the real story. It was happening elsewhere. Where? From the eastern coast of Florida in the 1500s, the Spaniards did conquest with vengeance against natives first. History went to Virginia. The Jamestown debacle—at first, lost itself—was a horror, to become a victory of blood won with disastrous, relentless and violent retribution against savages over time. The New Amsterdam story had hollow words of equal settlement promised to all, but it was the indigenous who were wiped out. He heard every tale. He knew wrong things were happening, but inevitable. He thought into the early sunrise and cried.

Plimouth was tame ground. The beauty of Misquantum, Squanto, validated by Massasoit, created a peace that gave survival to Plimouth. Yet, the idea of a Plimouth townsmen settler, Caleb, and a full-blooded Wampanoag, Wetamu, marrying was a concept not accepted in Plimouth. Caleb was clever. He had an idea. He heard tales. Actually, it could be sanctioned by church, by a congregation, certainly not all. If Wetamu agreed, it would not be sanctioned by public opinion in Plimouth, but, perhaps, elsewhere. It was a folly, but maybe not.

The Pilgrims and Puritans were nasty fools, always drab-clad. The ministers were white-bibbed, falsely pious conquerors when in officious garb. Bigots. Almighty, temporal, and unholy—religious, but not spiritual. They were unforgiving in their control; cloaked in righteousness. Salem was to prove that later with unaccountable shame. They were beyond self-understanding of their lustful will to steal a country from Natives for gain draped in God's name. They were totally oily in their denial of blame in the name of God's glory. They coveted for glory – their own. Nothing good was going to happen. Caleb saw it, limited as an unschooled lad may be. A relentless tide was afoot. His newly found "people," small in number, decimated by foul European germs, frightful of the guns, were doomed. He wept, tears falling on Wetamu's hair.

"Habbamock!" Caleb called over a slight wind to the *sachem* standing yards away watching sunrise on the sand spit.

"K-lib!" the chief called back smiling, awaiting his hug.

Talk between them was no longer an issue. Caleb knew the tongue in a weird way. He could only speak as a six-year old from his time, but his time with the tribe put him in situations where he heard vocabulary far beyond a child. It was a mix. Caleb could express the pronoun universe—I, he, she, we, they—and follow with many verbs—want, need, love, hate, seek. That established, he could use common gestures he and Habbamock adopted to express absence of language. It was sophisticated.

"My brother," Habbamock said as they embraced. "Why here?"

"You and I. Alone."

Habbamock nodded and looked to the sea.

"I want to marry Wetamu," Caleb said in Wampanoag.

"I know that. We all know that. Your *wetu* speaks."

"I am not tribe. Is this accepted?" Caleb said in the tongue.

"I will think on it for both of you. Such a marriage is not common."

"I know nothing of tribe marriage. What must I know?"

"It is not complicated, but serious. When do you wish?"

"In spring, after wintering and the hunts."

"Is it our ceremony or yours?

"I am Wampanoag in my heart," Caleb said with resolve. "The answer is both."

Habbamock waved his hands in front of his face. Their sign: *I do not understand.*

Caleb waved the same way back to him. It was complicated.

He started to turn from the *sachem* but said back over his shoulder, "It's to make Wetamu safer. A person with rights." His tongue could not hash to communicate all, but he knew Wampanoag for "safer."

Habbamock simply nodded. "Say nothing until I teach you our ways."

*   *   *

The winter move for the tribe was handled seamlessly. It was ancient and practiced. The distance was only two miles inland to a forested grove in a leeward depression by a small lake and away from the ocean wind. Perfect in nature. The summer "root cellars" full of corn, sundried vegetables, smoked, dried, and salted meats were emptied. The summer encampment was cleansed by sage ritual and closed down with attention to winter maintenance. All clothing, necessary mats, cooking vessels, and utensils were moved. The winter site had two *wetu nush,* longhouses, allotted to the two represented clans. They were oval and 150 feet long. The matrilineal clans were separated, but not in any way opposed. The longhouses were surrounded in a total circle by a wooden, palisade stake wall. It was practiced winter domesticity.

*   *   *

Before leaving, with Habbamock's teaching, Caleb followed protocol. Wetamu's parents died of the plagues just after her birth. He asked her guardian, her clan, and the community for marriage to Wetamu. No problems at first. He paid a dowry considered very generous. He had wampum, a currency that confused him, but he knew it was "money." There was a small feast with Habbamock to announce the intentions before leaving summer camp.

What followed was some bickering and emotion beyond his linguistic skills. Caleb had no standing in the tribe for property or resource rights. Wetamu was owner of her family land, food stores, and *wetu*. That was known. His only contribution was as a good, productive soul. People wondered how property would transfer in marriage if married to a settler. They wanted their ways. No book was written. It had never happened, marriage to a settler. It was uncharted territory. Habbamock listened and gave all their say. He spoke.

"All is different than we ever thought it would be. It is hard to think the Great Spirit would leave us, but Great Spirit has hidden the intentions. We no longer know how to be among new people who have come and will come. Look for new guidance. K-lib is the best of them. He will always do the right thing."

The *sachem* had spoken. The people unified then in ancient ways of cooperation. Everything was changing, they knew. The winds had not brought all to them yet, but they sensed it. New settlement on ancient sites, land taken, a foreign society exerting relentless muscle in the face of their decimated weakness. They assented with faith.

Wintering that year on the interior Cape was god-gifted— mild, an occasional nor'easter blizzard storm to remind them, but gentle overall. The tribe was protected in their compound from crazy storms. The hunts had been productive with raccoon, beaver, deer, turkey, and one moose. There was no hunger or disease. The longhouses were filled with story-telling, song, dancing, weaving, and tool-making. The Spring New Year ceremony arrived. It was time to head back to the hummock on the salt marsh, to the *wetus,* to planting and fishing and the coming marriage.

*   *   *

A very dark and sorrowful cloud filled with death and dissolution for natives of whatever tribe was afoot in the region. The troubles started years before but accelerated in 1636. It stemmed, like most things, from commercial interests. In this case, it was the fur trade. The Pequots of the Connecticut River Valley were an aggressive, warrior tribe. They pushed the Wampanoags, Narragansett, Mohegans, and Algonquians back from lands to gain control of the fur trade both with the Dutch in the south and the English to the north. The intrigues were too many with too many enemies. All unraveled as the Pequots brought the wrath of God on themselves through venial, violent raids on settler villages, Indian villages and traders. They had no friends and burned all bridges. A force was sent to destroy them that was three-quarters Natives.

The Wampanoags, like most tribes, had runners. The men were chosen for their athleticism, endurance, and character. They could easily cover forty miles, much farther if needed, in a day. They brought news a force had been raised, including Wampanoags from elsewhere, that marched against the Pequots. The forces torched their main fortress at Mystick in a genocidal frenzy and continued to kill on the withdrawal. It was a continuing massacre. There were a few survivors then sold to slavery or moved to household servitude. The mighty Pequots were declared extinct as an entity—that quickly, that soon.

The news did not change the rhythms of seasonal rebirth on the salt marsh. *Wetus* were restored. Raised planting beds to honor the belly of pregnant earth were fertilized and seeds planted. Fishing for spring fish migrations resumed on the winter-chilled waters. A marriage was afoot and the celebration planned.

On the day, Caleb and Wetamu went separately to the nearby pond to cleanse themselves in nature. They donned traditional doeskin garb made by Caleb in the winter, adorned with beads and shells. Habbamock called the community. There was a pipe-bearer with tobacco. A background drum beat a deeply resonant rhythm. When Caleb saw Wetamu, his heart and soul bounded. She was a beauty not of this earth. He knew her body naked and lithe and found her the most beautiful doe in the forest. Her mocha skin and almond eyes of deepest brown with an oval face were more than he deserved. He thought himself blotchy and clunky. Somehow, she did not.

Habbamock invoked the Great Spirit, Kiehtan, to be present. He asked her guardian and clan for blessings for the couple. They assented. He reminded the couple pre-marital cohabitation was sanctioned, but future infidelity was an unpardonable taboo. The pipe was lit. First to Habbamock, then to Wetamu and to Caleb. The festivities began and were joyous. Special stews, spit-roasted, prime-cut meats, cornmeal berry slumps, singing and dancing. There were many jokes on Caleb being a "white Wampanoag." If there was any discomfort, it never showed. As much as he loved them, they loved him too and were proud to have him.

In the days following, the "ways" were colliding for better and worse. It was inevitable in a rapidly changing world. Painful.

Caleb was training young Petonowit in the leather trade business. Caleb kept precise records of last year's production of fur pelts, cured hides, leggings, tunics, shawls, and coats. He created a list of how many deer, beaver, bear, and raccoon pelts they needed to match it and showed it to the teen. Petonowit's slowly arising dismay struck Caleb like a hammer. He was not about growth. The deer people. The beaver people. The bear people. The tree people. The cloud people. The bee people. The ant people. They were not numbers. They were life and people of their own kind. Caleb tossed the list. Whatever came, came. In a part of his mind, it was a shame. We, my people here, could be big. He knew that was not their way.

He sought Habbamock. They met on the spit with an embrace.

"I know your problem, K-Lib. It must be frustrating." Habbamock used a frenzied, side-to-side tearing motion with his hands for "frustration."

"No, *Sachem*. The Wampanoag way is pure, but it doesn't know what is coming. I lived in one, single town with many, many more people than all Wampanoags. There are many, many towns like it, too many, all over the foreign land. Many of them want to come here. They will never stop."

"You are not wrong, K-Lib, in teaching Petonowit. I know. I see the value of strong trade for us. We are confused by the sacredness of an animal kill and its trade value. We love the wampum but have a shame at the gain."

"I will no longer ask for kills for trade. I will take it as it comes."

"For now, best. I have experienced omens. I know your truth is pure."

⋆   ⋆   ⋆

Caleb had an unsettled but firm idea from his first knowing of wanting We-tamu in marriage. It was bold, unimaginable really, but based on real stories. He wanted her to have standing in the colonial legal world like a few other Native women in distant colonies. He knew little of it, but he knew "legal" was a gripping concept even with his naiveté. He knew the English to be ridiculous over "legal."

During the winter in the *wetu nush,* he had taken his walking to Sandwich. A Congregational church was starting but not fully formed. Caleb knew nothing of one church from another, but knew the Plimouth colonists' or the sterner Bay colonists' religious beliefs held nothing for him. He only knew from Aptucxet that the Congregationalists were freer and open. The people within were pushed out of settlement religions in their beliefs of a loving, open God.

Brushing snow from his doeskins, he knocked on the door of a small cabin. Two rooms—one larger with seating for a small group.

A man answered. "Welcome, traveler. Come in. Beset ye the cold behind ye."

They settled in a room cozy with a hearth fire. A bark tea simmering in a side pot was brought. Caleb wasted no time.

"I have come, Preacher, to ask a Christian favor, though Christ is not my savior."

"Your name?

"Caleb Farker of the Plimouth Colony.

"I have heard of ye, the walker and trader. You are known. Prithee, do ye have a belief? I heard not."

"I do."

"What is it?"

"There is only one Great Spirit. Religions divide, but the Great Spirit lives in us despite it."

"Ye are heretical and out of sorts with the times."

"Not with you, Preacher. Ye and I understand. That is why I traveled fifteen miles in the snow."

They both smiled.

"So what do you seek?"

"I will be the husband of Wetamu by Wampanoag marriage in spring. I also seek to marry Wetamu in a marriage sanctioned by the colony."

"I am not sure this has been done."

"I know that, but your congregation can sanction it. That is my belief from uneducated thoughts. The power of God is within your congregation, not dictated by others."

"True, but I must consult our small following. Are ye a worthy person? Ye arrive from afar asking strange things."

"I will reveal all. Please, let me get more wood for the fire."

Caleb did.

Caleb told it starkly real. He told his leaving Brighton with theft and shame. He wept at his low status on the boat and a painful climb to Plimouth recognition. He waxed about his walking as a passion. He confessed finding his Wampanoag people and experiencing love and acceptance. He told it with tears and steadfast resolve, no word untrue.

"I will consult for our common will here under God. If sanctioned, I will marry you and Wetamu with powers vested in me."

"When is the decision?"

"Tuesday morning."

"Can ye laugh, Preacher?"

"About what?"

"I will have a runner here taking your decision the same day to me—true, at your doorstep, twelve noon. The Wampanoags are amazing. I beg the understanding of your office. Godspeed."

Caleb walked the path home in a pleasant, light-falling snow, relieved, hopeful, and confused. He wondered most what the marriage of he and Wetamu on a colony civic register would mean. He could not know. So much was not fathomed. Two societies, one dying, the other growing, with little understanding. He shrugged his shoulders while striding. *Can't hurt.*

He awaited Tuesday afternoon in peace. All talk was about the return to the hummock. The children were the most antsy. *Wetu nush* life had too many stories and not enough play. They wanted shoreline freedom. Caleb wanted the privacy of the *wetu* with his soon-to-be wife.

The runner, Nanapashemet, arrived. Habbamock, at Caleb's request, had dispatched him. He carried no fatigue from his travels. He quickly gathered himself and delivered a message from his sack. Caleb unfolded the parchment with boldly written, scratch-ink pen:

"The Congregational Church of Sandwich to be under Plimouth Colony Charter and Mayflower Compact as of 1638, but now functioning as a sanctioned First Church, accede to the marriage of freeman Caleb Farker of the Plimouth colony and Wetamu of the sovereign Wampanoag tribe at a time of your choosing. At the ceremony, there must be four witnesses. For the civil record, I recommend at least two settlers."

His plan had happened, whatever it meant. He asked counsel with Habbamock with Wetamu by his side.

"Wetamu and I can marry in a settler legal ceremony," Caleb informed them.

"Why, K-Lib?" the *sachem* asked.

"I fear the future, father. You know many things about your world. I know another world. There are so many people. They will come year after year. They do not know our ways. They do not respect them. I want Wetamu to have her name known to that order."

"Why?"

"I am not sure, but Aptucxet stories say it can be helpful in that world."

"Your thoughts, Wetamu?" Habbamock asked.

"I am sad. I am happy for my near-husband but sad. There is so much change we don't understand. K-Lib and you talk even though he is childlike in our language. We share a *wetu*. We talk as deeply, too, in funny ways. I know K-Lib's heart is with us. I cannot believe the world beyond of which he speaks. None of our stories talk about it, but you knew, Habbamock. You and all the Wampanoag *sachems* knew bad things were coming—from visions, councils, visitors. You protected us because you did not know what to do. There was nothing to do. Nothing stops a bad storm. If K-lib thinks this settler marriage is helpful, I go to it with all my heart."

Habbamock took a pause that each of his followers felt as an almost imperceptible display of emotion. It was not his way.

"Of course, I knew. The foreign people brought death. At first, we did not understand. We thought bad spirit for our failings. When all *sachems* spoke as one, we knew foreign people brought bad spirit and unbelievable death. No warriors were necessary. Just share a pipe or breathe their air, and we died by thousands. All was dark. Then K-Lib comes from the forest. He was so goofy, it was a joy. He made us see. He was a link to things we did not know, and we prospered. I go to it with all my heart. K-Lib, who are your witnesses?"

"I know my tribe is here. I will have to travel for the rest."

★ ★ ★

Caleb, now married in Wampanoag ceremony in summer camp, went afoot for settler witnesses. His first stop was Aptucxet. Caleb was a profitable mainstay there. He had shown his honesty and trading prowess for years. The post manager was a friend known to be familiar with the drink. Caleb entered the empty post.

"Goodman Lester, how goeth the battle?"

"Goodman Farker, had no keen there was one."

"I have a favor to ask and your shut-up."

"Interesting, but not sold."

"Hear it out."

"Tell!"

"I am marrying a Wampanoag. I need ye in a hike to Sandwich, for which I will pay ye, to witness my marriage."

"How much?"

Caleb pulled generous wampum from his shoulder sack.

"I am there, Pilgrim. I have no slump with the Natives. Give me the details."

Caleb walked north on a path familiar to him to the Plimouth colony. He had not set foot there for a year and a half. He was a different person now with no need for deference and less need for pride. His doeskin garb was rich in style.

Much was the same in Plimouth, but some improvements were evident. The well was better fortified with new sheltering. The meeting hall was expanded and refurbished. The few Pilgrims outdoors barely looked askance as he walked with purpose to the hut of Goodwife Collins.

He called out:

"Goodwife, are you there?"

He heard a shuffle within the hut and saw a hand pull back the door blanket.

"The Lord bestows," she cried out. "Caleb of the wandering people. Come in."

He entered the hovel where all was familiar, nothing different. Her hearth had a side pot of tea which she quickly poured.

They sat on a small bench next to each other. It was the only seating available.

"I come to ask a favor of ye, Goodwife. Not of a kind ye will be familiar."

"Why thinketh I different? Ye never were cut to our belief."

"True."

"With glory to God, ye have made a name for yourself as a heathen. Is that true?

"True."

"Why, child of Christ? Born to salvation?"

"Because other people love and honor the same spirit in a different name. Their spirit is the same and not punishing."

"Ye worship a different God?"

"I worship the same God. There is only one for all people."

"What asketh ye of me?"

"I asketh that ye, Goodwife Collins, witness a wedding in Sandwich at the founding Congregational Church, where they have sanctioned a wedding between me and Wetamu, a Wampanoag maiden."

The woman hunched over and prayed.

"It is too much for my simple life," she said

"No, it is too simple for your good life," Caleb coaxed.

"I cannot abide. No history honors this."

"Ye are here, now, Goodwife. We make history in this land. Have ye passion against the Natives?"

"No, but they frighten me."

"Do I frighten you?"

"Never for a moment."

"I, Goodwife Collins, am the same as them."

All came to a halt in the moment. The hut and all it meant to be in the colony flooded her brain. The years of scratching survival to simply exist from nothing came back to her. Her sense that the settlement had finally made it but only after so much initial loss turned the Goodwife's thoughts. The Natives had been distant but good friends. That much she knew. They thrived in a peace of which other colonies knew not.

"I am a fool but will witness. I warn ye women are not much of governing account here. My witness may be of question."

"I thinketh not. From Plimouth meetings, I know ye have legal right to sign certain contracts, sustain inheritance, and own property. Ye are a friend true."

Caleb hugged her on the bench. He wondered on the potential troubles her decision might trigger.

"I shareth with ye a sense of the Wampanoags. In many villages, women are *sachems*, tribal leaders. In all cases, property flows from mother to daughter, not father to son."

"Can I join?" she laughed heartily along with Caleb, her few teeth bobbing with guffaws in her jaw. "Tell me."

"We will marry on the New Moon of May fourth in Sandwich at the site of the Congregational Church. It is an easy walk, but long, Goodwife. Probably a day, maybe six hours. I know you to be hale and feisty, but I knoweth I ask much. Please accept this doeskin tunic for your good heart."

"The Goodwife would do it for no regard," she said as she unfurled a tunic of fashion and passion, festooned with colorful shells and dappled with gems. "The piece is a creation of God, the Creator and Almighty. Your work is coveted and known to be inspired. We all see it, know it, buy it. Every garment fits like a glove of love. Your "God" is unknown, and it troubles us here. Ye say we are, all of us, struggling in this land—one. I will tell you, Caleb Farker, we are small, and ye are large."

"A runner, Annawan, will come for ye outside the Village by the cornfields. He speaks some English. He will guide ye gently to Sandwich. Walk well. I have arranged comfort for your stay. Stay as ye wish until you feel the journey back to Plimouth sensible."

"Crazy fool, Caleb. Taken away by a savage on an overnight journey. That is not of our stuff. The Lord here offended, but I am old enough to abide the new. Nothing was as promised. All is what we make. I quake."

Habbamock, Wetamu, her guardian, and Caleb arrived after a long walking to Sandwich in the morning hours on the New Moon. Goodman Lester and Goodwife Collins, the Goodwife resplendent in her new tunic, stood speaking before the "church." Preacher Braddock bade all welcome and invited them inside.

Caleb did introductions among the parties. It was a nervous moment. Goodman and Goodwife had never met a *sachem,* one who stood solemn, stoic, observing, and in command of his thoughts. They had never met a free, beautiful, heathen woman who stood strong in her marriage dressage. Caleb sensed the awe of the colonists and knew it as his own. Ancient wisdom, patience, and wild freedom were right before them. The Indians were gracious and reserved in their greetings, Habbamock nodding tribute and Wetamu smiling to their souls.

The ceremony was brief, but wordy about husband/wife things that flew in the face of the reality of K-Lib and Wetamu. No, she was not bound to her husband's will. No, she would not obey and please. Yes, they would love and honor. Caleb knew Habbamock did not understand every word but caught him with a smile on his face at times. They nodded in conspiring at the insanity—almost laughed.

Preacher Braddock produced the papers for the couple and witnesses to sign. Caleb signed for Wetamu (wife), Habbamock (*sachem*) and guardian instructing them to put an "X" after their names. Goodman Lester signed with flourish. Goodwife Collins hesitated.

"Let the God of us all make this worthy," and she signed.

Caleb quickly translated and they all, Preacher Braddock and Habbamock included, laughed with understanding. Upon leaving Sandwich, Caleb confessed to his travelers he knew not what was accomplished. He said simply:

"Wetamu is known in the coming world. She has standing."

★   ★   ★

The rest is beyond sad in the short days after.

The massacre of the Pequot at their Mystick encampment was followed by the frenzied, brutal, withdrawal killings by colonists and Indian allies. It was savage and lasted months. The Pequot were not beloved, but they were people surviving in their way. No more. Killing frenzy does not subside easily. It lives among the doers because to let it die means to live with the disgust in their souls. Keep on it. Anything—rum-crazed drink, talk of "brave" life-taking, continuing the "higher purpose"—was better than confronting ghastly slaughter. Yet another galleon had set sail from Mystick, north along the Sound, past the Cuttyhunks, seeking Pequot survivors to enslave or kill.

As it entered the bay by the tidal settlement, everything said "bad" about it. It was not festooned with color on sails or sailors waving. The ship meant no good.

Three long boats were dispatched to the shore, each of twelve men. They were armed. Thanks to historical sensibilities, the Wampanoags had mustered two dozen armed braves themselves to meet them.

Habbamock, Caleb, and all warriors gathered as the long boat crews pulled up on the sand.

"Greetings," their drunken, tottering leader said, eyes rimmed red. "Do you harbor fleeing Pequots here?"

"No," Habbamock said. "Ye have killed and enslaved them all."

Caleb was astounded. His English was perfect.

"We command to see your Village."

"No!"

"We do it under charter. Do ye defy the King?"

"Ye are a fool besot with drink and out of your territory. Leave!" Habbamock said with uncanny precision.

As moments of history happen, the next was tragic.

The longboat captain made a motion to withdraw. A drunken sailor took it as a sign to fire.

His flintlock ball hit Habbamock in the chest, yet he stood, shocked but stand-still.

A hail of arrows and a fusillade of newly acquired weapons launched as angry crows drove deeply into the confused boatmen. So many of the birds were mortal. Confused gunfire erupted, all of no impact. The mixed crew of English and Indians ran to their boats. They suffered more arrows and powder ball in painful retreat. The galleon crew was routed, running as misplaced fools in a nightmare. The skirmish was never reported in history, even with sixteen dead from the galleon pulled far upshore and left to rot on the beach to crabs— —only one Indian.

The colonial governments desperately wanted no more unrest and bad publicity and it was unrecorded to history. The galleon was without charter and toxic—but it was deadly to the hummock community.

Habbamock was mortally injured. All could see. They laid him down. The blood was copious. Every compress of seaweed at the shore was inadequate.

He called in a weakening voice for K-Lib.

"I have seen bear and moose and elk like me." He coughed some blood. "Dying. Pray, my brother."

Caleb did with a passion he did not know ever existed.

"Please, Kiehtan, please," Caleb sobbed. It was deep, sorrowful, and beyond his grief.

Habbamock passed on the beach, the *sachem* gone, all disrupted, never to be the same.

K-Lib had, in his mind, little standing in the funereal rights of their righteous leader. Yet all, both clans, somehow knew he had a say in the spirit of the *sachem*. They were as bereft and in sorrowful commitment as he and Wetamu. He did his best, guided by Wetamu with humility and sorrow, though he felt himself completely unworthy. The bereaved tribe listened.

"We will bury Habbamock on the bluff across from our hummock on the mat he last slept, with the bowl from which he last ate, with our faces blackened by charcoal in sorrow. We will hang his *sachem* robe on the nearby tree. It is a sacred point that overlooks us." That was all.

Wetamu told him it was the exact way.

★   ★   ★

That is the story. It was the place the bones of Habbamock were disinterred in the Village, 296 years later for a mansion. They were reburied one hundred yards away with no ceremony of memory.

K-Lib and Wetamu lived a Wampanoag life with children, a girl and two boys. All survived the bad times soon enough to come in the Prince Phillip Wars. The tides were always against the Wampanoags—"people of first light." Impossible odds. It never got better. The family did live, love, and prosper in dignity on the peninsula with K-Lib's skills and Wetamu's wedding standing and enduring charm. A walker and a heathen were fulfilled as best allowed in a changing time.

1923–The Rum Shooting

In the early 1920's, the local newspaper reported in a 4x6 dispatch an accidental shooting death in a cottage on the shore of the salt marsh bordering the nearby Village. In handing a self-cocking gun, butt first, to his partner, Alistair Keane was shot in the chest by Josephine Cleary. Keane lived long enough to confirm it was an unfortunate accident. An inquest was to be held in Buzzard's Bay.

*   *   *

The shooting event was tragic, ghastly, and suspect all at once for a place that knew little of violent death. There was likely no good coming from an inquest. The man was dead; he cleared the shooter. Case closed, nothing to prove or dispute. The relationship between Keane and Cleary was already unsettling in the tiny Village's understanding. It was awash in romance, willfulness, defiance, and love. The pair was not in keeping with the evolving, powerful spirituality of the natural Village spaces for calm and mindful, ecumenical Christian development.

The Village plot was purchased by an open-minded Christian group in 1871 from the Perry boys. It was useless to the Perry clan for farming, not much better for grazing, but it was beautiful beyond description for human peacefulness. The land deed for the 240 acre plot was its own tiny peninsula within the peninsula. It was bordered by salt marsh, ocean, and ponds, with each of the landscapes being a visible treat.

The Christian group launched well-attended camp meetings with a large prayer tent and quaint side-tents for visitors' dwellings in its center. They summoned the best of preachers and enlightened intellects of the region. A clapboard hotel stood at the green's south end, offering additional accommodation to vacationers and the new crowd of religious folk. The Village became a mecca of summer revival in the region.

Keane and Cleary were odd ones in paradise and made little attempt to hide it. Living in sin, they were a taboo. The two were the handsomest pair whoever walked the Village, sometimes irritating, too. They both had chips on their shoulders probably borne of bad decisions and self-inflicted inferiority. The source of it was unknown because their history, singularly or together, was sparse. They were seen as immensely kind, helpful, and charming one moment and resentful and chiding the next. Why have this untidy vibe in a place of peace? The Village was a summer place with, maybe, twelve weeks of keen activity until September. The rest was an off-season with scraping and scratching to survive. The answers hid in the long interlude.

To the simple, a gunshot felled a relationship many citizens felt doomed but secretly envied in its outrageous passion. The relationship was a game played way above their heads and not to be easily understood. Each, Al and Joe, had hang-on admirers from the beginning—some for one, some for the other, many for both, although they each could spit occasional poison and then apologize with charm.

Being of the Village, the denizens, mostly Christian summer people, a sparse few of them year-round and all sea savvy, knew tides. They knew high and low, when to launch a boat, when to oyster or clam, when the full moon may swamp the Village low road. They knew Al and Joe to be tidal people on the flats. There was ebb and flow, mostly gentle, and then storm-driven tides when the ocean was packing the marsh and bottling it up. The two lived in the cabin on the marsh where the tides mattered. They were on the edge of it.

Al and Joe's time had precursors, many for certain, but one was no small minnow in the shallows. Some embrace the concept of destiny. A slew of others think nothing of it at all. Why, in a time and place, do two indomitable, star-crossed people intersect and intertwine? It is clearly the Divine Perfection, something too strange to contemplate. The universe grinds on to natural laws.

It is perfect, not in fairness, only in that it is all that it can be in the moment, the sum total of all events. Al and Joe were that; the sum total of all events.

A new, unforeseen force had risen from the coastal waters that made the peninsula a "hot house petunia." Polite discussion refrained, but Prohibition was now the law of the land, and the entire peninsula was a natural magnet for booze.

Known as the "noble experiment" to reduce crime, spousal abuse, and solve social problems, Prohibition had deep traction from a Temperance movement dating back to 1830s. The U.S. nation always was a haven for zealots: religious ones, exiled ones, profiteers, and adventurers. The religious, however, had their dominating way and say. The Volstead Act of 1920 finally made it constitutional that the "manufacture, distribution and sale of alcohol" was illegal. The larger populace did not agree much, but sagged to righteousness. True, most said, some took booze too far, but most did not. The bare-faced result was years of corrupt, booze-running chaos that reigned nationally. It was far greater than abuse of the substance itself.

The generous coastal inlets of the peninsula were a perfect maze for illicit commerce. There were rum-runners and bootleggers. On the coast, the general term was "smugglers," but the operations were more complex. "Runners" bought and ran liquor to at-sea, drop-off people who had ways to shore, and "leggers" did the land-based distribution. It was not always that simple, but folks doing it knew the differences.

The runners brought it offshore to near Cape Cod by boat from all over––the Caribbean, Canada, and Europe. Captain Bill McCoy ran Rum Row, often off Nantucket, but also up and down the Atlantic, too, with near imp-unity. He was no slouch in intellect or taste. Top notch, clean whiskies, scotches, premium rum, and wines were his specialty.

He was handsome, educated, nautically trained, and thought himself a Sam Adam patriot fighting constitutional stupidity. Unseemly as this trade was, he never was to bribe the law, coerce the leggers or get involved with gangsters. The term, "the Real McCoy" most probably did not originate with him. It had deeper history, but in Prohibition, everyone knew the term. His booze was exquisite and never adulterated. In many a speakeasy along the east coast, a heartfelt toast to the "Real McCoy" was shared with a "huzzah."

The offshore Cape peninsula was perfect as a station. It was jutting into the sea, with hundreds of harbors, coves and inlets hard to monitor. The region had a flotilla of tough fishermen looking for winter cash. McCoy had many locals with boats, secret inlets, and "hidey holes" all wrapped up. In the words of a Cape Cod matron onshore to a reporter: "The blinking on and off of boat lights comin' in for drops was like fireflies in July. Booze coming in with a waitin' line."

"Drops" at Waquoit, Popponessett Beach, Cotuit, Point Isabella, East Bay, Centerville, the town dock in Hyannis, Hyannisport, Parket's Neck, and Harwichport were Coast Guard-documented in the mid-Cape. There was no place up or down Cape that was not used. There was no way to police the entry with a big ocean, intricate hook-ups to transfer at sea and hundreds of local boat captains looking for extra cash.

The peninsula was barren in winter with uncounted summer homes shuttered permanently for the harsh season. The runners were directed to slide to the coves and navigable marshes and deliver pallets to cottages and grandiose mansions with their locks politely picked. They would not be opened until Memorial Day at the earliest. The finest and less fine houses were free storage for booze with owners never knowing it. The owners occasionally questioned stamped out cigarettes on the floor and an occasional tossed bottle, figuring an interloper happened by. Few, if any, thought themselves a cache house.

The leggers had to distribute it, and there was no lack of demand. By far, the drops were not for the peninsula alone, although the Cape had a hollow leg for drinking. The cases went up and down the east coast to speakeasies and private stock with a fear supply could crumble. People loved their drink and thumbed their noses at the ridiculous notion of constitutional barriers to get soused or, at least, easy of mind.

The Village with the pliable, salt river marsh on the right flank was long understood as a premier drop off. The Village itself had no complicity but, like the rest of the nation, there had been an unwritten covenant, unbeknownst even to God, since Prohibition. It was this: We will sit on our porches or verandas at end of day and have cocktails. We will strive not to abuse, but screw you if you try to tarry with the pleasure. The Volstead Act of 1920 was a major insult and few held prejudice for those trying to make a living if it kept gin and tonics flowing.

Many wanted to pin the liquor flood through the peninsula on Joe Kennedy. They never could or did, mainly because it never happened. Ol' Joe wasn't the man. It was Bill McCoy and the Nantucket Rum Row that were sure as a tide in all seasons. He was the real deal; his network delivered the goods. That much was known by the Coast Guard, the constables, and the populace. No secrets, but it was damn hard to cover and prosecute as he feasted on the marsh-scapes of Cape Cod.

It was fertile ground for the forlorn and wayward such as Al and Joe with histories to lose and guilts to expunge.

Al had, truth be known, been dumped on the Village or near it. He was puking and drunk when his WWI buddies threw him from the car. It was a 1918 Pierce-Arrow, gifted to his war-torn son, a trench buddy of Al, by a Lowell industrialist father hoping to get the boy on track. The roads were iffy on the Cape—a lot of dust and gravel in the day. Their journey was but a wandering of war mates to New England byways. The peninsula was no more than a bumpy lark to forget. Al was too much.

He was too much nightmare, too much feeling, too much of what they were trying to escape. Drunk and puking, they wanted no more of him and left him above the tideline on the sands of the marsh by the Village.

"Gotta leave him," Big Moke said to Quick Eddy and Lucky Joe. "He can't take a city or a lot a people. Maybe the sea will make sense. I tell ya, we gotta do it. We ain't worth shit to him. Got me? What a goddam soldier! He saved all of us time and again! We gotta save him."

They did. Al awoke on damp sand in 1920 with sand grains pressed on his cheeks and a coating of sand like a sugar-rolled donut all over his clothing with seventy-five dollars pinned by a Silver Cross to his chest to afford him dignity. Seventy-five dollars was big, large for a starting. They were good men who knew.

Al came out of WW I nearly catatonic, but no one knew "battle fatigue," and he had it for sure. Al had enough medals to forge a chain-mail vest worthy of a knight. Campaign medals, service medals, bronze star, silver star (two), and purple heart (three), and a Medal of Honor under inquiry. It seemed unreal to him because he had only fought to stay alive and protect friends. He had seen more than he ever wanted to know about human stupidity, and his body told every truth. It was compromised with metal frags, though his face was pure and vibrant as "Danny Boy."

He carried the metal in his body and, unfortunately, a big snort of mustard gas that hit a brief second before he could don a gas mask. The mustard gas was a nasty, lethal, destructive puff. No easy breathing came after, no matter how pure, refined, or natural. It was never the same after for unbothered breathing. He had a cough nothing could heal, yet he soldiered on denying it.

He had suffered the waste of brave souls on both sides. He saw American, allied, and Bosch dead in heaps that amounted to nothing he could decipher. He chose to keep killing as best he could to stay alive. There was no purpose he could discern. God had abandoned all.

At the time he fell by the Village by the decision of friends, he had no belief in anything but a laughing, leering, vengeful God that offered no redemption from the killing of charging men from trenches. What God did that? Who could conceive the carnage of brave men mangled and dead for purposes barely defined? He collected a belt buckle off a Bosch corpse: *Gott Sei Bei Uns* was imprinted. "God is with us." Al did not thinks so, nor on similar words on his own paraphernalia, in English, "God is with us" either.

Alistair was not a violent soul by nature, but may be now, perhaps, he thought. Maybe he became one.

He came from a family with a stone-cold, drunken father emigrated from Ireland to Boston. The "affliction" crossed the Atlantic boundary with the man and the man never made an admirable lick of himself. He had an engaging, small charm to give hope, but then he would steal it away like a magician's trick, pulling table cloths under table settings—enough to hope, not enough to trust.

His Gaelic pop could show just enough love that Al could adore him—no one better at Christmas, Easter, birthdays—and then the man could turn mean with drink and frustration. Al was a confused, feeling kid, always uprooted because of wanting. He always hoped and got disappointed. He was shocked by physical cuffing and belt work for no reason. What had he done? He loved his pop and hated him. He only ever wondered what he, himself, did wrong, but he knew for sure he was no good.

His mother prayed the rosary beads. She wore them dangerously thin; "them" being made of soft pinewood from a Portuguese holy site. The beads grew thinner. She was seeking relief that never came. There was routine—best meals, clean laundry, tidy house—that was good enough to avoid the anger most of the time. Pop's anger came from a source undefined and deep—ancient resentments, frustration with his drink, and could not be soothed. He viewed his father as a dog on a short leash, chained to a post, barking at the sky in his alcoholism.

Tough. Tough was the word. Be tough. Act tough. Ignore the pain of the household where your barely employed and mercurial father ruled with random abuse. Carry the pride.

Al never got that, never felt it. What pride? He did not know the pride. Just don't let others know there was hell in the kitchen. That was the hell, being forever dishonest and silent. It did not play well in his mind. He wanted to tell his story. No one cared. No one asked. Ever. He enlisted at eighteen, without passion – but to get away - and became, probably from genes, a killer soldier. He was crafty, gifted and lethal.

Al awoke wanting to drink water, even salt water in his dehydrated state, knowing it poison. He did from the shore if only for a gargle cleansing. He ripped off his clothes for a dunk, and then took a sip to his mouth, and another for a quick swish for cleansing. Reassembling his clothes, shaking off the sand, he quickly saw the money pinned to his shirt and knew his buddies jettisoned him with sorrowful regard. He was not worth the continued support of those with whom he rose from the trenches, but they had said in their way, "God-speed, Captain."

If there were salvation, he had no clue. He had only war skills for killing people and none for living among them. His very name, Alistair, meant "defending men," and he knew little else of commercial value. He had not a sensible clue as to how to live the very day that was upon him.

A strange thing happened.

Walking the beach with no destination and bereft in his heart in the early morning, he passed a man-jack of about his own age. The guy was a working man and purposeful. They shared glances and, though Al wanted no contact, the man altered his path and veered toward him.

"You lookin' for something? You ain't from here," the man said with a calm Al could accept, distraught as he was.

"Willie Stockhausen," the man offered, still too far to extend a hand and with no intent to do so.

"Al Keane," he answered.

"Look," Willie said, "isn't nobody walking the beach with money pinned to their chest with a Silver Star. I ain't seen it."

"I'm okay."

"Hard to believe, sir, but I take your word. I'm not the most regular."

Al took his measure of the man-jack and got it immediately. No agenda or motives. A simple soul, he had a touch of being sensible within himself.

"Given how you see me, I am even far more irregular than you know," Al offered.

"Maybe so. I don't get into people much. I do listen. Know stuff," Willie said.

"The War. I am fucked up. I may have been before, but worse now. Unsettled and a drunk."

"It looks it. I can't tell you much except this," Willie said. "If you ain't got no skills, rake clams and oysters, fill baskets. It goes all year, and you can survive a little. I got extra rakes, baskets, and floats. I don't use them anymore. Did once. I do maintenance and odd-jobs now."

"Why?" Al asked. "Why would you do me for?"

"I don't care for you much. Don't know you. Just helpin' a soul. You served your country. Some buddies pinned cash to your chest with a medal. They were sendin' a message. Said you were worth somethin'. That's it."

Al met with Willie on the beach the next day, having slept in a shed on the marsh. He accepted the tools: waders, float buckets, and two rakes for clams and oysters. Al offered money.

"Nah," Willie said, "They was nothing waiting to happen. Glad they're gone. Go East Bay first. You don't know shit, but it ain't complicated. Oysters pay. Listen now. You gotta find a bed, a reef. You gotta feel and adventure a bit. They cling, but bust 'em up. You got nothing there? Quahogs and clams are dumb. Rake 'em in the salt tides. They'll pay a little. Get this. Ice and burlap. You got more money pinned to you than I ever got. Keep everything iced in burlap. You can probably stay in the shed there. Been here a while and nobody claims it. Good luck."

The man-jack moved on and, although Al saw him more than often in the Village, all he ever got was a nod of hello. Willie was not a needy sort. He gave and left, clean in his doing.

Al was inspired, and he jumped on it. It didn't take all that much but gumption. Oysters were the royalty. He found a nearly endless bed in Cotuit and harvested bushels. He busted them from the substrate and disrupted their clinging together until they dropped to his rakes. Clams were less easy, but rake-ready. Al had to hitchhike from his marsh shed to new sites with his ice and burlap, and, on a slow day, it failed. Never perfect, the advice still suited him. He was as disciplined as a top-notch soldier. Up and out, oblivious to foul weather. Relentless. He was really good. He courted endless inns, restaurants, and food shacks on the mid-Cape who wanted shellfish.

The raking and the hits defined his hunting. He quickly came to know the burying grounds and shallows as a diviner of mussels, oysters, and clams.

He supplied mid-Cape hotels and restaurants with shellfish bounty in abundance, bushels. Wading year-round with no, or when necessary, wader protection, he provided meaty, tough Quahogs for chowder, little neck steamers, and juicy oysters. The weather-driven turbulence, tumultuous at times, was a playground for Al. He loved the surf rolling on his thighs and up to his chest. He filled the bags.

Each of the mollusks was entirely different. Quahogs were stupid and lay for raking. As such, they were not much money unless you had good volume. It was basic chowder meat and Al delivered the meat. Clams were similar, seeing the puffing blowholes was easy enough, but not transparent when underwater, he learned. Oysters were the real find. Diamond Jim Brady was slurping them in New York by the dozens a few years before. Getting the oyster gold was an art. You had to find the bed or reef.

Al was a shellfish savant with no training. He was a shellfish machine of driven merit. He was familiar to the mid-Cape local bars and restaurants. He delivered the mollusks of every species on time and in plenty. At the Village clapboard hotel, he became known as a reliable supplier, known to take drink of smuggled booze too far at times, but he was amiable and polite, even while stumbling.

Al stayed in the shed and began improving it, making it habitable. Though he had no knowledge, it most probably belonged to the religious group that bought the Perry farm. They had no interest. It was too tidal and of no value, especially in bad storms and they had bigger fish to fry with real estate in the Village.

*　*　*

That was where the union of Al and Joe took hold.

Josephine Cleary crept into the Village in 1922 with no measure or recommendation. She had no past anyone could reckon. To most, it was clear she was running because not a single comment advanced her arrival. People clammed up on that. She had a great merit, her exquisite beauty. She was dark-haired, Irish with slim body, ivory skin, and a perfect, angelic face, though she was far from angelic. It is said the Irish have a sense of crazy, some maybe more and some less, but they know. Joe's was an unknown, but a few said crazy was palpable. Call it pain or manic joy or loving or hating, she was a tough being hidden by the startling beauty that drew you in.

Josephine, in fact, came from a respectable home in Salem, favored by little strife within it. Her father, Liam, was a garrulous, friendly, Salem tax collector and a favored story-teller in the pubs he frequented, a conscientious man. He had undoubtedly kissed the Blarney Stone because he could charm and cajole in equal measure.

Her mother, Saorse, was a loving, sometimes fretful homemaker who made chicken pot pies, clam chowder, and beach plum jelly to magnificent taste. She had immigrated from the "Emerald Isle," as she called it, based on a Drennan poem, due to an arranged marriage to Liam in 1890. She called upon her frets, "the nerves" she said, and took to her room silently when the mood hit, not wishing a foul-temper to show itself. She longed for the "ould sod" where family worked the green hills. All the leaving did not work for her.

Josephine, the daughter, was a mix of the steadfastness of her father and the longing of something by her mother. She was wickedly brilliant in her passion and intellect. She was studious, serious, and angry. She was a "suffragette" to the core as a teenager, aggressively, and felt women to be painfully discounted at the time. The movement now held moment, and she had fire. It built resentments toward just about everything she saw. She suffered the humiliations while trying to pursue her passion for biology in school. Joe was denied studies as a serious future scientist. She was "guided" to less intense pursuits and seethed like a clan queen at the rejection.

The fate of women and ignorance of their capabilities never abided within her.

Her uncle was a drunken, ne'er-do-well. It was her father's brother, Sean, who caught her while socializing at a family gathering. Using his blather, he lured her to an upstairs room on the pretext of a gift. The gift was rape. Joe was amazed at the strength of an evil man and of her own helplessness at the taking of her virginity in her own house. Totally distraught and traumatized, after guests had left, she told her parents. Liam and Saorse looked to one another with deep pain.

"Joe, you must never speak of this again. It will destroy all of us," Liam said. "Sean will be kept away, forever."

She shut down, forever. The bastard was not "kept away" and leered at her in gatherings. Her ancestral Irish hatred knew few, if any, bounds. She was Queen Maeve of Connaught, vengeful, proud and fearless. The man would die, yes, he would.

Joe was both deeply scientific and with Irish wrath.

She went to the library and studied poisons. She stalked it as a highly intelligent and clever girl who knew how to be subtle and scholarly. She was polite to librarians and beloved in her intellectual intensity by them. If only they knew. She would have revenge. She was that way.

She had excelled in biology classes, though now redirected. Joe would use it. She researched toxicology and settled on tetrodotoxin, the amazingly powerful poison from abundant puffer fish on the seacoast. She went to the wharfs and asked for puffer fish. They made fine cooking if you stayed to the meat, but most knew not mess with them. They were considered junk fish and throwaways; no one liked them. Everyone knew they had bad poison. Few ever considered eating the catch. With little knowledge except the poison was concentrated in a specific gland she self-studied by dissection, she compressed and gathered a fair vial of organ juice.

At the next family gathering, with Sean being soused as usual, she dumped it on his serving of scrod. In but a few seconds, he went paralyzed and unable to breathe. He died on the floor, partially under the table. Joe was elated but professed horror. She had poisoned him by her science and laid a bad man low never to recover. Dead. There was never to be a blame. Sean was a drunk, tetrodotoxin disappeared in moments, and forensic pathology barely existed.

Poor Sean, dead of his excesses. She rejoiced.

After Sean's funeral with a falsity of statements about what a great man he was with very little evidence in the ceremonies, Josephine packed with little and took off. She was failed by her family and school, had taken her vengeance, and had nothing left to do with Salem.

She left a murderer, though no one could pin it on her. She left with scorn of a prideful family who looked at her in their own shame and sorrow for her lost innocence—raped and cheapened. She had not an ounce of remorse. That was the way it was. Tough. She saw Sean, his breathing shutting down, gasping, in total fear on dying, eyes bulging. She laughed. Fuck him.

*   *   *

The most beautiful Irish girl ever seen in the Village came looking for work at the hotel, nothing recommending her but beauty.

"Got a job? Cleaning, cooking, serving?" she asked the manager.

"Any recommendations," he asked.

"No, sir, but you can hear I speak intelligently and look you in the eye."

"Well said. May not be enough, but see me tomorrow."

Al was sitting at the upstairs, no-alcohol bar and heard all.

"Jake, give this woman a break. You know you got need. Say, yes."

Jake didn't right then. Al was a regular and a pest, but Jake knew no beauty like this had crossed his path before. She was "front-piece" and out to the public. Tomorrow she would be on at the hotel. Glamour counted, and Josephine had glam.

Joe turned to Al and saw what she knew not.

He was beautiful, weathered, old and young at the same time, a sufferer and survivor. She needed that badly. Her instincts fluttered. She knew right off he was no predatory guy. He was as gentle and hurting as she was, but she knew of her grit. She was a killer. She said to herself, *Do not destroy this man. He is pretty good.* She did not know he was more than a match.

And, so it started.

"Got a place?"

"No, not yet."

"Need a place on a couch?"

"Maybe."

"I got one. No baddies. You'll like it."

"Okay, thanks."

It was the salt marsh cottage, not owned by Al. No one knew exactly who it belonged to, strange as that seemed. No one had an interest in figuring it out or was pressing for ownership. Deeds and ownership were not easily decipherable, and the parcel was too endangered by tides for passionate claims.

Al had raised it with friends on a solid Belgium block foundation with weep-holes a few feet up from tides, using some jackscrews Willie lent him from a friend. Few words were exchanged, but "stayin' high" was a known need. Willie knew. Al had tapped a spring pointed to him by a Wampanoag to hand pump water to a kitchen and toilet. He block-lined a septic with exit. He hand-built, with fairly good craft, an extra room and a porch overlooking the marsh.

Joe entered the cottage with unbounded joy at her luck. She felt it.

It was a place to be with a gentle man, and Al was that. Al never pestered her for days.

It was she who unleashed the desire. She could not imagine sex was a forbidden garden. She was beyond law. Why should Al ever be denied? And so it started. She came on to him slowly, barely dressed in dainties she had hastily packed in Salem and hand washed in the sink.

"Why do you come this way?" Al asked.

"Do you really have to ask?"

"I am not normal or reliable. I would prefer to do no harm ever again."

"Perfect," Josephine said. "Neither do I."

The connection was beautiful and conflicted with each working out demons. That was their way of sexual intimacy. They needed the unguarded, physical contact of each other in their damage with each not knowing what the other's horrors were. Beautiful people making impassioned love on the marsh, abandoning themselves to its peace.

Al was known as a "supplier." He found the blocks of oyster reefs where no one could. He busted them, took the adults carefully, and laid back the young'uns to grow bigger. He raked the Quahogs, the hard shells, and coveted finding the soft shells for steaming. A good day was seven to ten bushels, and he rarely fell short. Restaurants warred with each other for his relentless catch. It was a sparse living but consistent and paid every bill. His pockets clinked with cash. He owed no one.

He bought Josephine two long-waisted gingham dresses that showed her figure to work the hotel. She had no coin but would eventually. Al never thought about it. Life was flowing as tides, and Joe was Joe. No questions, no answers, no telling. It was just a no-judgment feeling of acceptance among the two. Why tell? What was the gain? Live in your pain. No one would care.

★ ★ ★

Prohibition had its naughty, nasty, and violent ways as illegal enterprises usually do.

Joe was working the hotel front with unfortunate ga-ga eyes at her beauty. It could not be helped. Many well-to-do men checking in with their wives would have chucked them in the harbor for a fling with her. She found it mildly flattering but too stupid, having murdered Scan. She was forever changed and hardened. She was now a gangster Hester Prynne with a red "A" that said "no redemption," just don't screw with me. Not a one them was Al who was precious, beautiful, and urgent to her desires.

There was a "speakeasy" downstairs at the hotel. It was beyond scandalous for the Village in its natural piety, but the hotel had residual, legal rights under the Village purchase deed to run its business. It thrived in a secret; a naughty denial for the locals. No booze-lover was going to sacrifice knowledge of the cache and place , and it was a good one. It served top-shelf, McCoy booze. It wasn't for the drop-in, unknown sojourner. One had to say, "The governor sent me." With that, a dreary path down a dank staircase led downstairs and opened to opulence. It was a mahogany-lined room with a burnished oak bar and a bartender waiting to serve. There was little fear of a law bust because most of the constabulary were drinking there.

Al frequented the comfortable confines of the bar, mostly waiting for Joe to go off-shift and descend the steps. After a long day in the hot sun, or when the colder elements in later months that defined the peninsula lashed, he was prone to excess. Sun-struck sometimes, chilled and shivering sometimes, he drank and waited for Joe. He was appropriate as best as possible, created no uproar, but drank to a level beyond most. He was liked, but the locals knew when the war talk emerged, he was either quiet or belligerent. There was no middle ground. At his best, he said, "We won." At his worst, he said, "Fuck you. You were there? Ever see a slaughter of good men on both sides?"

The war was over, and no one cared. All was crazy "upward," with everything but Prohibition stunting the glide. The emerging stock market, flappers with bobs, the Charleston was a rage since 1913, bathtub gin, new jazz, and investment speculation ruled, and, by late1922, the belief flowed that the worst was behind.

Joe, with a humanity she so wished to deny and ignore, as it made her weak, soothed Al after turbulent nights at the speakeasy. She realized he had witnessed, caused, dealt with, and regretted death. Hers was a one time—personal, with cause. His were many—impersonal. Was there a connection? There was. It was anger, injustice, and survival. Joe swore, as best she could, she would let him suffer no further.

Life on the marsh, an idyllic life reigned between suffering people that was close, tight, and understanding.

On a quiet night with peepers in harmony in the marsh, Joe decided. She told Al she was the murderer of the uncle who raped her innocence. All sentiments told her to leave the topic alone, but she could not refrain. It was an exculpatory need to try and free her from blame.

"I must tell you something, Al," she said, holding his hand in her lap. "I was a quiet, studious girl. I had passion for issues emerging about science, women, and their rights. It seemed everything worked against me."

"They killed my passion, saying I was not equal in pursuing things I knew I was total tops in. Tops. 'Go be a secretary,' they said! I was really angry."

"Then my uncle, at a family gathering, raped me in humiliating ways. To then I was a total innocent. I was a virgin with no knowledge of sex or what it meant. My will had been taken from me in a violent, involuntary act. I wanted justice. I told my mom and dad. They said, 'Shut up about it, Joe.' This will destroy us."

"You know what? I killed the fucker. Poisoned him in a scientific way. Blowfish poison. I cannot tell you how exacting I was. Lab work. I totally did it. You have no angel here, Al. A murderess with no remorse. You want to kick me out?"

"So you poisoned him with blowfish juice?" Al asked.

"Yeah."

"You actually have my respect," Al laughed with gusto. "Really, nasty, but too good. Brilliant really. Laying a bastard down is beautiful. Tough burden, huh?"

"He was a son of a bitch. He tore apart everything and exposed the fraud of my family."

"Gracious, love girl," Al sighed. "You are tough Irish bitch, a queen, whom I love. Congratulations," Al laughed. "You, yourself. It is a gift."

"You are mocking me, you bastard. I planned and killed a relative with malice."

Al laughed again.

"Sorry if you are sorry, but you aren't. I know you—beautiful, smart, and never a fool. Fuck the asshole. You nailed him."

"That I did," Joe smiled.

"I love justice, Joe. I do. If I knew his grave, I would dig it up and stab him a few times."

"That is really silly. You don't hate me?"

"Only if you do it to me," he smiled. "I gotta watch my fish. I love you." They embraced.

Al then went quiet and told Joe his war past.

"…it was horrible. Billy Odom was by best friend since kindergarten. We signed up together. The nature of the war was gruesome. Fetid trenches, calls to charge into a blinding, insane hail of bullets and cannon shots. Craters were blooming from mortar shots like evil flowers. Billy got himself gutshot, and we fell into a bomb crater.

"There was no recovery for him, and I held him for a day until he died bleeding out. I couldn't leave the crater for another because of the action and watched as he rotted. That was the worst, but by far not the least."

"The trenches were like you descended to hell. Rotting flesh smells, nothing but a helmet full of water to wash the lice off you. It was always tough to stay sane watching rats eat bodies. It killed my soul."

"After that I was a killing machine. I had to get out. I was crafty, knew the angles of attack, knew the sounds of danger. I got wing shot but didn't care. Press on and kill. The bullshit rifles we were given were inferior. I took an Enfield off a dead limey with a boatload of magazines. Fifteen shots per minute, and reloaded a mag."

"I was crazy invincible for no reason. I put so many Bosch to spirit. Fifty at least. Maybe more. More wounded. I came upon a few lying there I knew my gun killed and looked at them. They were me and Billy. No different. I cracked forever, damned to hell.

"The last shot that got me hit was my hip. Bad, still got frags, but it was over for me. Sent home."

Joe grabbed him, hugged and shouldered his head, kissed his forehead. She finally knew his soul and hugged him with a fervor that surpassed his own mother for him. Joe never knew compassion deeply. Now she did. Now they both knew how deeply they hurt. They knew each other in the raw, in the beauty of fighters. They cried into the night. They were damaged people and owed nobody anything with so little given to them. They were a pact of the misbegotten, and their love was impenetrable.

It was one night in September, just after the season closed for the Village. The hotel was now low-grade, few visitors, but still year-round. A big, handsome, confident man walked into the place. He flirted, intent at Joe, and she was smitten. The man was beautiful. At heart, she was still a "suffragette" and not a fan of "men," but the man's appeal was powerful and alluring. She shuddered and withdrew in her sentiments.

"Hello," he said to Joe, "Captain Bill McCoy, and you would be?"

Joe gathered herself.

"Joe's the name, and what would you like?"

"You."

The boldness totally turned off any charm she may have perceived.

"Sorry, sir. Not on the menu and won't be. Anything else?"

He laughed, not used to rebuke but amiable to it.

"The governor sent me."

"The governor is open to friends," she said.

She guided McCoy below and left him at the speakeasy entrance. She nodded to Al with a, *Whoa, wake up, buddy,* in her expression. The man was affable, in charge, and friendly. No fear. He knew who he was. That night, he wasn't on the Atlantic with a ship hold of liquor running the Coast Guard. He was a citizen on a night out looking for business partners.

Al was in fine fiddle. He had not imbibed yet and was more into listening to the folk Irish band playing in the corner. A fiddler, a mandolin, and a guitar were juicing it lively, sounding happy.

Al was a bit concerned when the captain, after taking greetings all around, approached him, specifically, without hesitation.

"Al Keane, I believe," McCoy said. "Bill McCoy." He extended his hand.

"True, though I do not know you from Adam," Al said, accepting it.

Al was lying but took it as a very venial sin.

"You don't need to know much. I have heard good things about you."

"That would be a surprise," Al responded. "I know few and impress fewer."

"People say you know mid-Cape coast better than anyone."

"A lie," Al retorted. "I am a clammer. That's all."

McCoy accepted a hefty shot of Irish whiskey neat from the barkeep and took a sip.

"Look, Mr. Keane, I don't fool around. You sit here drinking the booze I run, and it is no easy enterprise. Prohibition is a disgust against the inclinations of America. I could use your help. Do you want to make some good money beyond clamming?"

Al thought, cooly, before answering and left McCoy sipping. McCoy had ordered a top notch single malt scotch for Al, and when placed before him, he knew it to be a ridiculous sum to pay—the ultimate from the shelf.

"I got no love for Prohibition," Al said. "I got no love for jail either. I want a peaceful life, Captain McCoy. Had enough in the war. I heard of you, straight up enough I guess, as a runner. Why fuck with a small fry like me?"

"Decent question, soldier. You know an operation and can keep your mouth shut. I know operatives who get the job done and like the money. Mission. That's it. I need safe drops in quiet places. Booze unloaded and put in safe places. That is all there is. It's two hundred dollars a drop to a safe house."

Al was serene as frozen ice and mindful of consequences.

"I gotta think about it. I have a girlfriend whom I know—word leaks downstairs—you were schmoozing with. Never do that again. Got that? I will kill you. I will. I gotta talk with her and let you know."

"Sorry about that," McCoy said, "She is a winner and best to you. Little could help me comin' on not knowin' you. No harm intended."

"So said. Never do it again. Answer tomorrow," Al said.

The night faded and all went home.

"So what the hell did McCoy want besides hitting on me?" Joe asked.

"He wants me to be a drop finder at two hundred dollars per."

"You kidding me, baby," Joe enthused. "Two hundred dollars per. We are astronomical. Ten drops and we're in the Village in an awesome, nice house. Really nuts."

"Nothing comes without risk," Al said.

"What risk? Joe asked. "No one cares about running booze. This speakeasy is full of law men."

"Yeah, they do, Joe. Some care," he said, seriously. "A lot of them, and they come from both sides of the law—the white hats and black hats. The G-men, the Coast Guard, and the bastards."

"What do you mean, Al?" she asked.

"The local constabulary cares less. Half of them are drinking here tonight. The G-men care, and the Coast Guard does too. It's their job and probably drinkin' off-duty too. The game is the bad guys will steal drops, not hard, and kill you if needed. Money."

"You wanna do it?" Joe asked.

"Only for you, babe. I'll live as is."

"You confident?"

"It's all luck and fortune as it turns. We have a good thing. It could be awesome with this, but know it ain't clean and tidy in any way."

Al contacted McCoy through a fishing boat at dock he was directed toward, the captain of whom no longer fished but ran whiskey. He told the captain to tell McCoy he would handle three drops per week into the mid-peninsula to safe, shuttered houses he would scout for storage. Al knew the lay of the land. He knew who was where and who wasn't. He had a sense for those who checked on their summer property and those who did not. Finding houses was the easy chore. Avoiding mishap was a crap game.

It was a hard decision. Al accepted his life as a productive shellfish producer, honest, straightforward, and free. The Village speakeasy was a salutary home.

All was good enough for him. He knew, or thought he did, that Joe wanted more. The marsh cottage was simply not enough. She, maybe, was nesting, not social climbing. He trusted her desire.

The first drops were so easy that it seemed heaven opened its doors. A night boat blinking, just barely, came cruising toward an inlet of his choosing. The captains were able and never grounded their propeller screws in the sand. There was a transfer of cases handled by able men in shallow water based on tides using pallet floats. It was a true lug from the beached pallets to shuttered houses in dark places. It was seamless. Two hundred dollars cash was delivered to Al's pocket when the cases were placed.

It was a money machine. One thousand, two thousand, three thousand—then four thousand. Twenty drops and rolling. Four thousand dollars on top of Al's clamming and Joe's salary. This was bounty. Al and Joe could buy large into the Village. It was an emboldened time for risk-takers.

The effusive flow was unparalleled. Joe's appetites were the same. She gave in all ways bounteously: love, sex, home skills, her job contributions from the hotel. She was insatiable in the joy of her manful man and the fortune he provided. She was a woman on fire. Every dream was now in their grasp.

It was a gibbous moon. The nastiness of illicit commerce was always lurking in the shadows. Bad people of lost soul always lurked with evil intent, and no one could ever know when their weak souls might arise. They smoked up in poisonous zephyrs like demons from a very bad place.

Al awaited a boat he was instructed to meet from a runner for whom he had no love. "Stompin' Cal." The man was a bully from the Hyannis docks. Al sensed him as a weak opportunist. Rumor was the man was a sucker-punching coward who bullied the town docks without bravery, always sly, and a cheap-shot and then kicked the unsuspecting victims silly when down—a man with no honor, but a boat-load of hate.

It was remarkable such a coward could survive, but he was just, plain and simple, a man of no merit. Cal would stand to no man straight-up. He had no skills, even his boating. His arrogance was born of his sense that few, if any, could know how dangerous and cut-throat he could be. He believed in his evil as a charm.

Somehow bullies fail to realize brave men will kick their cowardly asses.

Al could not pick his partners and acceded to McCoy choosing his navy. He had a bad feeling about Stompin' Cal. He hated at this very moment what he was doing. Nothing good was happening here. Every instinct in Al was arisen. Taking a drop from a sleazy guy on the Osterville Neck shore? He cringed.

Al always kept a crowbar back-slid in his pants, only the hook visible when doing drops. He felt in him: *You never know.* It was tool of immense use with lifting crates, jimmying doors, and leveraging pallets. It was, also, his only weapon against possible violence.

Stompin' Cal's boat laid proper to the Centerville tide outside the Village. The mansion chosen was up-river, closer to Osterville. A scruffy crew of two wharf rats pulled cases off the boat deck, wading them to shore on floating pallets. Al watched and directed the activity to a mansion on the salt river over-looking the marsh, upriver from his home. All was as planned. Drop delivered.

"Okay, clammer?" Cal said derisively.

"Just as soon as your ass is gone," Al said with conviction.

"You don't know who you are fucking with," Cal said, handing him McCoy's two hundred dollars.

"Yeah, I do. I want no trouble. You pull out, I'm good. Deal?"

"Good."

Stompin' Cal backed off, but Al knew in his gut there was a bigger game afoot. He knew the tingle. He never would have stayed alive if he did not have it.

He left the opulent mansion and went to the bushes. He waited and watched, listening for the boat screws to signal a departure. A half-hour. No engine sounds. Then voices. People coming back to the drop.

It all meant nothing to Al. He had his two hundred dollars and no responsibility. He had zero allegiance to McCoy and no regard to the outcome of stealing a shipment.

Yet, somehow, in his improving but roiling brain, he was not letting Stompin' Cal have a free pass on stealing booze on his watch. It was visceral—war gut. He hated everything about the guy. It was too emotional. He "trenched" once again.

All was dark. All was unexposed from the main road, visible only to the sea, the definition of most safe houses.

Al walked straight in the front door and saw the wharf rats stacking cases to take out back to the boat. He saw Cal sitting on a leather chair in the drawing room on the oriental rug next to the liquor.

"I guess you're fucking McCoy," Al said.

"Not the first or last," Stompin' Cal said with nonchalance.

"It is here," Al said with a killer coldness that made the coward tremble. "Bring it all back and go away."

"Okay, Okay, I got it," Cal said. He was clearly shaken at the intrusion. "You gonna tell McCoy?"

"Got no reason to if you get the hell out. This ain't a chosen life."

"Let's shake on it," Cal said.

Cal said it with one hand reaching and the other for something from his jacket pocket.

Al was hyper-vigilant since the war, paranoid on potential violence. He was still sick, never unprepared. He had hand-eye coordination that should have put him on the Red Sox. He deftly pulled the back-slid crowbar, smooth and quick on the draw with the tool, and brained Stompin' Cal to mushed watermelon as the man's weapon fired in his pocket.

There was a crack of a pistol and a whump. The sound was the deathblow of a caved cranial cavity. The sound spoke death, ugliness, and a lot of blood from ears and nose. Cal's men, alarmed to the pistol crack and thump, looked in on the scene and ran toward the boat, terrified their bully was dead carrion.

"Self-defense, assholes," Al yelled, figuring no one heard.

Al shook with the iron in his hand. He had feared this very situation. He knew it was possible and probably would happen. He had wished he would know better what to do. Events did not afford that. He now had a body in a princely home of which to dispose with witnesses on the lam. He cared less for the carcass, a bastard who someone should have killed before. Dead meat.

Getting rid of a body is tough business. Making it disappear is never as easy as it seems. Weighing it down and dragging it to sea? That needs a boat. Carry it up-coast and bury it where crabs would enjoy the feast? That needs transport. He weighed his options. The sea would be best, rocks in bag, but he had no boat. Up-coast sand was inferior.

Bigger yet was the runaway crew of two. They were dock lowlifes, petty criminals. There was zero chance of them keeping their mouths shut. They would tell the drama, if ever confronted, to say with swagger how brave they had been or to cop a plea for petty crimes they probably were facing, spilling what they saw.

It all depended on how it played out. What was anyone involved willing to say and for what relief?

Stompin' Cal was, at the moment, a brained head gourd stealing a shipment. It wasn't complicated. Al was running booze. Cal was trying to steal it. Al was defending the cache for little reason, and there was a confrontation. Disaster has simplicity.

Al decided to find a boat—a dinghy, a dory, a half-assed raft—and dump the body in Centerville Harbor, a mile out. The night was now quiet as if no violence had ever occurred. He had the luxury of finding conveyance. He was fixed on the mission and devoid of regret of the confrontation. Stompin' Cal was a miserable man and worth a good riddance.

He found a dinghy with oars inside, turned upside down to weather, under the deck of the very house of disaster.

Al was methodical in his shock and sorrow. He dragged the dinghy to the water's edge and filled a large canvas bag he found nearby the boat with a co-pious amount of beach stones. He dragged Cal into the dinghy and lashed the bag around him with rope he found in in the basement, as in mummy ritual, using every knot he learned in basic training. He rowed for an hour out to sea, double-checked the rope and knots around the carcass, and dumped Stom-pin' Cal. Cal sank like a stone.

Al rowed back to the house. He replaced the dinghy underneath the deck with exactness and tried to figure how to get rid of the blood upstairs. It was a copious bleed on the oriental carpet. It was that fact plus a ton of booze cache that was laying on the carpet and would have to be moved to remove the rug.

He moved the cases with grunting labor, agonizingly beset with pain from war injuries. He rolled up the rug. With great luck, the fine carpet completely absorbed the blood horror. No floor residue. *God bless the Arabs.*

Al went outside and cursed until he found gasoline in a farther side, out-side shed. He lugged the carpet far uphill and leeward with the gas can. He doused it with meticulous care and set it aflame. Al waited, morbid with all he was doing, until it was total ash and then swished the ash with marsh grass until it was nothing but an innocent, barely discernible beach burning, not uncommon.

There was little, if any—really no—physical evidence except booze and the word of miscreants who ran. Could he depend on that? He thought not. They were loose-lipped and easily tipped to whatever may favor them. They had little guilt in the game. There was a storm coming. He hoped not, but luck never really ran in his favor—except avoiding death bullets in the war.

He returned to the marsh where Joe was up, very late, way late, and brewing tea. It was dark dawn. She knew something went wrong.

"How did it go, love boy?" she asked.

"A disaster, Joe," he said. "Less you know, the better."

Joe was so into Al, she just knew. She felt it as if she were an appendage of him, most probably his heart.

"Did you have to kill?" she asked.

"If I were a smarter man, sweetheart, probably not, but I did," Al said sadly. "He pulled a gun. I had no choice except to back down. I could not. I see that and react like a trained idiot. I don't back down. It was a royal fuck-up. I didn't want to, but my nature is not to be killed. My thinking was not good. Shoulda walked. Not my problem, but I made it mine. So sorry, love girl."

Joe broke into tears that flowed and could have raised the marsh.

"I am so sorry, sweet man," Joe said. "I pushed you to all this. So sorry. So sorry. I thought all this was a cat-and-mouse game no one gave a shit about. You said different."

Joe went her analytical way and focused as her deep intellect afforded. She had stopped crying and was now an avenging angel for her man.

"Tell me simply what happened in detail—every detail, love."

"I had bad feelings on the drop guy, Stompin' Cal. I saw him as a coward and a cheat. He and two minor wharf guys made landing. They transported the booze okay to a mansion on the neck. You would know the place. I got paid, but I knew he was up to no good. Shoulda left it. Couldn't."

"And then?"

"I went to the bush and watched. Sure enough, they never left. They were going to steal a drop, probably planning to lay it on me. I came back in. Cal was always a coward and a bully, but shocked. I told him, 'Get your ass out.' He said, 'Okay, only if I had no word to McCoy.' I said, 'Don't care about that.' 'Shake?' he asked. Problem was he was reaching in a pocket. I knew it was a gun. Don't ask how I knew. It was. I was quicker on the draw and brained him with my crowbar. He shot himself in the leg really bad, never gettin' the gun out."

"And then?"

"His boys didn't see it exactly, but they rushed in and seen Cal laid low, bleeding like a stuck pig. They ran. I should have run 'em down and killed 'em, too, but the killing was gone in me. I found a boat and a bag for rocks and rope to tie it really good. I rowed him far out and dropped him. He sank. Rowed back, place the boat right as rain, and burned the bloody rug way up beach to scattered ash."

"And then?"

"Nothin' more, love girl."

"You are a reckless, fucking brilliant nutcase. We don't let shit go ever, do we? They have nothing. Words of drunks on the wharf. No body. No blood. Self-defense. You are beyond it, babe. My hero."

"Get a grip," Al said. "We will find what we need to. I could not find it to let an asshole push me around. No sorry from you, ever. Just my own. I kinda told you. Nothing works easy."

"How bad, Al?"

"Don't know, sweet girl," he said. "The man tried to kill me. I brained him with my crowbar. His crew, two guys, ran. I deep-sixed him and figure it will hold. No body. I cleared evidence, but the clearing is a sign of itself. It's all about the crew. My sense? They will be spilling their guts all over the docks tomorrow. Little nobodies with no liability and a bar story to tell. Way it is."

Joe took his hand and put it to her cheek.

"Al, I gotta tell you something. I was waiting. It is the worst time I can think of, but we must figure. I apologize, but I am pregnant—yeah, I think—with our child. Missed three periods and having the morning sickness. It should be a joy for us, and now I am sorrowful for my man in distress. I am puking in the morning and feel a belly rising. What do we do?"

*   *   *

For a few days, all went as every day. Al clammed, delivered bushels, and calmed himself in what he knew. The McCoy connection went dead. McCoy was paranoid about failed drops, though he knew many. Al was relieved, glad it was over, but there was overhang. He had brained a "son of a bitch" person in McCoy's defense. It was never asked for. Entirely stupid.

Joe was upstairs in reception; Al was downstairs but not drinking, listening to music.

McCoy came in, guided by Joe. She left. He walked to the small table Al occupied in a corner.

"So what happened?" McCoy asked.

"Don't know what you're talking about, Captain."

"Rumor is the drop went wrong."

"Still got your booze in the Osterville Neck?"

"Yeah, but people talk."

"Get it out of there then before talk takes action. Ya hear?"

"You got nothing to say to me?" McCoy asked.

"Yeah, I do. First, you hire thieving nobodies. Second, in your words, you hire someone with a sense of 'mission.' How is that supposed to work? Nothing more to be said except you fucked up."

"Anything else? You know I can't use you anymore."

"Use? What a great word from a national criminal! Else? You betcha. I want fifteen thousand dollars on this bar head tomorrow or I will spill every captain, every drop site, every communication protocol I know to the G-men. You want peace? Do it. Man of my word. Do I strike you as a squealer? Never was and couldn't be. You want war, I bring it. I stood for your stupid-assed drop out of an unknown loyalty to your cause. I served you; now you serve me. Total silence."

"Done, soldier," McCoy said. "Barkeep, pull the finest single malt and fill this man's glass as much as he wishes. He is a war hero and knows no quit."

Al declined the favor and shook hands.

"No ill will. Do it," Al said. "You will never hear anything again. Promise."

★   ★   ★

"So what happened?" Joe asked.

"I told him $15k on the bar head tomorrow or I'd dump to the G-men. He's a businessman. Not a killer. He'll deliver."

"Love boy, with that we got over twenty-two thousand dollars. That is rich by any standard around here. Fuck the Village bitches who look down on us."

"We deserve something, Joe. We never hurt the innocent except me in war to stay alive. Yeah, Cal was an exception, but he was no innocent and trying to kill me."

The next day, a packet arrived at the hotel for Al Keane. He was clamming that day in the October cool and forgetting as much as he could of the disaster and its trauma—the braining, the weight-down, the rowing, the dump dug into him. He delivered fifteen bushels. He went home and cleaned the sea muck from his body, washing his waders.

Joe held the packet out to him as he walked into the hotel foyer. He splayed it open in the vestibule with his pocket knife for her. No one there was watching in the slow season. It was hard to count then and there, but it proved, on kitchen top counting later, to be, fifteen thousand dollars.

McCoy was over. They had way more than the means to buy into a lakefront Village home, make it their own, make it winter-proof. They would have to work, but working was never their problem. They found the perfect house.

It looked over the pond and had magnificent bones—sturdy, tight, nothing dank on the bluff. Al started figuring how to make it year-round.

In late October, a constable came to the marsh house. Joe was queasy with the morning sickness but bucked up with resolve.

"Is Al Keane here?" the constable asked.

"No. He's a clammer up and out. Why are you askin'?"

"Got a few questions for him."

"Fine, sir. Try me for a few. I know what goes on."

"Where was he October thirteenth in the evening?"

"He was here fixing a balky toilet."

"That so?"

"Said so."

"Okay, I still want a talk with him."

Joe was shaken the law showed up. She had stonewalled like Andrew Jackson but knew more questions were coming. Mouths were running, and truth was an elusive mistress. What did anyone have or know? She gave up on the questions. Joe could not answer except to lie, which she had done. Boo-hoo. She would protect Al Keane until death.

"The law came today," she sighed to Al.

"Anything said?" he asked.

"I was stupid," Joe choked. "I said you were here on the marsh on the bad night fixin' a toilet. I should've said he's a whoring son of a bitch, and I never know where he is."

"So, why bad?" Al asked.

"Because you were seen at the drop. It's just one word against another, but lord knows what the lackeys are spilling."

"True, Joe. I don't like it. Still, it's low-lifes spreading lies."

"Lies?" she asked. "You killed the bastard and deep-sixed him."

"Nothing pretty, but he tried to kill me. Truly. Self defense."

"I know, sweet man, but you couldn't let a drop go bad. Could you?"

"Not to a man as evil as Stompin' Cal. To make a point, you couldn't lay off your uncle either. You laid him low with scientific intent. I applauded you. Kill the bastards. No one else will. No one has the guts."

"I got life in me, Al. Everything is different. You and me and the baby are growing. You were you, and I was me, and we both are killers. We murder bastards. Now a gentle baby? Would I kill again? In a second, if anyone comes close to taking my loved ones. I am an animal with claws, fangs, a brain, and passion."

"Well said," Al laughed and hugged her fiercely. "We will figure this out. We got dough. It will play. It may be odd, but it will. We are not bad people, just different."

The marsh was peaceful that night with gently swishing tidal flows that ran the rocks and tickled the grasses.

The constable showed at the marsh house the next day early. He knocked, and Al answered having seen his mud-smeared vehicle from the window.

Al pulled open the door and stepped on to the makeshift porch.

"You Al Cleary?" the man asked.

"The same," Al answered.

"We have a report of a missing person you might know."

"Doubt I do. No one I know is missing, but I'm willing to help if I can."

"Do you know a Calvin Stronson?"

"I can't say I do personally. I know he runs a fishing boat off the town harbor."

"How did you know that?"

"I clam and know the harbor where I drop my bushels. I have heard of every boat, every captain. It's all scuttlebutt."

"Do you know Calvin Stronson is a missing person?"

"Never heard that. Fishing is a dangerous business."

"So is bootlegging."

Al was cool and did not bite in the least.

"Stronson was a bootlegger? Who woulda known?"

"I don't know from shit, and Cal was known as miserable," the constable said. "He is missing, and good riddance, but you are not clean. There are witnesses who say you may have killed him."

"I appreciate your honesty and diligence. I will defend myself against anyone who tries to associate me with Stronson's disappearance. No relationship to the man."

"Two witnesses saw you October thirteenth on a boot-legging drop site on the Osterville Neck. They never saw Stronson again."

"I was not there, but it may be likely they killed him. It is an iffy thing to run booze, I would guess. Tell me, was any booze found at the site?"

"Not my place to tell."

"Anything else?"

"Yeah, one thing," the constable said, steady and gauging. "You know Captain McCoy?"

Al was waiting for that and did not flinch. He had rehearsed his answer a hundred times.

"A little. He shows at the hotel in the Village occasionally. Friendly guy, always willing to buy a drink for conversation."

"Folks said he liked private, in-the-corner conversations with you."

"He did that with everyone. Quit your fishin'. I got nothing to do with a missing person and less with McCoy."

"Witnesses said Stenson may have tried to kill you. We found a bloody bullet in the hardwood floor. You got self-defense and bootlegging. I doubt there's much time there. You want to own up?"

Al knew he had to keep the pattern of denial even and steady until he could process all that was revealed.

"Own up to what? Something I didn't do? Why?"

"There's more you don't know."

"Then arrest me, now."

"Trying to give you a chance. People say you deal square, but everything has its limits."

"Done, constable?"

"Done."

Joe had left early in the morning, pedaling her bike to the markets in town. It was an easy pedal on the flat lowlands—enjoyable with the thought of a baby in her belly and her stand-up guy. She pulled into the cottage front-way, her saddle bags full. Al met her at the door and helped carry the purchases in.

"You're not out today. Not like you. What's up?" she asked.

"Had a visit from the constable early after you left. Tough stuff."

"Let me make tea and we'll talk, baby."

They sat on the porch with cups of tea, the sun shining and the marsh river water sparkling its wavelets like a broken mirror.

"So—tell," Joe said.

"I'll try to be logical. Just hear me out, love girl."

"Tell."

"Whoever Cal's guys were folded when questioned on his disappearance. We knew that would happen. They aren't credible, but...they are two. I'm betting six ways to Sunday there was no booze in the house when the cops got there. The guy wouldn't say, but I told McCoy to clean it out. They found a slug in the floor with blood on it from Cal shooting his own damn self. The cop said the witnesses heard a shot. He offered, 'self-defense by you and boot-legging if you want it.'"

"What did you say?"

"No way. I wasn't ready. Wasn't there. Didn't do nothing. I have to tell you, Joe, they sussed out a lot, and this guy just had the calm demeanor of a bettor with an ace up his sleeve. I've been thinking all morning about what it might be. It likely ain't stone cold solid, but it's something to spring like a trap."

"Any ideas?"

"Just one. McCoy would never turn and doesn't have to. I would go 'trench' with him, true, but he has an organization. People who do things. The G-men are all over McCoy and trying to nail him. Where do they start? Lower down. Get weaklings to turn with prison threats."

"You amaze me with your thinking, even if it's paranoid. Who would know anything about Al Keane?"

"Ya know those two hundred dollar envelopes that came with all the early drops? They were unmarked, clean and cash. McCoy sure as hell didn't stuff them. Someone did. Do I think they kept a ledger that said: Al Keane – Osterville Neck – 9/19/23 – $200? No way. Do I think someone may have had a lot to say if they turned coat? I do."

"So, baby, what are you saying? Play it out for me. My head is spinning!"

"Mostly, no bootleggers die in these parts. I think the law is framing a weak case to show the evil of all the booze running to put heat on McCoy. They will put me in handcuffs on weak stuff in suspicion of the death of a 'brave' fishing captain bootlegging to support his family. They will parade me in front of journalists who will write impassioned Prohibition articles to look good and crucify me whether they get a guilty verdict or not. I am guilty only of self-defense. That won't matter. I think they got enough circumstantial to say I served McCoy."

They sat in silence, the gulls wheeling and squealing overhead.

"Got a plan?" Joe asked.

"I do, but you are not going to like it."

"I figured that. Run. Hide. Clam down south?"

"No, I don't want to be a hunted man, Joe. Can't be. Doesn't fit. It's simpler. We got the twenty-two thousand dollars plus the five thousand dollars saved from my clamming and your stuff. It's a small fortune. It's yours—"

"The hell with you," Joe screamed, "I hate you!"

She leapt up, tore off her clothes and ran to the river crying, plunging in with no regard to the baby. Al watched. Tears he had never shed over years of war and drunken travail were falling from his eyes in a torrent. He was a confused, simple man, yet his resolve stood in his mind.

Joe left the river naked, her baby swelling defined.

Al had grabbed a towel for her. He wiped her body.

"Look, Josephine Cleary. You got the clearest vision I know. Your brilliance is a gift. You dazzle. Gonna listen?"

"I hate you."

"You gonna listen?"

"I hate you even more, but say your piece."

"The money? Keep it cash. Secure it in a bank box. Trust it to no one. We are going to create an accident—"

"Can't. Won't ever, you stupid idiot!"

"—an accident where I die."

"Nooooo. No way, ever," she wailed.

"It's gotta be for you and the baby. Get rid of Al Keane. He had his run and made mistakes. I fucked up. I will not have my sweetheart and child living under a shadow. I won't."

"I hate you more than ever, you coward," she hissed like Maeve.

"Nothing good is coming. Someone has gotta grow up. I am marked for life no matter what—guilty or innocent. Living peaceful in the holy-roller Village? No way. You and the babe can be better. You so know that, murderer girl, who I love beyond question."

"I am so scared of losing you. You were the only person who ever understood my evil and called it righteous. I don't know how to let go. I can't imagine a world without a guy who never quits against the assholes. I just can't. Let's all go together."

"It is all okay, loved one. I should have been dead a hundred times and lived. It was only that luck that gave me you for a couple years of joy. Now, I gotta give it back for us and the baby. Trust the stupid soldier."

"You stupid man. I hate you."

"I got that point by now, Joe. Once we iron out the plan, I am gonna hand you an old army pistol, butt first. Tell 'em, 'He was tryin' to teach me to defend myself.' This is tricky. You gotta shoot me where I bleed out. No heart shot, baby. I gotta stay alive to say it was an accident. Nah, let me rethink...we can do it, but I'll aim the gun and pull the trigger. Lord knows, I've seen enough shots to figure it. I'll help it."

"I hate you, you bastard."

"No, you love me too much. That is the sorrow. Let me sacrifice in love."

Al laid out the plan with military precision.

"You're gonna buy a car when shock dies down and pay someone to teach you how to drive it right away. You need wheels. You're gonna birth the baby here with a midwife and get a paid Wampanoag girl to help you get strong again. The midwife will know one. You are gonna leave to one of the up-coast, fine towns like Natick, get a place and enroll in college, maybe Wellesley, or a ton of other places up there. You got the money, Joe. You're gonna get a home, help to raise the babe while studying and become the genius you are. Do I gotta repeat? Tell me no. Tell me!"

"No, got it. Not stupid. Star-crossed people. I am closing my eyes," she said, "I love and hate you so badly."

The shot exploded. Al pulled the trigger of the gun in Joe's hand.

The shot sound over the marsh was so unpeaceable as to quiet everything. Silence. Al had the shock in his eyes of the trauma, but he knew the plan was working. Joe bent over him and gave him the sweetest kiss. All quieted. It was as if nature was witness and could not respond to the sorrow.

She ran, as told, to find medical help. It took an hour for help to arrive. Al had a sense of bleeding out, didn't mourn it, and hung in.

The crude ambulance arrived by a hand-cranked marsh ferry, the only connection to the main road.

"Are you okay, sir?

"Not hardly," he barely gasped, leaking blood. "I am saying this (cough, cough) is a totally stupid accident. There was no intended harm. My partner is an angel (cough and drizzle of blood). No fault but my own in teaching firearms. I wasn't careful. (Gasping) Joe is a great girl, and I love her. My fault. All mine."

He went to spirit.

They took Al's body to Fall River. Joe didn't want it and didn't go. Village talkers gossiped at the trollop's seeming indifference, but she had said her good-byes in the most intimate way. They buried him in a plot of a family origin she knew nothing about. The inquest amounted to nothing.

A few strange things happened. An unmarked envelope arrived at the hotel for her. She opened it and it had five thousand dollars in cash. A note said: *For the soldier!* She obviously knew.

The constable stopped by. He said, "Sorry for your loss. Al was a noble, brave guy. I liked him a real lot. He would have had some trouble, probably some jail time. He was righteous."

So her man was right in his knowing.

Another envelope showed at the hotel reception. She opened it.

Al was our captain and leader. He got us through the war with bravery and cunning that saved our lives. He was hurt by the war. Please accept this in memorial: $2k.

And so the plan played.

Josephine got her car and learned to drive it expertly. She gave birth to an angelic baby girl, Persephone, and was nursed to health by a young Wampanoag, Weetamoo. She had a tidy sum and a bastard baby.

She chose boldness for Al. Joe never suffered a moment of financial insecurity again. She went to Newton and bought a house. She fought her way into Wellesley and studied biology to a B.A. magna cum laude, then to a graduate degree at Emerson with the same. She never married, though she dabbled. No one could match the force that was Al Keane. He was a crazy knight, handsome, brave, and too much for the world.

Joe made a great mark as an educator and innovator, but never reconciled with family. They failed an innocent, virgin girl and turned her to a murderer. She never had any remorse because Al said, *Good job.* What a relief! She felt the same for her dear, moral hero. Their, Al and Joe's babe, Persephone, was a feisty, loving, genius mess of humanity. Ph.D in neuroscience at Brown, the only woman in an emerging field. She was a force of nature and giant in her publishing. No quit. No back-down. Deal straight or die. It was their way. A history of loving desperadoes. It was the only way they could be.

1958–The Game

In a 2x2 small column in sports, the local newspaper reported the upcoming final between the Beach Guards and the Inn staff in the Village for the Pilgrim Jug.

*   *   *

A corona rings it from the setting sun sinking below salmon clouds over the marsh, the white orb rising to an apex seeming to halt for a slight pause before its descent to gravity. It was the set of a volleyball coming from the least proficient of the Inn team players, yet it rose to soft and appropriate height. It rose and fell into the wheelhouse of the most violent yet gentlemanly spiker in the Village's volleyball history.

Jack Rhodes, of the perpetually losing Inn team, climbed the ladder his long, rangy legs afforded him at six-four. He swung his striking arm from below his waist and palm-smacked the ball with the sound of a rifle shot across the green. Birds flew. The ball compressed then exploded toward its destiny at the Beach Guards. It was match point in the final test of the season—teams tied for the Pilgrim Jug—and the first chance in untold, actually never, seasons for the Inn to triumph.

Rising with a leap on the Guards' side was the equal six-four frame of Paulie O'Brea, arms up, massive hands with sinew-stretched fingers spread. It was only the two—all others were of fervid, but not transformational talent.

71

Offensive strength, defensive will. Bam. Bam. Defend or die for the Guards, smash and win for the Inn.

The volleyball pitch was sand-based with limed boundaries, a stout net and a referee's ladder at net center set on the south end of the Village green. On this evening, it was ringed three deep, about 275 people positioned two yards off the lime to thwart injury from diving players. The crowd was a mix; scores of children adoring the Beach Guards, diffident Inn visitors, strangely aroused Inn staff, and the whole complement of Villagers looking for Thursday evening excitement. There was little TV then in the cottages, none at the Inn, only small black and white boxes and a handful channels grabbed by rabbit-eared antennas. The action was here.

For years, the weekly clashes were mostly ho-hum, barely competitive events with the Beach Guards taking the nine-match summer season by margins of 7–2 or better. The Guard losses were mostly from weeks when their guys had to go to winter venues for family or school business and rag-tags, aged old Guards with paunches, filled the gaps.

The matches were a weekly highlight in Village fun, mostly ruled by sportsmanship, intense effort, and polite applause. That was the Village way and always had been. Not now. If ever there were a "blood match" in an essentially Christian enclave, this match was it. The season was tied 4–4 in wins, the Pilgrim Jug on the line. If mild-nasty ever might be raised in a place of no drama and Christian virtue, the Village boiled with it. The partisans were fueled.

When Jack Rhodes and Paulie O'Brea ascended, there was a hush on this small patch of the universe. Local. Minor. Inconsequential. Yet this was the vortex of Village life among those who knew with fervency this was no less than game seven of the World Series. Ninth inning, bases loaded, two outs, three and two count. The perennial doormats were perhaps now to take down the Lords of the Beach. Eyes widened, spectators inhaled, cries of support burst forth from either side that, with Jack's smack, sent the crows winging.

The dynamics of this powerful and strange moment lay in a history of peacefulness, restorative Christian campground serenity, and real estate plays. The Village came to being in 1871 through the purchase by a regional church group of marginal grazing land overlooking marshes, ponds, and the ocean from local farmers. It was a beautiful parcel of about 240 acres and included a brilliant beach expanse that kills with envy to this day. There was a singular intended use. Glory to God, revival, and a place of beauty to gather and build or renew faith over the languid months of summer and early fall. It was part of a movement only later understood as outdoor nature worship in a Christian context.

At first, a single big tent was erected on flat ground in the non-existent, mid-Village—the same ground of which the volleyball court was now a part. In the 1870s, a summer program of celebrity religious speakers, faith-based lectures, and community socials with song and feast was held. While Christian to the core, it was non-denominational, that being an amazement of the time. Catholics, Jews, Buddhists, Hinduists, pagans were never present, but acknowledged in respect.

As the seekers gathered in the first years, family camping tents surrounded the "core" revival tent. The Village, cut off by natural boundaries, supported no commerce save for a small store and some surrounding clapboard, wood-built "inns." The popularity of the site was soon spread widely as the most revered minister/academics came to preach and rejoice. The regional church body opted to sell parcels in the Village to raise money for infrastructure and to construct a Tabernacle on a hill at the apogee of the Village—a large, open-sided barn with sliding side doors to replace the Gathering Tent—and build new inn accommodations for the new pilgrims.

Those buying in over the years, be they of difference—actually a lot of Irish Catholic—in religious fervor of their way knew the place to be a "slice of heaven." The new Cottage Owners worked hand-in-hand with the founding body to maintain the peaceful, intelligent serenity that existed. True as it all was—and it was—the Village had new, decent blood that was different but not at odds with the purpose of spiritual revival, though the definition was not as uniform.

⋆　⋆　⋆

Then there was the Beach. It was part of the original Village purchase and owned by the religious group. It was prime almost beyond description. It was not about the mesmerizing, rolling surf and dunes on other parts of the peninsula. It was not about "sea-rising-to-mountain-vistas" as in Maine or California. It was the perfect swimming beach—south-facing, broad with beautifully textured beach sand, sandy bottomed, no radical drop-off, chop waves, devoid of rips and nasty currents. The arc was splendidly picturesque and the Beach lay at the center of spreading arms in a bay five miles wide at its opening. It was protected as much as it could be. Perfect.

At the Beach, something memorable happened. A beautiful, rustic, gabled pavilion arose on piers off the sand. To each side of the Victorian structure, boardwalks on piers extended parallel to the shore for 250 feet. The road-facing side of those boardwalks, a clabboard wall, if you will, was created by an unbroken row of closet-like bathhouses that tastefully shielded the beach from outside view. Charm could not have been built it better. As it stood, though small and unassuming, it was one of the most architecturally pleasing structures anywhere from Florida northward on the east coast—maybe any coast.

The volleyball game had roots here. The Beach, integral to revival and serenity, was the pagan Siren. All pilgrims went there every reasonable day: sunny, cloudy, iffy. When there, amidst its beauty, the spiritual rather than the religious held sway. Religion is for those afraid of hell. Spirituality is for those who seek something more. The two, spirituality and religion, were not natural enemies. Spiritual was more playful. There was freedom at the Beach. The Guards were of the Beach, not better in any way, just of the Beach. The Inn, though loving the Beach, was of the Village origins—more religious. It was not a nasty divide, just an artificial, not important separation, which at the moment of Rhodes's spike, was all that mattered in the metaphysical cheering section of mortals. The teams, Inn and Guard, were of relatively the same circumstance in life—pretty much of the same decency but, among all similarities, different. It was less than one might think but different—macho boys versus good boys, but all decent. The child spies knew it better than any elder.

The Inn staff was chosen from elite, religious-based colleges and the Ivy League. It was a premier summer job that called from the origins of the Village to those of tangible religious values and refined social skills, not elitist but engaging. The hires were not, for the most, religious zealots. The Inn staff was destined to be doctors, lawyers, politicians, and teachers. The lifeguards were by no means an underprivileged crew—more entrepreneurs likely. Their lot as Guardians was doled out by the patronage due long-standing, Village cottage owners or by recruitment of local talent under the direction of the Beach Director. He was a gruff, efficient, and joyless taskmaster, but ran a great beach. Still, by comparison, the lifeguards were pagan-like—destined to serve in Vietnam, start businesses, invent doo-dads, fight the tides they saw every day, and not always with wisdom.

The Guards had a lot of Irish Boston or other Catholic ethnicity. The Inn was purely middle-road Protestant. No one would dare speak of the contrast because decency and brotherhood were the norm of the enclave. That is, until the Christian/pagan, Ivy league/public college, good boys/bad boys came to the final kill shot. It was none of that by logic, but in every mind on the Green, the emotion says it was.

The Inn that year was led by the lanky and mysterious Jack Rhodes. Mysterious was not a term generally associated with or liked by the religious body that governed the common properties such as the Inn. He was quiet, handsome as hell, and took a job to work in the kitchen. People said he was from Oregon, never before a recruiting field for Inn help, or California, even more strange. Was he a "ringer," a hired volleyball gun brought to the eastern sea by the Inn, was a question sometimes debated over back porch cocktails by the cottage owners. Few, if even a one, believed it. Well, they didn't. It wasn't true. Only we kids knew anything because we, a few friends and I, were curious pests who asked, spied, and cajoled in kid-like innocence for information. Information—gossip, I suppose—was the lingua franca of the Village.

He was the coolest guy, actually cooler than any Guard. He endured our stupidities and lack of guile with a calm, half-smile like we were crazy. Something like acceptance. He would let two or three of us invade his tiny quarters and sit on the floor. The accommodations were lean—mattress on a spring bed, overhead bulb in a tawdry shade, a tiny side table, two-drawer dresser, coffin closet.

"So, Jack, where are you really from?"

"California? Everyone says you're from Oregon."

"Do you even know where that is?" Jack smiled.

"Not exactly."

"So why should I tell you?"

No great answers for nine year olds.

"I go to college in Oregon; it's north of California."

"What are you going to be?"

"A mortician."

We all shook our heads knowingly, knowing absolutely nothing.

"What's that?" someone had the courage to ask.

"I will take care of the dead and help their families bury them," Jack smiled.

The only sound was the clattering of pots and pans in the Inn kitchen twenty yards off Jack's quarters being washed for dinner. None of us had any direct experience with death. Those with deceased in their past had been shielded. None of us had seen a dead body or envisioned touching one. This extraordinary and creepy revelation was wildly upsetting by any reckoning.

"That is so weird," I finally said.

'You think so?" he offered. "Say your grandma or grandpa dies or a friend——maybe you—in an accident?" Jack asked. "Who handles it? Who takes charge of the body? Helps the loved ones through the hoops? Prepares the body of the departed being? Creates a funeral so people can pay respects? Think about it. A person dies. Do you have a clue about how that human being is handled and put to rest?"

"Yeah, I guess, but…so creepy."

"Call me the Undertaker."

Cool. The Undertaker.

Of course, little unbridled bastards we were, we had to supply the Guards with our intelligence to curry a favor so they would tousle our hair and call us "champ." They, in their own late teens, early-twenty metaphysical flux, had little more clue than us. Truth? Everyone knows the Undertaker in their way. Call it fear, but Jack Rhodes was dealing with the dead, and he liked it.

The rest of the Inn team, of which Jack was a humble and giant force, was a typical mix of semi-athletic or semi-spazz guys. They could not help it. They were hired because they were upright dandies. If that sounds like a put-down, it is definitely not. They were cool in a way we did not understand and scoffed at. They would be solid citizens, responsible, probably increasingly conservative, but pay their taxes, vote, and try to do right. The Inn girls? Librarian sexy bey-ond belief. A sense of female power and intellect did not exist in the enclave——Adam's rib and all—but they could melt icebergs in their demure ways.

The Inn knew its audience. The Inn people came, often in new model, re-spectable cars—Plymouths, Chevys, Fords—and checked into spartan quarters. How spartan? We knew because I and my pals regularly snuck into the Inn properties and reconnoitered. Bead board walls, shared bathrooms, minimal furniture—monk-like. They came for simplicity of soul but knew how to deck out with class.

Each morning, an Inn bell-ringer went past the Inn dwellings, the pure clanging announcing breakfast. People emerged from the clapboard buildings dressed as if for an admission interview with St. Peter. There were no shorts and t-shirts or ruffling track suits and sneakers for the adults. The women wore tasteful, sleeveless, slightly contoured summer dresses slightly below the knee. The men wore button down, pinpoint oxford cotton shirts with linen slacks and sports jackets with wing-tips or the occasional pair of two-tone saddle shoes. From the Inn dining room arose great communal song every morning––hymns, tunes of fellowship. Loud, fervent and fun.

After breakfast, the visitors repaired to the Green and its shuffleboard courts. Ka-ching! I and my fellows played shuffleboard endlessly in the hot afternoon hours when the courts were deserted with people enjoying the beach. Endlessly. We could ram 'em, curve 'em, kiss 'em like Olympic curlers. When games got tense, the Inn people had the option of paying, like a quarter, for a local to take the shot. We waited on the sidelines like respectful hyenas for the call. Different folks had different favorites. Whatever. Nine of ten, whomever was picked, nailed it to the marveled applause and delight of our benefactors. A quarter with a penny candy store across from the Green was a couple sodas and enough candy to make us sick. Some days we all scored.

The Inn thing was about decorum, Christian spirit and natural peace. As said, they hired students from the best colleges as chambermaids, wait staff, and maintenance. The girls' uniforms were a crisp, pale yellow, linen button-down dress with a white Peter Pan collar, augmented with an equally crisp, white, linen short apron. It is not overstated to describe the outfit as a vision of youthful purity and innocent sensuality. The guys' uniform was black pants with a short-sleeve, button-down collar white shirt. It was dramatically colorless in the sun-drenched days of summer with madras, prints, and pastels abounding. The get-up sadly contributed to the sense they were dull. Jack Rhodes wore cut-offs and hacked T-shirts like the Guards. He was kitchen.

The reality from the eyes of relentlessly spying, unknowing kids was bespoke, sensual passion in abundance among these mystical Inn and Guard elders. Beach or Inn, they were sex-oriented and inspired about it despite volleyball rivalries. They were canoodling, how chastely unknown, and drinking some beer (we found the empty cans). For all the religion, young, good-looking people wanted to be alive and passionate in a summer place of beauty. Such is the paradox of outdoor, natural worship.

To the game and spike.

The Inn basically had Jack and Eaton, a lanky Brown hire, who was deft of foot, could anticipate flows, saw the pattern and was a competent player in this small world. He was the field lieutenant under warrior Jack. Beanie Wells and Rodney Striker were marginally competent in that they did not duck if the ball came their way as others on the Inn side did. Beanie was a violinist in the Yale Symphony Orchestra and passionate to experience life beyond his intellect and violin. Beanie was clinical, striving in his efforts, but short of being a reliable shot-maker. Still, in his athletic flaws, one saw the intensity it must have taken to master concertos of endless pages and complexity flawlessly. He was frustrated his prodigious other talents left him wanting on the volleyball pitch, but he was game. No emotion of victory or defeat ever showed. I thought frankly he was a killer with no gun. Rodney Striker was the scion of a rich, west coast vintner, spoiled by east coast prep schools. His soul wanted feral but, given the opulence of his birthright, defaulted to languid elitism. Still, the feral soul lived in the fury with which he dove for sand saves on sinking balls.

The rest of the Inn team was marginal biomass. They took spaces in rotations and hoped balls did not come their way. They were not athletes and cursed the fact their employment—never stated anywhere—put them weekly six on six against the Guards.

A strange thing happened to this Inn haphazard amalgam. Few in the East had a concept, totally not in the Village, that out West they played beach volleyball with a vengeance, two on two, full court—inconceivable. Likewise, no one could know Jack Rhodes was a legend in two on two. The truth was, with a single competent teammate, he could slice and dice the Guards like a surgeon. Jack did not care to do that in the Village as a gentleman. He let the others dither and smack, win or lose. This was recreational volleyball. He did his thing in a laid-back manner, a universe above and away. It would take an awkward happenstance to unleash the Undertaker to full magnificence.

It is the identification of and proximity to greatness that sets dull passions to a hope, a belief. The Inn team—no hard athletes, no yearning jocks—saw in Jack they had the rare experience of teaming with an excellence they would not experience again in any athletic domain. In their limited ways, they got competitive. It was a revelation. They grew in a lethal manner the religious ways never taught. They wanted it. Oh, yes, they did. Kill the Guards.

The Guards were a strikingly different bunch on game days. You could hear them coming up from the beach a scant quarter of a mile away as tip-off loomed. Two rag-top Jeeps, horns honking, rolling into the Village like a conquering Mongol horde to wild adoration, most vociferously from the young crowd. They rolled into the Village familiar in body but dominant in thought. There was meaning in what they intended. For the series final, they had all applied eye black, war paint, in a strip across their cheekbones.

The Guards were the pop stars of a small, inconsequential ecosystem, but they ruled. Every kid wanted to be a Guardian. White, zinc-pasted nose , twirling a whistle around a finger on architecturally cool, wooden towers, warning swimmers against flaunting beach rules. No diving backside of the rafts where chains threatened. No swimming under the rafts where the weak could not resurface. No distance swimmers from adjacent public beaches seeking respite on beach rafts. It was a private beach, after all.

The Inn versus Guard fan hysteria was lopsided in the Thursday night competition. The Inn dwellers were diffident. They were two-week vacationers, a revolving population, with less-than-rabid volleyball passion. Their focus? The Tabernacle, spiritual revival and the Beach. The Villagers had daily, except for weather, interaction with the Guards.

All summer long, it was "Sarge, the wind is so strong. Can you dig the umbrella deeper?" or, "Paulie, my kid still can't swim to the raft. What are you going to do?" or, "Davis, I can't believe the seaweed at the shore, do you guys rake?"

Serving the members—constant, entitled, oblivious to the whims of the ocean, the Guard role was not the beauty one might imagine. The Guards knew at a tender age the wrath of the privileged. Still, they were Guards, a coveted title on a small slice of beach in a place barely known to anyone and then, very cool.

The Guards were in a macho quandary. The Inn "poofs," however limited, were not rolling over to past history. Through a closely contested season, on the Inn side of the net, there was not the bent-shouldered, telltale posture of subjugation of former years. They would fight hard for nothing more than to take the mottled, old corn liquor jug with "Village Volleyball Champs" in old script on its side as if it were an ancient Greek laurel wreath. It is called doubt. These Guards knew it. Doubt kills. It was to be a scrap.

Much as they may have wished differently, the Guards were no juggernaut. They appeared to be at times, but the current 4–4 tie in standings spoke of flaws. In the backwaters of athletic endeavor, minor glory is major and timeless. A glut of small time championships everywhere. It was impossible to know if any of their team possessed the insight this game would be an event remembered in quiet and unexpected reflection in their lives. Probably not. Life would only ever get bigger and better with victories of far greater moment.

The Guards had the athletically gifted Paulie O'Brea from South Boston. Though not to the mystical perfection of Michaelangelo's "David," his frame might have been a passing model. He was tall, powerfully proportioned, and agile. He was twenty, out of high school, working construction during the "off-year" and lifeguarding summers. The appointment was a patronage job afforded by his parents' long-standing beach membership. He was a former two-sport, all-conference athlete in football as a tight end and track, throwing the discus in Boston. He was quiet and at times abrupt in communication. He carried himself as if winning was an ordinary expectation. Paulie had no clue about a future life, just that he would figure it out.

He was flanked by two gamers.

A-tone, Anthony by Christian name, out of Worcester. A scrappy, pugnacious Irish mongrel born to parents, his mother of olde Erin wealth, his father brickyard Irish tough. Gracious enough from his mother's side, he still carried the warrior, zero-sum ethic from his father. He had no time, no way for those not striving. A-tone was a bristling, live wire, prone to manic joy and depressive moods. There was no quit, but there was flawed volleyball talent. Boxing? He would clear your cobwebs as a welterweight. Wrestling? Your joints would never know the pretzels they could achieve. Volleyball? Okay, not memorable except the way he would debase himself loudly, verbally at any failure. ("A-tone, you idiot. Rally! Get it together!") Yet, his Irish clan mania could make a dig, a set, a spike from nowhere in the clutch for the team—sometimes.

Pollack, Georg Wiz—no one could spell the flood of consonants and sparse vowels in weird combinations in his name, let alone pronounce it—came from Beverly. He was a tight package of muscle and agility befitting the accomplished gymnast he was. Compact, lacking height, he was an excellent setter and digger. Pollack had perfected the "skyscraper serve" where he put every taut sinew into launching serves so high and in bounds even the worthy blanched at the descending ball from the pine tops above. It was said the Wiz family was from Polish aristocracy. Looking at him, you might believe it. In the time, what was said was what was. "A Polish prince? Okay, glad he's here." Move on.

A fair-minded person would throw Sarge into the mix as a factor. The trouble was, at twenty-one and pre-med at Boston College, Sarge wanted to be a surgeon. He came out of Cambridge from a lineage of Peter Brent Brigham hospital physicians. Moderate of physique but canny and prescient, he always saw the play and knew where to be. Whether he was going to risk his hands to abet or thwart the attack, offensive or defensive, was totally in question. If the calculation were positive in his mind, he could make a deft shot. Hands at risk? No.

The other Guards were like you and me. They wanted it, had the desire, looked good in hacked sweatshirts and the loose cut-offs of Guard garb, but fumbled more often than executed the necessities of the fiercest exchanges. Caffs ate more sand diving in his passion for glory, teeth covered in quartz/silica, than anyone, mostly with little result. Davis, the gentle giant, lived knowing his size, to the surrounding fans, should ordain dominance, but the coordination and the killer being escaped him. He was among the kindest on the pitch—he was the best swim teacher, the calmest, non-macho (the term meant nothing then) guy with whom to talk about your swimming fears and much else. We wanted to protect him in a silly, we-know-nothing way. The court exposed him. He was barely passible.

The stories went deeper, but it was a volleyball match after all. The fevers and hopes of the lads are the basis of psychology and history. The match meant nothing and everything in the Divine Perfection, just as it is. Let it play. Let it go. Maybe, not easy.

The match was two of three games won to twenty-one points, need to win by two—same as always. Aldous Creen was set on the umpire's ladder. He was as fair as fair can be defined and a retired athletic director from a Little Ivy school. The man actually lived in grace. Peace. Justice. Passion. Compassion. No tainting as if there ever would be in the Village. He knew honorable competition and the deadly will of athletes. He was the judge and knew it, loved it. He had coached great teams and seen individual champions play with far, far more at stake. In his keen eye and "old soul" sense, he knew the match was a thing of beauty however small. It would be fair.

The first game was a disaster for the Inn. No sportswriter or poet could put a better spin upon it: 21–7 Guards. The feeling of subjugation, resignation, and anti-climax permeated the sand pitch. Go to game two. Go home thereafter. The Guards did nothing great beyond competent handling of serves, three-and-over to deep corners on the Inn side, and an occasional gnarly spike from Paulie on a good set. The Inn was comatose. Pollack launched a skyscraper serve that descended through the flailing hands of a biomass guy—name never to be known—and hit him on the head, knocking him to the sand. Politeness and sportsmanship curtailed excessive laughter, but it was comical. Beanie had the simplest of easy sets for Jack at the net, but the ball squirted up and back, requiring Jack to arch and reach beyond his control and slam the ball twenty yards deep out of bounds.

All was quiet on the exchange of sides and short time-out. The crowd held an apologetic silence in humane deference to the embarrassment.

Jack, out of character with his entire summer being, called the Inn team closer in a huddle. At first, it was a loose milling of elements around a nucleus.

"Get the fuck over here," he hissed, heard only by we spy kings.

The language was not of the Village or very Christian.

"Now!" The spit shot from his pursed lips. "Damn it."

The Inn team contracted into a tight mass around Jack kneeling in the center.

"Listen up," he said in a low, calm voice. "You go down like this to these bozos, you will go down forever to other bozos when the deal matters. Compete, Godammit. Call it going to the next level."

Then, Jack got better than fire and brimstone. He laid it out cold and challenging. His voice was a whisper, but it sounded like an orator at fever pitch.

"The next level is you leave your sorry thoughts and become your body. You see, move, hear with nothing, no other thought but doing the perfect thing in your power to win a point—one point. Get it. One point. One after another. Fail? Repeat the goal for the perfect. All the time. Every time. If I see less than that fire of commitment in your eyes, I, as captain, will kick your ass off the court. I am not a loser and will not play with anyone who is. We had it at times. Now is the only time. Get the hell out there and win!"

The Inn team seemed hypnotized and unrecognizable as they broke the circle. Unlike the Guards who broke with war cries, hand claps, and cheers, the Inn took their places in silence and awaited the Guard serve. Sarge launched a spinning cut to a biomass player who actually shifted his feet and arms and delivered a ball to Eaton in the front row. Eaton pumped the ball up to Jack about five feet over net height. Jack elevated and slammed the descending ball with a spike that had never been seen in the half-century annals of Village volleyball. The ball screamed off his palm and struck Caffs middle high on his no-sleeved bare shoulder, turning him, before squirting to the ground. Caffs laughed it off, but the redness flamed like a beacon. Something had happened, and any sentient fan knew it. Game on.

The Inn reeled off five more points for a 5–0 lead before the Guards regrouped in the face of the Inn's new intensity. It was not a 5–1 to the Guards because, under the rules of the time, a team had to win service from the serving team before it could score points on its own serve. The Guards took back three and possibly had a fourth point, but the Pollack bellied too close to the net and, barely, barely ticked the net cord on a return. It was so slight and may have been ignored in a match of lower stakes. The whistle of Aldous Creen shrieked, much like the Guards signaling an infraction at the beach. He awarded the Inn serve.

Grumbles of disbelief arose from the Guard faithful and mutters from the Guards themselves. Georgie Wiz, showing great sportsmanship, dispelled the discontent with an affirmative nod to Creen who, with his own almost imperceptible nod, signaled, *Well done.*

The Inn piled on three more points with simple, non-spectacular execution of dig, set, and place. Only Eaton could actually get up high to deliver a downward slam. Most on either side could not unless within a foot or two from the net. Eaton was on front-line in the sixth rotation and got two. Jack smiled at him in respect.

The second game was prelude to the match game. The strange and transforming ethos of the Inn was undeniable. Though the Guards could scratch back points, the Inn would add a few more with conviction. It is a sorrow those who never put themselves on the line in competition could not understand what was happening. It does not matter pro sports, college sports, intramural sports, pick-up sports, the Inn had gelled. Basically non-athletes as they were, they had a team ethic. What is that? The Inn, biomass included, had gone beyond fear of failure and humiliation. They scented winning and knew each had his own responsibility.

Game two: 21–16 Inn.

The Guards, though not voicing it, knew something had changed. A once predictable set of objects across the net had morphed into a group that responded to all challenges as a whole. No slackers. The Guards, gritty, smart, and proud—reasonably seasoned athletes—knew they had to answer.

In the huddle between games, Guard wavering eyes looking toward him, Paulie O'Brea said:

"I love this. This is what it is about. Every time the Inn falters, the Undertaker yells, 'Compete.' That guy is insane. He knows. Compete harder, you win. What do you got? Are the 'poofs' going to send us packing? When Jack yells, 'Compete,' we compete harder. That simple. Unless you want to go down."

Going into match game three, Aldous Creen knew far more than his visage would ever reveal. What did he know?

He knew Jack Rhodes could never compete in any college sport sanctioned by the beloved associations of which he was a board member. Basketball, football, volleyball, whatever. Aldous knew Jack would be near-pro as a college player, pro material except for the damn beach volleyball. Creen had tentacles so deep across the landscape of the entire U.S. amateur sport scene. He merely had to make a few calls. He knew Jack was "dirty." He played for money on the volleyball circuit. The darn thing was that Undertaker never tried to fool anybody. He did not play for his high school team, though he would have likely been all-state. He did not go for an athletic scholarship at his college.

No harm, no foul. Creen just shook his head and wondered what the boy's thinking was. One thing for sure, he violated no rules playing for the Inn, as if ever they might have known they had a money player in their midst. He liked the guy. Total class. Let it play, but Lord, he wished he could have shaped him.

Game three was a seesaw never before seen on the pitch. Back and forth lead changes. Lesser talents stepping up to no-mistake shots. The level of competition was so high from everyone, even from the untalented, that respect took hold. Something happened. It was the sense that however small and inconsequential many things may be, the heart says, *You don't want to lose.*

As if the drama needed heightening, strolling to the court at the first serve in her cotton yellows was Amilie. She had been detained by an Inn fundraiser serving Cape delicacies and wine, seeking donations for the Village sanctity, the Inn relying in part on her virginal loveliness to unleash the flow. It was not amazing how a woman, in her case a young woman, could create a maelstrom of chaste desire and the opening of wallets.

In truth, Amilie was, although Wheaton, average smart. Beautiful with honey hair and a lithe body, her voice was angelic, and chaste innocence exuded from her. As part of her Inn contract, she would sit on benches in the dusk of evening with Eaton and others and sing harmonic tunes a cappella, perfectly and with soul. It would be hard to imagine in future times, but Amilie, Eaton, with other crew, did actually sit on the green and sing spirituals, "Kumbaya," "Michael, Row the Boat Ashore," "If I Had a Hammer," with such purity it brought an already peaceful place into a slice of heaven. Amilie was, hidden beneath all of her Back Bay Boston gloss, of good nature, struggling with tartness, and an ingénue party girl.

Why did her appearance matter?

Somehow, the concept of medieval chivalry survived the onslaught of the modern age and, however faint, probably would forever. The fair lady seated above the jousting run offering a hanky to her beloved knight never died. Centuries later, the reference was bastardized, but quaintly intact. It was complicated as always. The spy crew would know.

There was a secret haven off an inconspicuous door on the backside of an Inn property, almost a cave, as it settled into the sandy turf with a looming, clapboard structure above. The religious founders and Village elders consciously, with wisdom and restraint, ignored it. It was the place where Inn staff and whomever else could go for a break at any time, a wise winking of the eye. We spies knew it intimately. It reeked of cigarette smoke. Playing card decks were strewn about. The occasional empty pint bottle of vodka could be found tucked under musty and stained sofa cushions.

In our omnivorous voyeurism, we actually found what seemed to be a woman's panties nestled into the cushions. Strange as it sounds, we were too young and naïve to put two plus two together. It really did not register some-one had them on, then off—why?—and forgot them. Someone had been doing something, but it was in a world blind to our innocence. Did someone wet their pants?

Amilie's appearance was like a spike of cocaine, which no one knew of back then. Snort it, jack up, and trill. The chaste party girl had not one, not two, but three on the line, it seemed. As always a woman of desire can inspire, and some guys had play in the game.

The Village oohed and aahed at Amilie and Eaton. Such sweethearts, hand-holding Inn stalwarts in their walks to singing sites around the Green. Perfect a cappella harmonies sung on slotted benches. Pure notes wafting over the Vil-lage eve. Chaste pecks on the cheek in parting. The audible, if you were hiding in bushes, was, "Love you," when heading back to their separate quarters. If heaven scripted a love scene, they were it. It actually rang true.

Paulie O'Brea was a Southie bad boy. We saw it and loved him for it. Peek in the rear window of his car, and a few brown-bottle Carling empties caught a glint of sun. In the unholy mess of the Guard's quarters upstairs in the Pavil-ion, which we dutifully raided whenever a Guard left a door unlocked, we found girlie mags by his bunk.

When the Inn staff got off in the afternoon and went to the beach, some-how Amilie, in an arresting but approved two-piece suit wound up under Paulie's guard station. She would chat up to him, smiling, smoothing her suit, pulling the bottom below her buttocks where it had been slipping up. He would smile and laugh, temporarily oblivious to the dangers of the sea. We never got the goods on them, but every instinct said attraction was palpable and most likely more. Why was she so shivery?

Jack Rhodes, so young, had a woman in his young time. Who knew? She was a forty-year-old divorcée, fading B-movie star who followed his beach volleyball career. She seduced the twenty year old like a biblical whore. He was not proud of it. He came east to get away from it. The allure of the Village position was spiritual renewal if he were to be true to his chosen profession. Amilie was a disruption in the design. The only sign of anything was when Artie the head cook in the kitchen let us collect the soda bottles from the refuse to claim a one-cent deposit at the Village store for candy. Sometimes, Amilie in her crisps and Jack in his whatevers sat in the kitchen with a cup of coffee talking, she touching his arm.

It was impossible to believe in a Village so very small and compact, eyes ever-present from the early risers to the can't-sleepers, that Jack and Amilie were undiscovered lovers, a naughty fling, not a passion. Betting odds would say they were the source of the "lost panties," but it was not proven and could have been any of them. Nothing solid.

Game three, match game, Pilgrim Jug at stake, a possibly soiled Guinevere, unfathomable to the public, waving her invisible hankie to whom was unknown.

The game will go down as the greatest ever played on that pitch, a paean to amateurs. All pretenses were gone. It was no longer "poofs" and "pagans." It was grim elation—eat or be eaten, conquer or die. No one saw it more than Aldous Creen. In his career, he had seen and coached national champions in their division. Never for a moment had he thought he would need to be at his best in a puny, recreational volleyball event. Only he could know this was as important as it ever would get athletically for almost everyone on the pitch. Playing for championships, no matter how small, especially in a heated environment, carried a big sobriquet—winner.

The point by point was gritty and sweaty. Sand flying, grunts, expletives that shocked the locals. Give and take, a few points to the positive for either, a claw back from the other. Aldous was mesmerized at the combat and knew he could do no more than call a fair game. All during the summer, he had ignored unclean carries and non-egregious net touches from the less talented to boost their self-esteem. Not now. It had to be clean.

A respect, actually the only way to describe it, had settled on court. No team was entitled. Each team was eating sand to win. A set went way backwards of Jack's normal reach. He overextended, reached back, and palmed it, firing across the net. Whistle from Aldous. Carry! Guard serve! Jack folded his arms and rocked as if carrying a baby to the laughter of the crowd. On a net on net, Beanie Wells went for a dink over A-tone's upraised arms. It fell daintily behind him for a point. A-Tone bowed, and Beanie returned—both laughed.

The Guards were up 17–15, and a force emerged. Jack came afire. He was not going to let his teammates lose and could not allow their failures. Never before seen during the season, he ranged wide and far, stepping into the serve's arc in front of lesser players, popped it up softly and said, "Give me a set, give me a set."

They did, and he delivered not without intermittent serve loss. He moved the Inn to 20–19. His nemesis was Paulie, playing like a demon with "no way" in his eyes, always killing his own spikes to get stops and stop the momentum. In his fury, Paulie drove one into the net, losing serve. Jack knew that kind of competitor and shuddered. The Irishman was not going down easy. Inn serve, one point from championship.

"Inn serve for match," called Aldous.

Who remembers or cares? It was a bunch of stupid kids—some high school, some college—playing volleyball. Truth? Most do. The serve went to Davis, who kept it in good play, to Sarge, who gave a set off-center, to Paulie, who could only punch it deep. Rodney Striker gave a deft riser to a biomass guy center court, who somehow lifted a heaven's arc to Jack Rhodes. Jack rose and smacked it into Paulie's block, not blindly but angled. The rebound ball crept along the net top and fell on the Guard side to a diving, unsuccessful save from Caffs. Game. Match!

The kids groaned. The adults clapped politely. Nothing changed in the universe. Maybe small things did change.

The teams never really met after games, but they gathered under Creen's ladder chair and shook hands. Most of the Guard's eye black had smeared, and the team looked fearsome. The Inn team looked almost sheepish and apologetic in comparison, having the rare experience in winning.

Creen had a way, a confidence, and a resume that made people listen. He simply said, "Fine a game as I have seen all summer, maybe all summers. All winners."

That was right before awarding the jug. The Inn team bunched up to accept the trophy jug like they were embarrassed for being the feral animals they recently had been. Jack was in the back. He called to Eaton.

"Hey, pick it up, raise it, kiss it. We won.

Eaton did most all, but did not kiss it.

Jack walked over to a sideline bench where Paulie was sitting.

"Nice game," Jack said.

"Easy for you, Undertaker," Paulie smiled.

"Don't be an asshole."

"You are killer, buddy."

"Truth is, you're better than me. More natural. You just haven't learned the game."

A hand from behind touched each of their shoulders with a gentle grip. It was Amilie.

"Wow, guys. So well played. Congratulations."

"Thanks, Amilie," Paulie said over his shoulder, only half-turning. "Could you go congratulate Eaton? We're kinda talking right now."

She turned on a dime and left. They looked at each other and laughed. Jack never could have been that tough, but he liked it.

Jack spoke first.

"West coast, two-man volleyball pays a wage. I got five grand playing part-time last season. I need a partner. Last one said I was too weird. Any interest?"

"You damn ringer," Paulie shrugged.

"Nope, came out here to get clean. I had no clue you had this volleyball ritual."

"True?"

"True. Interest? Wanna be a legend? Get girls. Work a job, but really do what you love?"

"Do I gotta handle dead bodies with you?"

Jack laughed harder than he had for the whole summer.

"Nope. I leave tomorrow. I can get you set up but you'll need a job. Tournaments are regular but spaced. If you want to pump formaldehyde into veins, I have contacts. Other opportunities. That's it, Paulie. Sorry for your loss."

"Fuck you, Undertaker," he laughed.

Aldous Creen saw them talking on the bench, waving Amilie away, their shoulders slumped, pitched forward, elbows on knees as teammates do. He surmised what Jack was proposing. Come out where it matters. Every match like this but for money and fame. He descended his ladder and walked over to pair.

"Thanks, Aldous," Jack said. "Well called."

Paulie grunted assent.

"Make the most of it, gentleman. Jack is honorably soiled with professional winnings, never professing otherwise, and you, Paulie, are not looking for college eligibility. Might I say with conviction—go kick some ass out West. I believe you can."

* * *

Our voyeur boy crew passed on to teen maturity with our own needy lives. I know a little gossip over the years and pass it on as a Village neighbor. Amilie and Eaton did marry, their happiness was true. Sarge became a surgeon in Boston, his reputation impeccable. Beanie Wells became a concert violinist of note in almost every major city orchestra he auditioned for, but never concert master. A-Tone was shot up in Vietnam and proud of it. Georgie flim-flammed a scheme that brought him time. Davis died young. That is about it.

Except.

About a year after the big game, I asked my hometown librarian for a copy of Volleyball News. She looked at this kid with a sense of incredulity and duress, having no clue such a publication existed. A week later, she said she could get some old copies from a local university sports department secretary. She did.

August 27, 1959

TopEnd Beach Volleyball Champions

In a tightly contested finals match on the Venice beach pitch, the Under-takers bested the Sun Gods 3–2 to win the coveted four thousand dollar TopEnd purse. Jack Rhodes and Paulie O'Brea, a newcomer to the beach scene from New England, displayed superior grit and resilience in the face of a thundering Sun Gods offense from Dirk Banes and Yevi Rostok. Congratulations!

1964–The Goddess

It was a tough thing "summering" on the very cool beach, a stone's throw from the tiny New England Village as a fifteen year old. Why? Try the nubile, tanned, coming of age, bikinied girls. The bikinis, more two-pieces, weren't as scant then, even though the famed "Itsy-Bitsy Yellow Polka-Dot Bikini" was extolled in song a few years before. Those bikinis, hot as they were, would be like a nun's habit now. Add to the equation incredibly few of the girls at the beach club, none in my knowledge, were putting out—anything. We are not talking about orgies, far beyond my conceptual thinking or social imagination at that point. How about some tongue kissing and body contact? The girls were beautiful, proper, sensible, and tighter than a tick. Nada.

The "beach" was not singular. There were four of them splayed in a row in the center of the concave arc of a wide, picturesque bay; all were renowned in their way. Two were public beaches run by the county and highly visited by locals, vacationers and day-trippers from the Boston surrounds. Two were private beaches. One, called Association, dated back to the late 1800s and had a center Victorian-style pavilion and rows of bathhouses neatly built upon boardwalks atop piers on either side of the main structure. That was my beach. It was not really all that exclusive for a little money, but it was stunning, old-timey architecture. The other was the "Club," way more toney, a lot of dough, and by invitation only.

The upstairs of my beach's pavilion had a broad deck and a large, wood-floored ping-pong room with two doors—one to each side—to bare, plank-walled lifeguard quarters with rough bunk built-ins. Many summers, an adult—the guards were not considered adults, merely idolized—never set foot up there. It made it an adolescent kid heaven. The Association was fenced off from the public beaches on each side. The Club was fenced off as well.

The other Club was august, landscaped, ever the clink of cocktail glasses chiming noon through the evening. Even if one had the money to join the Club, which most did not, the person would not likely feel comfortable there without some Brahmin lineage or claim of Boston-Irish royalty. It was dotted with judges, politicians, and an occasional monsignor or bishop of the church as weekend guest.

We had a gang who all belonged to our frankly impressive, yet lesser, Association club. Most of us lived summers in the Village on the bluff above the beach, and we blended in with a nice gang of local teens who had family memberships. We were about equal in number, guys to girls, an ambient group of ten to twelve teenagers depending on time of summer. We were reasonably handsome, pretty, and fun. We created a territory in a bay between bathhouse rows that was known forever as our space.

But...there was a fatal flaw like a bad family gene. In our midst, as hormones and sexual awakening boosted kid's play to what passed for racy innuendo, trouble was brewing. The bad gene?

Too close. We had been coming there for years, since infancy in some cases, to the same Village, to the Association Beach, to the beach locker bay like turtles returning to the same parcel of sand and water. We had attended early birthday parties for those who had a summer birthdate, wearing conical, elastic-banded party hats. We were documented with Kodak photos for posterity with smeared icing and dripping ice cream on our persons. We had taken the dreaded swimming lessons at the Beach together as pre-teens in cold, morning waves, standing and shivering on a bad day in shore seaweed so thick at times as to make us feel we were the meat morsels in a soup. We had thrown the innocuous "moonie" jellyfish at the girls who squealed. We had taken group tennis lessons on the Village courts with some skills but no visible Wimbledon star emerging, maybe third singles in high school at best.

We were too close for erotic encounters in that era, and "erotic" was something totally different then. In a quaint, almost forgotten language, like disappearing tongues of tribes, all of us knew the metric of scoring on the drive to fame. It was baseball-based. A first base single was kissing, and a long single included some tongue. Second base was breast petting with a long double being under-bra skin. Third base was hand on crotch with a near inside-the-park homer if you touched anything moist. A home run was if you actually achieved penetration. No one came close to the warning track. It was totally male-oriented, but it was the lingua franca of teen sex. The girls knew the metric totally, and everybody hit banjo—as in "plink"—singles. It was pretty innocent then. Today, forget it. I often say I missed that cross-over, but I knew boundaries then and cared.

Our little clan had a core, and it changed composition on the fringes, sometimes numbering fourteen. New guys and girls would show up, maybe to vacation a couple of summers with parents or aunts, and disappear. Our locals would bring in friends, too, which added some excitement. As we hit puberty, the new blood girls created a shark feeding frenzy—maybe, just maybe, a four-bagger. The problem was we were in a homeostasis. No one could break out to passion because everyone else would know in a nanosecond. Dabbling was fine. Home runs were not in the mix.

If you had the sex thing on your brain, it was tough. There was no porn, no magazines with pink back then by a long shot. You just had to imagine. Imagine what? You could go to a library and furtively look at medical books––pretty clinical—about the treasures that lay beneath lined, cotton two-pieces and bikinis, but no one was showing. What was a hormonally driven boy to do? Only the age-old option.

It was that crucible of forbidden lust that created my star-crossed love for Lexi Johansson. It is a story of crazy, insatiable love—me more than her, but not entirely—for the most beautiful, prescient girl in my lifetime. She haunts me in soothing and sad ways fifty years later, and I will never let go. The goddess who made me a man gently.

I do not know why, but I found women, girls, the most beguiling of creatures. I felt their power. I was saddened, as I came to understand later, that they, the original goddesses of ancient cultures, were subjugated and demeaned all around the world. In my brain, they held a wisdom I never perceived in my male buddies. It may be stupid to say, but I felt them more sacred, more put-together. That belief proved both wrong and right in life. There are crazies all over, regardless of gender, but girls generally less so. I loved them very deeply in an honest way. Actually, I wanted to ravish them and give all too. A little crazy at fifteen, that was me.

*   *   *

Lexi Johansson worked in the Harpoon snack bar across the beach road. I wasn't a rich kid, but we had money and had membership at the club. We had our own excellent snack bar there and I had a part-time gig. Showing teenage, pathetic bravado to the females in our gang, we would sometimes blow off our own snack bar, leaving the babes behind as if we were adventurers and go to the ocean-front strip. This was all of 150 yards away. True Shackletons were we. On a day off, I went alone.

The scene was not notable. A fifteen-year-old boy, sixteen in September, in surfer baggies of the time, T-shirt and flip-flops, comes to the counter for a clam roll. Lexi Johannson addresses him.

"Hey, what'll it be?"

The boy, me, cannot answer because every sensory input—vision, hearing, smell—is overwhelmed. Lexi is the most beautiful girl he has ever seen. If beauty transfixes, I can tell you—and I went on as a cinematographer in films with great actresses—Lexi was beyond stunning to my beguiled, horny teenage eyes. She would have been thus in any era. She was also clearly older by that slight but impenetrable gap between a graduated senior and a sophomore. Out of my league, me being C-league, her being Triple-A going to the Bigs.

Lexi had the most perfect mid-neck, vibrant blond, bob cut—a perfect corona—that could ever be shaped. Every hair fell as if placed. A Goddess helmet. She had wispy bangs and eyes so ancient, ice blue as to make one question his measly life. Every feature on her Nordic face was sensually symmetrical—eyes, nose, cheeks, lips, chin. Pure. Even then, I could not imagine she had not been snatched for modeling for all I knew of it. She wore khaki shorts, and her legs dropped from them like those of a Greek sculpture. Her perfect ass, which I noticed waiting in line, protruded from the shorts as she moved and bent to the roundness of an exacting hull design that could have been calculated by a master marine architect. Aerodynamic. Her tanned calves thinned to her ankles in that way of dancers and athletes. It was perfection in the eyes of a lusting, soulful teenager.

"I don't know," I stammered. "Leave it. Back in a sec. Gotta take care of something. No problem."

I could not even order food. The girl I wanted all my young, uninformed, immature life was before me. *Please marry me today and let me make you happy always,* was my first thought. It was not alone with other thoughts. *Please cop-*

ulate with me as a goddess until my eyes spin like pinwheels and saliva drips from each corner of my mouth and they take me away in a straight-jacket, was probably equally accurate. It is tough to be a teenager. I returned to the counter more sensible.

"So what'll it be?" Lexi asked.

"Clam roll and fries with a Fresca," I said not even registering whether I wanted them. I could have said a bowl of tar with a side of sawdust and a glass of Drano for all I was thinking about food.

I got order 546 and took it to an outside picnic table overlooking the ocean. A semblance of rational thought soothed my disrupted brainwaves much as oil on a churning sea:

Look, chum. You're fifteen, lie if you want. Maybe sixteen. One of a couple hundred orders in the day for her. Mr. Clam Roll and Fries and a Fresca. She didn't bat her eyelashes or say, "Hey, cutie." You did not register on her Richter Scale any more than a small wave hitting the beach on a calm day, meaning zero. She is at least two maybe three years older, probably has a boyfriend and a driver's license. You're not rich, have no accomplishments of note. The downside of lustful fantasy is embarrassment and humiliation. You did that already with Kathy Spring with your incoherent babble, speaking tongues at her locker. Thank your lucky stars you didn't start speaking in tongues when you saw this goddess.

I was halfway through my order, sitting alone at the picnic table. The others were full. The screen door squealed open on its hinges, and Lexi emerged into the sunlight. She had a BLT, a side of slaw, and lemonade on her tray. She squinted, adjusting to the sunlight for a moment, saw my table was nearly empty, and walked, glided in my eye, across the sand/seashell mix.

"Mind if I join you?"

"No," I answered. I begged my mind to think of something more gallant or clever, but at least "no" was sensible.

"Lexi," she said smiling.

"Dutch."

"Dutch? Never heard that one. Real or a nickname?"

"Real. You on break?"

Of course she was on break, idiot, but I would have asked any question to keep the dialogue alive.

She raised her BLT, which was half-cut and bit with dainty precision into it. She took a half forkful of slaw and mouthed it. I always watched how people ate. My parents were European and demanded fastidious table manners—neat, efficient, and respectful. Lexi was impeccable, enough to make my mom crumble.

"Yeah, on break. What are you doing? Vacation, local, day-tripper?"

"Vacation. Been coming here since birth. Cottage in the Village. Go to the beach club," I said pointing to ensure I was not talking the Club. "You?"

"Local since birth. A Cape girl."

We each took a bite of our fare and sat silently watching the clouds wash lazily over the water, seeing the change of hues of blue to green and darker as cloud rolls passed.

"So what do you do when you're up here?" she asked.

"Truly care to know? It's boring."

"Try me."

My brain was kicking in. It was more relaxed as I realized I was sitting with the most beautiful of girls, simply talking. I had made myself seem a somewhat bedraggled teen, but I was not. At fifteen, I could not score the second and third bases, but I was actually very smart—tops without bragging—in grades and athletics so far. It was not in my perception then, but I was college scholarships in the waiting. It was not a glimmer of a factor at that picnic table, so I told the truth without games.

"It's always been a beautiful thing. Friends. We always did and do beach, tennis, teenage parties in garages. Bottom fishing at dusk after rowing out to the club rafts for scup, blowfish, and sand sharks. Stupid races on sunfishes. Same old. Now it is trying to find adventure and action up in the big town. Our long-time group lies on towels, teases with no romance. I work part-time shifts at the snack bar."

"The club snack bar?" she asked. "That is the best food of all these dives."

I knew it was good, fresh food—top of the line—for a snack bar, but was taken aback with Lexi's enthusiasm.

"What do you do there?"

"Mostly prep, then bus, clean garbage cans, clean dumpsters, filter the cooking oil and swab all surfaces for tomorrow. The old man, Charlie, is teaching me the fryalator and the grill, but he doesn't trust me yet."

"What do you think of the food here?"

"Really want to know?"

"Duh?"

"Not too good."

"Why?"

"Well, take my order. The fried stuff is not crisp and light. Clams are tough. You pay more, you get more. Charlie has told me. These clams are not puffy and crunchy, too oily. The fries are not hand-cut from potatoes, just from frozen bags and fried. You cannot compare. Everything here has the same burnt flecks from the oil that hasn't been filtered for days."

"Do you like him?"

I knew he was a history teacher at the high school Lexi probably attended.

"He is horrible at times. I live in fear. He has that gimp leg from the battleship that got attacked in the Battle of Manila. He was head cook on his ship and fed hundreds every day. He has a pipe in his mouth dawn to closing. He wears whites always, always, dazzling clean in the morning, and a towel around his neck on the grill. He is impossible if you fuck up, but he is amazingly great if you deliver."

"Do you like him?"

What a pause. I tried to remember Charlie's castigations of me. *Left your brain home? You call that plating attractive? Wouldn't want to meet your girlfriend.* I realized at the moment it was no different from my football coach training a teenager to be adept, accountable and proud. But, Charlie got under my skin more. I wanted to please the bastard man.

"Yeah, Lexi. Not because I am a buddy. No one is. He has taught me more about cooking and kitchen skills than I could get in a lifetime. He said, 'If you can run a kitchen, you will always survive.' I cannot believe he has taught me knife skills that are amazing."

"Charlie is a teacher at my high school in the off-season," she offered shyly. "I was in his class. He scared me for reasons. Not bad. I was just not confident. He wanted more from me. Strength. Drive? They were tough because I struggled. He wanted me at the Association for this season. I chose this because he scared me."

Lexi finished the remains of her lunch. As did I.

"So what else about lunch?" she asked.

"You really want to know?" Spoken as both a brat trying to maintain contact with a goddess at any cost and hoping her interest was real.

"Charlie would never serve a half-cut sandwich. He makes us cut on the diagonal. He says it looks bigger and is easier to eat. He is all about dressing the sandwich. 'Leave the fixings exposed on the edges. Makes it look more inviting.' Your coleslaw was the creamy kind, which he hates. No mayonnaise for him. He has me shred ten cabbages at end of day into a huge bowl. He never measures but adds olive oil, rice vinegar, lemon juice, garlic, thyme, salt and pepper, and throws in caraway seeds and raisins tosses it, and lets it sit overnight. Really tasty. He is always doing something different."

"Maybe I should've taken him up and worked there. Learned something."

"You can if you want. We're down a girl at the counter. The one who left was a ditz. She splattered frappes all over the walls because she didn't secure them."

"I'll think about it, Dutch, but don't be a stranger here, even if the food sucks. Thanks for the info."

With that she stood, emptied her tray into a trash barrel, and went back in to sling snack bar fare.

I returned to the bath house bay and found the crew sated from lunch. Some had brought sandwiches in insulated packs. Some were back from the snack bar.

"Hey, Dutch! How was the big wide world?" asked Mikey Garragan.

They were all lying on their stomachs or backs on towels, some with heads propped on palms looking out or up, depending on position.

"Who is this Lexi Johannson behind the counter at the Harpoon?"

It was a question not a pronouncement, but on a windy day with four-foot swells, at least two crashed before anyone spoke. It was only the locals who eyed each other with mouths in an unsymmetrical "O."

It was Danny Briles, Mikey's buddy, who answered.

"She is the mystery of the high school. Beyond knowing. Every jock, class president, mover, or shaker wanted to tap her. She's nice. Smiles. Offends no one but is out of bounds. Untouchable. She hangs with biker guys from Scituate who come to the Cape on weekends. What the hell is your question?"

"I had lunch with her. Who is she?"

"Oh, no, no, no," injected Danielle, a saucy and petite local with promise but inelastic Catholic values. "You get no answers until you tell us about lunch and why she was sitting with your loser self."

"I will ignore the insult. She found me unbelievably attractive and took her lunch break with me."

"Oh, yeah, mmm, mmm, mrrmrr," emanated from the group.

"Okay. She had a break. There were no picnic table spaces except at mine. She asked if she could sit with me. 'Oh, no,' I said, 'I need this space for me and my clam roll and Fresca.' Yah, right, dolts. She sat and we talked. That's all."

"What did you talk about?" mouthed Mikey.

"Nuclear physics, fuck up," I said with a sense of cool. "I don't owe all of you a blow-by-blow of my life."

"Was it juicy?"

I turned to my stomach on my towel and slept. Why I slept for so long, I will never know.

It was Sara, another local—actually the next homecoming queen-to-be — —who tapped my shoulder. The umbrellas were stored, the guards off-duty, the sun dropping over the marsh to the west behind the beach.

All of us in budding ways had loved Sara. It was beautiful and ridiculous. She accommodated each of us with kind, mild attention over the period of our teens. She puppy-loved each of us serially, only one per summer, like she knew we pimply, neo-males needed validation to become our eventual meager selves. If it were your turn, it was a summer of beautifully desperate teenage kisses that suggested more but never evolved. She was quite beautiful, very mystical, definitely Wiccan through her family lines from colonial times—but that was unbeknownst to us as fact at the time.

"Dutch, Dutch, wake up! Time to go home."

I was in my own thoughts in that state between sleep and wake, sand plastered to my forehead as I arose.

"I want to say something about Lexi."

"Look, Sara. This is ridiculous. I had a random lunch with an older goddess who totally slayed me. Out of my league by leagues."

"Shut up. I want to tell you something."

"What?"

"Lexi was the most exciting, creative force in my boring life. She was two years ahead of me in school. I adored her," Sara said with an intensity that caught me.

"In the field days at the end of school in ninth grade, she outran all but the best boy quarter-miler. Tops. In swimming, she actually beat all the boys in an ocean distance swim. People were talking possible Olympics. Of course, the boys hated it."

"Hold it, here." I said, thinking about the girl/goddess I had seen. "She beat the guys?"

"Totally. She was so pretty, yet powerful. She was always joshing girls, including me, to get off our asses and compete, but there were so few sports, even for her. She totally could have run men's track or swam if we had a team. She was a thoroughbred without a racetrack, especially up here."

Sara said it with a passion and a sadness that, given her empathic gifts, gave me uneasy pause.

"Then, all of a sudden, something very hush-hush happened. We're old Puritans here. There was no information. All I know is Lexi went into Child Services and disappeared for two years until this spring to graduate. She came out silent, lower energy, with no desire to be in the high school mix. She wanted wilder. Definitely not interested in our little knicker-butts anymore."

"Sara, I had a sane, normal conversation today with Lexi, who popped the lid off my head. There is no more. She was as interested in me as a fly on the table. She was just, I don't know, nice."

"Drop it, Dutch. She will hurt you. There is a hurt that happened. She is a biker chick."

"You are a horrible witch girl who makes us all love you with no return."

"I give what I get, immature boy."

I pulled myself off the sand and took the short walk up the bluff to the Village wondering what the hell was up. Lexi Johannson, a biker chick, away from whatever joy drove her youth.

★   ★   ★

I had a full shift at the snack bar starting the next morning at 6:30 A.M. Charlie didn't arrive until 8:30 A.M. I had a checklist and improvised on my own. You had to be aware of the weather. Good, go max—iffy, go moderate—rain, go light on the prep. It was a total go day. I made sure all the garbage cans, inside and out, were emptied and newspaper-lined. It was not plastic back then. They weren't lined, but I wasn't going to rat out Gus for the sloppiness of his job.

I re-swabbed the floors and counters. I turned on the cooking oil, making sure it was strained and turned it to fry, and then the grill to 350. I turned the ovens to 375 because we had to bake today. I took fifteen lettuce heads, twenty tomatoes, three packs of carrots, three red onions from the larder and rough-chopped, grated, and fine-chopped into five big bowls for salad and mixed two cups of home-brewed dressing with Charlie's recipe and doused lightly––very lightly. I medium-diced five large yellow onions, tears running, for hot dog/hamburger condiments and sliced another three dozen beefsteak tomatoes for hamburger dressing. I took in vendor deliveries of clams, lobsters, haddock, and potatoes. I three-quarter fried four pounds of bacon on the grill for BLT's, early breakfasts, and bacon burgers and put that mass in the no-cook zone on the grill for early use. I took the twenty-quart pot, filled it with hot, hot water for head start, and covered it, and when boiling, threw in the lobsters for ten minutes and drained. I set up the various prep bowls for cooking. I checked inventories for critical items. Charlie kept the larders stocked, but it was not scientific.

Amazing, I thought, but I had been trained.

"Think about a couple hundred fightin' men," Charlie said. "You gonna say 'Sorry guys, runnin' late?'"

Charlie burst through the back screen door in his whites with the ubiquitous sweat towel draped over his neck and shoulders and pipe in mouth. "So who lit a fire under your ass?" he said. "Nice job."

"Thanks, but it is what it takes."

He grunted and started giving orders.

"We need fourteen lobsters boiled, shelled, and chopped for lobster rolls."

"Boiled, not shelled or chopped yet. I have a question."

"We don't have time for too many, but what the hell is it?"

"We're short a counter girl with experience. I met a counter girl with experience on the strip who wants to change. Are you open to that?"

"A dime a dozen, but the best are good. Who is she?"

"Lexi Johannson."

Suppose you are young and uninformed, brave without recourse, and saw madman Charlie blink; the only time I saw him do so.

"She wants here?"

"I think so. She wants to learn."

"Tell her to see me."

"I may be a kid, but I understand there is a lot going on I do not know."

"So," Charlie said, "you fell in love. Everybody does. Just beware."

"People say that, Charlie." He let his staff call him that. To anyone else underage it was Mr. Stafford. "Why?"

Charlie was in his peripatetic mode about the kitchen, rolling doughs for pies, filling bowls with pie fillings, stocking the grill shelves with spices and condiments for cooking, shoving filled pies into the oven. He was mixing dozens of eggs and milk for early morning scrambled eggs to be refrigerated for later use and a healthy portion with a little beer for batter and dusted flour for fried sea food. All at the same time, it seemed.

"You're standing doing nothing. Work! I pay you! Do something," he barked.

He was right. I was half-standing my rear on the ice cream cooler.

"I will tell you so you do not get your sorry, privileged ass flayed in this. Now you work. Got it? The girls aren't here for another half hour. Finish your prep."

I started straining the quart cans of high-quality clams and saving the juice for chowder.

"I don't trust you, Dutch. Not yet. At your age, you could not keep your goddamn mouth shut if some juicy tidbit made you look like the beach king in front of the broads. You are a horny kid with no sense of dignity for anyone else yet. If I say what I know to save your ass and it ever gets out, I will castrate you on this counter, and the daily special will be Dutch meatballs. You think not, but my wife died, I have no children, and I will do it for fun."

Charlie, his pipe chuffing smoke, towel over shoulder getting damp, crisp whites getting a little soggier glared at me. I knew, even if he did not castrate me, which he could have done with surgical precision, my mouth must be sealed. I knew it must be for Lexi.

"Treat me like a goddam adult, Charlie. Just tell me."

"I pay a fortune for those lobsters. Get all the meat," he growled, as I was careless in the lobster shelling.

"I'll tell you something first. On the spit here, we live a lot off of your kind coming. We don't love you or think as highly of you as you think of yourselves. You are here one or two months; we are here twelve. We survive. It is a different world than you know. You could take a sleeping bag on the Beach Road outside the Association off-season and nap for a few hours with not much chance you would be run over. It is close and private here."

I was trying to extract maximum lobster meat from highly resistant crevices and getting a decent yield. You can't do it without a little blood sometimes. Doing lobster yield, you bleed.

"Not bad," Charlie said, filling more containers for the grill. He stood, wiped his brow. "Keep working on the lobster."

Silence.

"Lexi stabbed a well-known Lutheran minister a town over in the chest."

The claw I was working on clattered to the floor. It sounds too dramatic, like I intended it for effect. I didn't. It bounced under the chopping counter.

"He barely survived, collapsed lung and all. He did bad things to the disgust of people who knew what he was like, but almost no one did. He was an ass-hole as it turned out. Nobody knew shit then. It was Lexi who was initially blamed as 'disturbed.'" Charlie paused and relit his soggy pipe.

"Her folks were Scandinavians. Hendrick, her father, is a Swedish carpenter. Those guys worked as a team and could pound out a typical box house framing in a day, so long as there were two cases of beer. He was heavy into booze, went to the Compass bar at quitting, and was big into the Taunton dog track. He lost regularly on the greyhounds. Her mother, LiLi, was a waitress, also into booze, and lived a life as far away from Hendrick as was possible on this postage stamp island. She was known as loose, if the scoop were true. The mix was nasty, and cops made more than a few visits to the home for domestic stuff. Lexi was always the sensible presence telling them all it was okay."

At this point, I was—best word?—numb. My goddess beset with violence, dysfunction, and shame. What happened or how it mattered, I could not figure. I wanted to leave the kitchen, throw up, and then rescue her.

Charlie kept prepping his grill set-up. He was twenty-three years removed from his past where he started the day organizing an efficient miracle with a staff of twenty, mostly black sailors, to produce three feedings for a couple hundred sailors on high and dangerous seas. Probably it was with a life vest on when told Jap subs were in the waters. He did not look up. He kept on.

"The minister was as honey-lipped as the worst politician, but really good at it. He even did a service or two over the years up in your Village at that barn church that conducts them every summer. He came from somewhere else but took this region by storm. Civil rights. Programs for the poor. Opened the church doors for AA and elderly programs. Good things. He won some regional holy man award. He wasn't married but could have been, the way the lady parishioners were falling all over him, so I have been told."

Charlie disappeared and went into the larder. I knew I better keep working my ass off, or he could lose interest. I put all the culled lobster meat in a huge, stainless bowl, mixed in the diced celery with a bare hint—his instructions—of diced onion and diced pickles and a dollop of mayonnaise for each of the four pounds with pepper, salt, and a sprinkle of chopped basil. He re-emerged.

"Done?" I asked.

He took a small spoon, dipped. "It'll do." High praise.

"So what happened?" I asked.

"About what?"

"Lexi's thing."

"You are an annoying kid."

"You said you would try and save my sorry ass."

"A mistake from an aging man."

"It is too far gone for that, Charlie, and you and I both know it. I know you most likely won't castrate me, but I promised no telling, and I am good with that."

He dropped the larder goods on the table and told me to prep the haddock to portion pieces, portion the shrimp and the drained clams, and fry-coat them all with the batter for the day and refrigerate.

"Lexi's old man went so-so to the AA at that church. He did a lot of external painting there, including the steeple—tough. Lexi showed often to support his AA and watch Hendrick rappel the steeple. The minister was all over it. He asked Hendrick if his daughter was interested in church and parsonage cleaning—for pay, of course. Hendrick, facing long months of no building or painting, was looking at winter dollars. LiLi was not in the picture."

In today's world, anyone, even a teenager, could see what was coming. It was all more innocent then, and I did not have enough dots to connect. I did not.

"Lexi worked for the minister. Four hours, three days a week. We failed her. She did not know he preyed—no pun—upon single woman parishioners. In our world, Hester Prynne is not uncommon. Know Hester Prynne?"

"Hell, Charlie, you're a genius?" I said very cheeky. "I have the picture. He came on to her, and, unlike Hester, she knifed him."

"Pretty much it, but she paid for a while. The minister said he caught her stealing and confronted her. He said she went crazy and stabbed him. The fact that most of the blood was in his bedroom raised eyebrows. He was the reputable "holy-roller" and she was a thief stealing from the church. No contest. She was taken away and put in a juvie psycho unit. Then it got interesting, but it took time to straighten it out—too long."

"A respected, heroic woman around here came forward. Thank God, she had dough and clout and told a story. As the tale was told, she was going to the minister for counseling on a bad marriage. He would sit beside her, arm over shoulder, and say, 'There must always be room for Christ between us.' That was until, days later, they were in bed, and she said, 'I don't see much room for Christ right now.' She said he was a fraud."

"Did anyone listen?"

"They didn't have to. A few others told a similar story. Mostly single women without much to lose. This wasn't played in the newspapers. They weren't into smear stuff. Mouth-to-mouth. It was clear to us the minister was a piece of shit. The Lexi juvie crap turned around but the legal machine ground slowly. We may be slow, but we are fair. We, not all, applauded her innocence in silence. She was released to a broken home. Hendrick was still often drunk and ridiculed, Lili doing who knows what."

"She met some tough customers in juvie—guys and girls—and though separated upon her discharge, they knew how to get together and they did. Lexie is not the same beautiful girl of all our hopes in this dead space. She is empty. We failed our best. She is angry. I know. She told me."

I had started early, and we were pretty much on top of the prep. The waitress girls would come in and do set-ups for ice, drinks, frappes, and condiments, get the cash register set with rolls and backed to zero, and then slice pies.

"Charlie, she said she wants to come here. Do you want it? I'm off at eleven anyway."

"Tell her she has a job. Monday."

Leaving the beach snack bar, having fulfilled my duties, I hurried over to the Harpoon Snack Bar on the Beach Road where Lexi worked. It was a hot day and the place was mobbed. All the counter girls had a sheen on their skin from the heat of the grill, the fryalator, the humidity, and the crowded snack bar with little wind to push through a breeze.

Lexi spotted me in the back by the door. She mouthed silently, *The same?*

I nodded and mouthed back silently, *Your break?*

She gave me a five and five with an upraised hand. Ten minutes.

I went outside and staked some picnic table space. In those ten minutes, I could have written my very meager memoir. Ten minutes can seem like a long time when you are packed with news.

Lexi breezed out the screen door with our lunches and sat down shoulder-to-shoulder at the table.

"Chasing your girlfriends?" she asked.

"Trying not to kill them, actually. Full of themselves."

"That would be harsh. Girls have to protect themselves from horny boys like you."

I thought quickly on that one and, with what I knew, I got the point. True. I was nibbling at the crisps of the fried clams, not digging in.

"Charlie wants you to start Monday. You in?"

I did not expect what I perceived was a pained look on her face.

"I don't think it would be good." she said, sipping on her straw from a cola can.

"Look, Lexi, Charlie told me everything about stuff with the warning he would castrate me on the chop table and serve Dutch meatballs as a special if I opened my mouth. I won't. He will do it."

She arched her head back and let out a laugh. It was hearty and feminine—full of fun.

"Charlie thinks everyone failed you. It eats him up."

"Charlie is a savior guy. You're a savior boy. I don't want saviors. In this little world, I am marked. Not rich. Not all that smart. A high school graduate. A killer tart. We are small people here."

We both ate in silence. It was a "silver day" where the sun-blunting haze, mild wind and humidity cast a balmy hue over the bay.

"Does that mean you're in?" I pushed.

"You are a true pest," she replied in a way that said, *Yes.*

A throaty roar of two unbaffled Harleys pulled into the sand and clamshell parking lot. Two guys in cut off leather vests and jeans with laced boots dismounted.

Lexi looked down and said, "Gotta go back to work, Dutch. Thanks."

"Eight A.M."

★   ★   ★

I went back and told Charlie Lexi might show up on Monday. He was grilling sirloin steak sandwiches for a group from New York—why not seafood? He did not turn, just nodded, and crisped them to perfection, charred outside, juicy inside, grilled bakery bun, lettuce, tomato, two strips of bacon, special mayo. I saw the group chow down in swooning congratulations on their choice.

I showed on Monday earlier than ever—6:00 A.M. I wanted to make sure everything flowed and Charlie would not be gnarly. I was just a part-time grill/prep boy without much status, but the crew got the sense Charlie gave me a little power. The crew was its own mix of counter girls, both local and those planted for summer jobs by beach regency. Charlie had a "sous chef" of questionable value—a son of the beach manager. He rarely showed, and I was pretty much taking on more hours.

Lexi arrived through the back screen door at 7:55. Charlie was already there and simply nodded toward the linen cupboard for aprons. I eyed her, and she smiled a hello. From that moment on, everything beautiful, horrific, and things in between took over. A freaking teen tragedy.

She flowed among stations making sure set-ups were perfect. She deferred to the established counter girls on stocking and back-ups of all stuff incremental to delivery of the days service. She engaged customers. A new face, especially hers, was noticed immediately. The punky teens, including my gang, and the hot dads were taken by this late summer, new beauty. Crisp, efficient. She totally invited jealousy and envy from the regency counter girls who had no clue how seriously she defended herself and had been damaged. As much as a kid could, I saw a lot of no good coming. The local girls bathed her with teen girl love, their queen come home. A rift with the bitch girls fermenting, I asked a question.

"Charlie been okay?"

"A peach."

"The girls?"

"Good and bad. The girls I know are so cool. The others are flat-out nasty. I get it, but don't. I have nothing to do with their privileged lives."

"I can only say this. It is not simply you are stunningly beautiful. It is that you are competent and carry yourself with dignity. You stoop to no one."

"Wrong. I do."

"The bad boys with the hogs?"

"The bad boys."

"Why?"

"It's my only way. My mom is on the crazy farm. My dad is a juicer in rehab, barely holding on to our house. These people support me. Enough said."

She spat it out at me in a way she had never addressed me before. It was sad, cruel. She went back to work.

Two weeks in, near end of summer, third in August, only a week until shut down, all hell broke loose. I look at it today as a ridiculous, self-righteous scenario of times gone by. It changed everything in a sorrowful and deadly way.

With my expanded hours, I was there when Amanda Dolan with an out-of-place, wide-brimmed straw hat came into the restaurant— Charlie wouldn't let us call it a snack bar. Amanda was head of the beach committee with her daughter, Pheign, working the counter. She called out for Charlie who was doing prep. He came over to the counter.

"Do you realize you have an employee who stabbed a revered minister under nasty circumstances working here with these girls?" she said with venom oozing.

It was early, and no customers were in the place, but almost everyone working had come on shift. Lexi was not—day off. All in hearing distance turned; those out of it swiveled by the sheer force of the silence. A pin dropping would have sounded as a cymbal crashing.

"Your point?" Charlie asked, his pipe steaming.

"I want her fired immediately. She is a danger to the girls who work for you."

Charlie took a suck on his pipe, exhaled, and took on the hard steel of his feeling.

"You are the danger," Charlie said, evenly. "This talented, unfortunate girl is a heroine. She is the victim. She is a winner—always was."

I was cringing seeing a conflict among larger powers. It was a small, insignificant world but the largest adult contention I had ever seen in it. What followed would define me forever.

"You get rid of her, Charlie. Today. I won't put our girls at risk."

"Your girls are fucking the lifeguards every night on the guard towers, legs spread. Both your daughters leading the pack."

"You are a crude, hideous man. Lexi is gone. I remind you that you serve under cancellable contract of the Beach Committee."

"No problem, Amanda. I quit, now. Fuck you, bitch."

"You c-can't," Amanda said in exasperated confusion.

Charlie, the last time I would ever see him, threw his neck towel, his apron, and headband on the counter. He walked, gimp-legged with a determination of pride and everything Navy about him, out the door. Goddamn, did I love him and know what true grit was.

Amanda was shaking in the face of the disaster that led to unsolvable mayhem from her imperious beliefs. No restaurant, no superb food, nothing. She turned to me, a fifteen-year-old kid, and said,

"I guess you will have to run this for a while," she commanded, obviously knowing the manager's sous chef son was permanently AWOL.

"Does that mean sacking Lexi?"

"Of course. We must have standards."

"I quit now. Fuck you, bitch," I said, mirroring the words of the best and most horrible guy I ever knew. I left the bacon sizzling and hoped the place would burn down. The restaurant/snack bar had a sign taped to the entrance: CLOSED FOR REPAIRS.

Lexi was terminated. The snack bar—no longer restaurant—went to absolute hell in a hand basket. I knew. I belonged to the beach and could go in. They brought in some alcoholic short-order who failed everywhere. Everything that was fried was soggy, wilted lettuce on sandwiches, "maybe cooked" hamburgers or hot dogs came off the grill with indifference. Members were appalled. Just fill the belly on the beach did not cut it. There was an uproar.

I rejoined my compatriots on the sand, all incredibly persistent on knowing the story of snack bar debacle. Strangely, knowing all in technicolor, I said nothing. The people I loved were too dear. My loyalties meant everything.

My parents told me I had to apologize to Amanda Dolan. I refused. They threatened all the standard parent retribution—no driving privileges on my birthday in the fall, curfew on all weekends until my social security date, no phone privileges. They had never seen such resolve and could not understand my rage. I did not care. I would not cave. They cringed.

I conceded I would apologize for bad language. I did say, "Mrs. Dolan, I am sorry for my bad language."

She waved me off like a fly. She got nothing and knew now her daughters were splay-legged, willing sluts and beyond the confessional. I thought them admirable. Wish I had known.

I was two days from going home for double sessions training for football. I so wanted to get into the pain and sweat and hope for a good season. Lexi showed at the beach, just briefly, on the boardwalk right above the bay where the gang gathered. My buddies palavered, my girl buddies sucked in their tummies and made nice. No one could totally process Lexi.

She called me up to the boardwalk. I met her on the planks.

"I know you are going away," she said. "I want you to meet me at the Sands Motel up island. It's a party 8:00 P.M., and you have to get there. Come if you can."

"Christ, Lexi! I'm fifteen. You driving?"

"No, you have to grow up, Dutch, if you really want to understand it all——me. Do you want to see it? Understand it? Everything ain't pretty. You are crafty."

Crafty I was. I was not an innocent. Sexually, yes; otherwise I always had daring balls. Always did. I led a small, disciplined, pre-teen crew that broke into institutional spaces—schools, buildings, even a courthouse late at night—never to destroy or vandalize but to show we could. My method? Tape the least used exit lock open at end of day. At night, we romped, sitting in the judge's or principal's chair never caught.. I had commandeered family cars when my very wonderful, social parents were out partying since I was thirteen. I picked up friends and drove a fair ways. I was a bad boy. I called it fun but think the be-havior totally unacceptable now as I view my kids. Yet, I was never enraged or destructive. Now, I would be for Lexi.

We had two cars in the Village, one in the driveway slot outside the cottage, another in a parking space in a lot downhill about seventy-five yards away. It was no trick to take a family vehicle from below, out-of-sight, when the family played Scrabble in the cottage, sipping beers or wine and then turning in. It was not as if they were coming upstairs to tuck me in. Still, I was fifteen, no license, and stealing the family car to drive twenty miles up-peninsula to a probable drug-laden motel room. It was new territory. I knew zero about drugs or thugs. Introspection is not high on the list of qualities of a teenager over his head. This? I totally questioned my sanity. Still, Lexi, my goddess, called for me, and I would figure it out.

I went mission and did not care. I was dressed in khaki shorts and a madras short sleeve shirt with top-siders. Pseudo-prep wimp exposed, but I wasn't buying leathers and military boots for the evening. To my parents, I feigned fatigue from pre-practice conditioning at the local high school, rifled the keys, went upstairs and out the window, down the porch pole, and heisted the car.

I knocked on the motel door and was answered by Lexi at its opening.

"Wow, a little gangster," she laughed in a way that made me love her more. "Stolen car. Driving without a license. Consorting with a juvie slasher."

"Shut up, Lexi. I am so far from my comfort zone, I want to run. This is for you."

"Relax, Dutch. It will be cooler than you think. Thanks, gangster-man."

She bent forward and kissed me, lips only, and withdrew. The first. From that point, I would kill police for her.

I entered a "double suite." It was two rented rooms, two beds apiece, cheesy cigarette-scarred furniture and rugs, with the connecting door between rooms splayed open. It was an odd mix of people that confounded me. Big, hairy guys with bare-skinned torsos in leather vests, dirty jean pants and beards, college ingénues in tight, cotton Bermuda shorts and cute, pastel, cotton pullovers or halters, skeevy girls in short-shorts, teased hair, and tank tops, guys in suits, no tie, neck-opened shirts, and buffy shoes. It was not Kansas, Toto. Ice coolers abounded with beer and a pleasant smell I had not yet encountered, marijuana, wafted in the place.

"So who the fuck is Little Lord Fauntleroy who just showed up?" bellowed a big dude, whom I recognized from the snack bar parking lot, toward Lexi.

"He's a friend of mine," Lexi said in measured tones. "Any problems?"

"Crazy chick," was all he said.

It was a party of the likes, at my age, I had no reference. I was pretty much a potato chip and M&M in bowls with cokes on ice kind of guy.

Frankly, I never saw the same of it again. Crude, macho, debauched, unholy. Guys and girls were drifting off to dark places outside or in bathrooms, leering and sniffing. Somehow Lexi held herself separate through guile and fierceness. A true statement? She was not one of them. She played off all comers, knowing they were too stupid or drunk to be of meaning. I endured the party-goers trying to ply me with beers, which I secretly dumped. I was already screwed, and the last thing I wanted was a DUI on top of my driving without a license in a "stolen" car.

Without intention, my age became a focus. The girls—some women—wanted to mother me. The guys—some men—wanted to tease me.

"So what's a good-looking young man like you doing here?" a wobbly college girl asked me.

"I have no fucking idea," I responded wanting to sound tough and cool. "A friend invited me."

"High risk behavior, short-pants," she said. "This crowd is crazy."

"How do you know I'm not?"

"Because you're not," and she moved on.

The big dude finally focused on me and came over.

"What the fuck are you doing here?"

"Lexi asked me, and she is a friend," I answered, no longer afraid, more disgusted.

"You know what she does?" he said with a leering hanker. "We own her ass."

"I really don't care. She is a friend."

"Cheeky fuck, aren't you? Should I beat the shit out of you?"

A surprising, calm awareness popped into my brain. I recalled my gay (but we did not make those associations then) freshman English teacher who spent two weeks trying to have an unruly mob of teens understand rhetoric and its modes. It was the art of effective persuasive speaking or writing.

"It is all about forceful, sensible persuasion," he had said.

I dug in to the blowhard.

"I really hope not. For what purpose? Short of killing me, which seems extreme, it is just more jail for you. You are in the company of scores of people who are witnesses. Too many. Any story of a beat down of a kid will not serve you well. My parents—dad's a criminal lawyer (he wasn't, but I did not see a fact-checker before me)—will make you miserable. Right now you are free, running a criminal enterprise I do not give a shit about. Enjoy it. Leave me the fuck alone."

I was shaking with true piss dribbling in my shorts after that delivery. I wanted so out of there.

Big dude grunted, gurgled the remainder of his beer bottle, and left.

Lexi came over.

"Man, you rocked Big Danny. He was shaking his head. Didn't know what to do. Who the hell are you, anyway? The party is moving upland," she smiled. "Gone. Will you stay a bit?"

"Lexi, this is beyond ridiculous. I'm just a kid over his head and so screwed because by now my parents have probably figured I am driving a stolen car without a license and have an APB out on me. No. I gotta go."

"It's only your parents. I doubt they'll do that. They know you are nuts in a Dutch way. I would place a bet they know their darling boy and let it play. Stay with me for a bit."

The crowd had dispersed like cockroaches under a spray can. It was amazing how the idea of the next drug and sex-fueled venue had such a cosmic draw. Ffffft. Gone, like the sound of air into a vacuum.

The silence was intense given the cacophony of drunken laughter, muted moans and bad guy bravado before. Silence.

"Come here, gangster-boy," she said moving to one of the beds. "My shit may be screwed, but I want you to know important things about women. You are so sexually frustrated and deserve something. I'm not the kind old whore. Let's play your bases, Dutch. I am no virgin, but I don't give it up ever to anyone cheap. Never did. Pretty pure."

"A question? If they come back, will they kill me?"

"Not coming back. No chance until their next episode."

"I don't deserve anything. It all started with ridiculous lust about you, but I know more now. I desire you, but I don't want you doing things for stupid reasons. That is over. I actually love you in what I know is a ridiculous way. I just feel stupid."

"Here," she patted on a bed.

I joined her and lay back on a flat, ratty pillow. She put her head on my chest with my arm around her shoulder. The feeling will never leave me and has haunted my dreams. We rested, sharing the peace. We did so for minutes until our breathing synched.

"First," she said, "most cool women would like to be reassured through talk and gentleness. So talk. You are a big talker," she laughed.

As beautiful as the moment was, and it was, the mood was not sexual for me. I had seen too much and wanted to save this darling girl from further damage. Feeling sorry for someone is not an aphrodisiac.

"Here's a path." I said. "You find a way into Springfield College—all our best jocks go there. Greatest for phys ed in Massachusetts, or try Cortland in New York, but that's out of state. There has to be a way. Lots of people would help if you ask. I know it. You run track. You swim. Maybe you're great or just okay. You get a phys ed degree. Get a job. You coach girls like you can. You rise to AD and make a change for girls' sports. What's wrong with that?"

"You are too beautiful. Sounds dreamy and right. Trouble is, I could get scooped up with the sleaze in the investigations going on. It hasn't happened, but I'm told there is pressure. I am not clean. Do you hate me?"

"How bad is it?"

"Facilitated drug transfers. Just a messenger girl. I had possession while doing it. No using ever. I'm not a college wonder."

"Man, I don't know. Have to talk with my dad. Seems small."

"Don't! Bad people. Do not get involved."

"Lexi, please…."

"So anyway, gangster boy, have you ever unhooked a bra? You have sold me on the four-base theory," Lexi asked with a kind voice as she pulled off her T-shirt.

"No."

"It is important to be smooth. Go round back and see it. It's all snatches with a snap."

I was ambivalent, but her beauty overwhelmed me. I was no industrial engineer as I looked but understood the design. Slide. Free. Pull off. The first vision of heaven I had ever seen. Forget religious pictures of rapture. Lexi Johannson's breasts bobbled free in the instance.

"Do you like that, Mr. Gangster?"

"Speechless."

"Well, to do the bases correctly, we skipped to second. We have to kiss with tongue," she said leaning softly toward me.

I tried.

"Hey, you. Your kissing is too aggressive," she said as I lay a quarter way on top of her. "I don't like big tongue down my throat. I want nibbling of lips, tongue touches, and a sensuous exchange. Not an assault by a guy tongue muscle."

Best advice ever given. I became known, hence forward, as a "good kisser."

"Second base, love boy? Okay, how to treat them. Do not pummel and mash, the word is 'fondle.' Massage gently, caress and suck nipples like a baby. Treat with beauty and respect. Do it right. If the girl is right, it is really stimulating."

I passed that test simply with Lexi's approbation and a sigh and was practically hyperventilating.

We were both breathing with a husky sound.

The grand prize, of course, was Lexi's instruction on her lovely nether region.

"I am not going all the way with you, Dutch, although I am totally aroused. Third base is a prize, not given easily. Never expect it. Earn it. You are an incessant, undeniable pest. Still, this stuff takes its own course. You get some, but not all. I want you to be virgin lover for the right girl."

I was pretty insane at that point. Erection was in pain in my underpants. I then shed my shorts, and she reached below to provide some stroking relief.

"How are you not the right girl?"

"I'm just not, you nut, just not," she hissed. "We are going to third base. Here! Kneel between my legs. Look at my stuff," and she pulled back her legs. "You have not seen this before, but you have to if you want to be a lover."

All mysteries were revealed, and I was never more awestruck at the beauty of what I had wondered, lusted, snickered about. It was the complexity and beauty of something so private and tucked away—secret, undistinguished under clothing, even bikinis—and all of a sudden to be an anatomical wonder with tens of thousands of years of magic to incite lust.

"Just beautiful, Lexi. Thanks. This is so surreal."

"Let me put your fingers where they matter. Treat your girl right with massage, not force. Here."

I did, and Lexi was wiggling and breathing heavily.

"Enough," she gasped. "Stop."

My masculinity was surging now, and I did not want to stop doing something that was obviously turning her into a beautiful, lustful woman/girl. But I did.

"Phew," she said. "You're good, Dutch. Too good. Follow instructions. Figured you would. Stupid me. Okay! Last thing. The prize all you guys want is penetration. It's down a bit further."

I slid my finger lower and it slipped into, was vacuumed into, the warmest, lubricated pudding a finger could feel.

"Gentle."

Lexi allowed me to explore in measured moments with my finger.

Over. Horror.

"Go home, gangster boy. No home run, but third-to-home in your language. Almost there. Don't think it was easy for me. I coulda done it."

"Lexi, I am crazed. You can't cut me off now."

She reached for her bra and hooked it on. She found her panties at bed's edge and slid them up her legs. She pulled a mid-drift halter over her head and slid her shorts into place. It was an act of disappearing that made me wonder about the wonders I had seen and experienced. It was as if I could not remember the magic.

"It is time for you to go, Dutch, to the cool life that awaits you if you don't fuck it up."

"Nooooo," was all that came out of me.

Lexi kissed me in the way she taught and was walking out the door. She turned, came back, and gave me a tender kiss.

"You already know how to treat people. Now you know how to treat a girl. We're different."

I made it back to the cottage and parked the car below. I had no clue it was 5:30 A.M. I figured it a disaster of recrimination in the morning and climbed the porch post up to my bedroom, expecting to awaken the household. It did not happen and no next day disaster. No one knew a thing, that I was gone. Not knowing that in early morning, I lay there stimulated, crushed, and defeated. I understood I was too young, living in a "foreign" land states away to influence anything for my truly beloved Lexi.

★   ★   ★

114

I had a pretty good game against our big rival on Homecoming Day. Seventy-eight yards rushing, 26 yards receptions, 5 tackles. A 20–13 win. Nice game in a good season. The craziest thing was less about football. Lexi had taught me so much about female power and cool that I was hot. More importantly, gentle. Chicks were all over me as we kissed in post-game parties. I was a gentleman. It all did not matter. The only female in the world that could rock my solids was Lexi. I religiously called the number she gave me. No answer. Wrote to a known address. No reply.

Lexi called that very weekend. My mom answered and handed me the phone.

"Some girl," she said with a distaste of the times of such forwardness.

"Hey, gangster boy. You tearing them up?" she sounded slurry and not crisp.

"Doing okay, but no marvel."

"You were a marvel to me, Dutch." She started crying.

"Shss. Shsss. It's okay. Shss. Tell me, sweet one."

"Sweet one? So Dutch, so beautiful and so nuts."

"What's happening?"

"Falling apart. Arrests. Plea deals. People copping. Not good."

"You?"

"Okay, so far, but you never know who caves to save a few years."

"What can I do? Tell me. I will do it, Lexi. Anything short of murder."

"Just know you are the only man, a boy—man—I have ever loved. Ever."

"Lexi—"

Click.

I was distraught and had no way to know where she was. I used the local vacation phonebook that my family took back home each summer to call handymen, beach people and locals we knew. No one knew how to get in touch with her.

*   *   *

Our team was playing a rival in a critical game heading toward the league championship. I was a vital player and a teammate, but I was a "savior" boy. I promised myself I would practice hard and play insanely through Saturday with passion for Lexi, heist the family car Saturday night, and go looking for her on Sunday, getting back on early Monday A.M. There was no way that absence would go unnoticed. I understood my parents would be demanding I go to a shrink for disruptive behavior. It was a small price in my anxiety. They still had no clue on the Lexi connection.

I did not need to endure it.

A call came into the home phone on Friday from Josh, a likeable, going-nowhere-fuck-up in our group. Nice kid. I answered it.

"Hey, Dutch. Josh. How you doing?"

"Same old. Why are you calling me as a never event?"

"Thought you may want to know Lexi is dead. I know you liked her."

I detached in a numb, psychotic, paranoid, denying way. I simply remember grief and violence in equal measure. Nothing would ever be the same, not for me. I knew more at the moment than I ever needed. I would never forgive.

"How dead? Why dead?"

"Very dead. Overdosed most likely," Josh said, shaken in his own way. "No one is saying as usual up here. She hung with a bad crowd. Guess it caught up. Her wake was a zoo. Biggest thing in a long time."

"Did she die alone, Josh?"

"Don't know. They found her in her little car at the beach parking lot by the snack bar."

"Our beach?"

"Yeah?"

"Thanks for calling. It means a lot."

I was too young to grow up, but at that moment, I did. I saw how Fates can conspire to turn purity and beauty into ugliness with absolutely no fault on the part of the victim. I saw immense promise turned to ashes from negligence of responsibility and from predatory evil in the heart of people. I saw a nasty wasteland of the corrupt self-righteous and their hysteria at order undone. I saw a brave girl awash in a nor'easter sea, struggling to stay above the caps and simply be as magnificent as she was. I never saw life the same again and forever forward hated Pollyanna feel-goods—male and female—espousing ebullient, positive thinking.

The next summer, early morning, I went to Lexi's grave in a Barnstable cemetery by a historical church that included colonial ancient and modern tombstones. Lexi's stone was small, barely above the grass, but beautifully placed at a crest overlooking the bay. I approached alone. I was relieved because I was crying so hard. I had brought flowers and placed them on the stone.

"I thought lust, Lexi, but you taught me sweetness. I thought about me, but you made me see it was about whom I love and how. You taught me like an acolyte about the mysteries using your beautiful, Goddess self. What a fuck-ing coach. You would have been the best coach ever and so young. Love you forever."

I still go there once a summer. Lexi's beauty remains timeless to me while mine suffers the incremental indignities of aging. The first, last, and only god-dess. I am decently centered, productive, a faithful husband with a remarkable wife and great kids and grateful.

If Lexi arose from the grave—alive and as beautiful in spirit as we left each other, I would throw it all away in a heartbeat and run with her to nowhere.

1968–KEYS

Willie was an old gaffer who walked the same route along the water's edge every day of the summer. When he was younger, he walked in the soft sand above the tideline. Now age, like an undertow, pulled him to the wet, packed sand where the footing was easier. His shoes often got damp, and he had taken to keeping an extra pair in his shed in the Village.

Tourists, strolling the beach and seeing the trail of their footprints erased in the backwash of waves, created metaphors about their lives. The old man was not given to that poetry. He gave the ocean respect, but not foolish sentiment. Were the ocean a person, Willie would share his whiskey but not his secrets. He heard that from a fisherman at the Compass Bar and knew it to be the opinion of people who depended on the ocean for a living.

Willie was a dependent. Indirectly anyway. The salt air blistered paint and dried out window caulking. It made gardening an art. The ocean stirred summer breezes alluring to vacationers and snorted fierce winter winds that yanked loose buoys, banged shutters, and chased all but the heartiest inland. The churning sea around the peninsula launched a three-front attack, weathering anything that couldn't crawl indoors. Someone had to make amends for the elements. It was Willie Stockhausen. He was the jack-of-all-trades for the tiny Village on the bluff and had been longer than anyone remembered.

Longer than anyone remembered.

Willie wasn't used to thinking in those terms, but it was fact now. Dirty Gertie had passed away at the beginning of August. She was the last one to have seen enough calendars to finger the year when a coveralled young carpenter, poor boy cap tilted low on his brow, entered the Village looking for work. Today, maybe tomorrow too if he took his time, Willie would close her home for the season. Gertie was dead; closing her home was a wake of sorts. Likely as not it would be sold over the winter to one of the Village smilers trying to curry her favor when the slide downhill started. With the passing of the key, Willie would be as timeless as the little lake that rippled on the flank of the Village.

Willie fingered Gertie's key in his pocket as he veered up the beach and on to the packed sand path to the bluff steps. It was an old key, heavy and smooth with an eyelet at one end, a thin shaft, and a notched piece at the other. In the days when the thunder of Gertie at her piano could cool the dead air of late July, he had an O-ring of such ones. They jangled merrily wherever he walked. The sound was prosperous and clinked of importance. The Village mayor, people once called him.

Lately, Willie had been keeping the keys in the buttoned breast pocket of his coveralls. This did not gnaw at him. He was an old man, and his needs were not great. He could live off the income of five keys. He had ten. After today, maybe tomorrow if he took his time, there would be nine.

Willie reached the bluff stairs at seven every morning and climbed. Years ago he had to if he wanted to finish work and catch a beer at the Compass by five. Nowadays, it was the sun that pressed him; noon was his quitting time. Willie wasn't worth a toothless rake when it got hot. In his rented room down the beach was an alarm clock, an ancient one with bells on the top and a clapper between them that rattled like the tail of an angry snake. It had been years since he set it. Age woke him before the gulls started bickering and set him afoot down the beach.

Dirty Gertie. *What a crazy cuss she was,* Willie thought as he pulled himself up the stairs. The name spanked of a children's rhyme. Even the old-timers in the Village couldn't agree on the origin. Most of the theories were idle gossip. Only two had much substance to them.

Once, at a cocktail party, Gertrude Miller, distressed at the line before the bathroom door and squirming at the pain of gin in her bladder, thumbed her nose at propriety and sought comfort behind a sweeping willow on the front lawn. On the far side of the tree she chose, behind the draping tendrils, was a band of Village brats spying on their parents. The original group was five. At least twenty-five in that age bracket, now middle-aged themselves, had since laid claim to witnessing Gertie relieve herself. Some say she simply squatted. Others say she stretched her legs in front of her and held herself off the ground like a gymnast on parallel bars. The wildest tale had her stripped naked, dancing around the tree, yelling for her friend Bela Bartok. With Gertie, all were possible.

The other theory involved her lifestyle and appearance. She was the daughter of a wealthy steel man. In the tradition of "fallen" debs, she did her best to annihilate the association. In her late teens, she brought the Woman's Suffrage fight to the sleepy lanes of the Village. At twenty she was running with a loose crowd of Bolsheviks and bohemians. Autos and ragtime were their passion. She smoked cigarettes and drank with men. Even age never quite subdued her. She drove a dusty, black '38 Plymouth with suicide doors and running boards until the end and lived in a house where the shades were drawn all day simply because everyone else's were open.

Gertie had been a tiny lady who lived to eighty-six and outlived her concern for fashion. The frowzy, black, front-button dresses she wore hung on her petite frame like a marathon dance partner. A black felt hat with a battered silver feather was the trademark capping her cultivated drabness. However neat, Gertie looked like a smudged chimney sweep.

A mystery dies with its answer. The secret of "Dirty Gertie" was not a closed book. There remained a person who, with a few chosen words, could turn years of speculation into solid fact. The person was Willie Stockhausen.

Willie knew where the name came from.

There were plenty of people who, over the years, had deluded themselves that they coined the actual moniker. None did. The summer folk were an aristocratic clan, fast with a clever put-down. Rich and successful, most of them, they came to the Village every summer and involved themselves in its affairs in the persistent manner only those familiar with country club politics could know. What decisions there were, from placing traffic signs to fees for the tennis courts and beach, were debated with raised eyebrows and snooty comments. Most issues were moored in social status and were dealt with in ways that left little doubt as to who stood where. Even the largely ceremonial post of association chairman was sought with intrigue befitting a palace intrigue. The Village had its tribal elders.

Gertie could have been the Grand Dame. She was two-fold wealthy, both by lineage and profession. She was a concert pianist who played the great halls from San Francisco to Vladivostok going east. Her Chopin waltzes were once described as being "pure as gently lapping ripples on a lakeshore in the crisp, cold Northland." Stravinsky had called on her in Paris and pinched her buttock furtively under the canopy at the entrance to Maxim's. Henry Miller made affectionate, obscene gestures like lapping his tongue every time they met, in public or not. She knew Berlin and Cohan and Tucker. She was the off-beat belle of a new age in sound and a new freedom of expression. She was also as zany as the plinky-plink of ragtime she loved so much as a hobby.

When it was fashionable in the Village to buy wrought-iron numerals to embed in one's chimney to flaunt the age of the cottage, Gertie tacked a huge, pre-Mayflower 1619 on her peak. When the Chronicle Society, a covey of matrons nosier than a tax man at the racetrack, appeared to cull biographical tidbits about their illustrious citizen, Gertie tousled her hair, sprinkled Beefeaters on her dress, downed a swig, and breathed generously on their faces when she told them her career was due to knowing "where to pass out the goodies."

Dirty Gertie. Willie could remember the very day he first heard it. Most likely, he would never forget. The name came from the old hummingbird herself.

It was a hazy, hot day in June about forty years before. Willie was laying a flagstone walkway through the tangle in Gertie's front yard. The house wasn't quite twenty yards off the road, but on a misty day, no one could blame the postman for missing it. Trumpet vines writhed around and over the beams on her porch. Clutching like tentacles of a squid, they pushed in screens and crawled on to the porch roof. With the full green leaves and conical orange flowers blooming on the vines from June until August, her privacy was a contract with nature. Landscaped by the caprice of wind, was a snarl of thorn bush, forsythia, a few cowering holly bushes, and two dead trees covered with creeping ivy, the yard was chaos save for a thin trail leading from the road to her porch. Walking home late at night from dances at the beach club, Village kids ran past the house.

Willie was working in a sleeveless undershirt. Back then, his shoulders were broad, and his limbs were sinewy-strong. Sweat glistened on his arms and neck, the flush of heat firing his tan. He hung the border strings and was digging the shallow pit for the stones when Gertie called him.

"Mr. Stockhausen!"

Willie had been handling her maintenance for years and, to his recollection, this was the first time he had ever heard her voice. His employ had been arranged by a local realtor. She paid with checks that arrived monthly in his mailbox. The only contact passing as personal between them was the annual Christmas card he received. It was his only one each year, and he kept it on his bureau until spring, mostly because he forgot it was there.

"Mr. Stockhausen!"

Nobody called him that. Just Willie.

"Come in and have something to whet your whistle."

Willie was a mite suspicious. He wondered how long she had been watching him. The more you looked at something, the more faults you could find. He didn't want any lectures or advice from a middle-aged spinster eager for a listening ear.

"No thanks, Miss Miller. I want to finish this today."

"Get in here, you damn fool! It's a hundred," she said sharply.

Willie dropped his shovel. The Village was a polite place—in public anyway. Maybe from surprise, or owing to the Christmas cards, he walked to the porch, wiped his shoes on the edge of the top steps, and went inside.

Dark. Darker than dusk. What little light filtered in wasn't equal to the gray of a foggy day. The illumination was more like a long cellar with small, single pane windows at either end, shaded by bushes.

"Well, have a seat," Gertie said gruffly, as if he were questioning her hospitality.

"I can't see, ma'am. A little sun blinded."

She stepped behind Willie, spread her hands in the small of his back, and pushed. Willie stumbled forward until his legs met with a chair.

"Okay, okay, I'm here."

Gertie was still pushing like a wind-up toy against the wall.

"Why didn't you say so?"

"I did, ma'am."

"The name is Gertie, Mr. Stockhausen. Gertie."

"Mine is Willie, ma'am."

Gertie, Mr. Stockhausen. Gertie."

"Willie, Gertie."

"Willie? That's a name for delivery boys and doormen. I'll call you Mr. Stockhausen."

Willie felt a pain in his toe as if someone were stepping on it.

"All right, ma'am."

Gertie laughed.

"You catch on quickly, Willie."

As his eyes adjusted to the light, the features of the woman on the divan grew distinct. Her skin was pale and white as the foaming caps of waves. She was bewitching—impish and teasing even in the way she sat, legs tucked under her body, the top buttons of her dress open and daring. Her hair was pulled into a thick, tight bun that yanked the skin on her face taut as perfectly hung wallpaper. Though the skin was tense, her eyes and mouth were flexible, playful. Nonchalance leaked from the corners of her smile. The smile itself was slightly curious, a child looking at a favored puzzle.

"What'll it be, Willie?"

"Lemonade? Tonic? I don't care."

"The hell you don't." She raised her eyebrows. "Why, Willie, there isn't a cottage owner who doesn't know you head straight for the liquor closet when closing their house. Why do you think most of them are hiding it these days? Now, what'll it be?"

"Now just—"

"Come, come."

"Yah, I nip a bit." He smiled. "How about some of that good Irish you got under the sink. One cube."

"You nasty thief. That's my boy," Gertie said, reaching over and patting his hand approvingly.

With the first drink, Gertie sniped at the neighbors, jumped up to do an imitation of Willie swatting mosquitoes as he worked, and told him she never wore underwear. Along with the second came the story of the Miller Million and how it evaporated like so much Lafitte-Rothschild in an open vat.

"You know what a couple million dollars is, Willie? A couple of three day bashes with all your friends invited. A villa in Spain managed by a gigolo para-mour. A few pretty rocks, a fur or two, a New York apartment, and buckets of champagne. That's all." Gertie sipped her gin and tonic casually.

"Of course, I had a crooked accountant too. Every time I would go in for a grand, he'd say, 'I'm sorry Miss Miller, but in anticipation of the Crash, our money is no longer liquid. It's frozen in art and real estate.'

"I found out what he meant by 'our money.' One day I said, 'I better have a thousand watery dollars in my hand by tomorrow or—' Right then he broke down and started whining about his embezzling. The money was frozen all right—in horse manure. The ponies ran away with it. I asked him to show me the books. When he did, I started laughing like a psycho. The worm ran to the corner of the room, afraid I had blown a fuse and was going to pull a pearl-handled derringer or something. Actually, I was laughing because the balance was three times what I thought I had left. I took him to dinner."

Willie's dehydrated tissues were sucking up the booze like a thirst-crazed nomad.

At first, the dark sitting room seemed a cool cavern in the woods. As the whiskey aged in his veins, he realized he was amidst elegance. For the first time, Willie admired the rosewood paneling and the tarnished silver service atop the walnut buffet. He lounged in a sinfully comfortable chair, calloused hand wrapped around a cut crystal glass. Gertie prattled on and flitted from chair to chair, spinning around him like a dark moth. Her ceaseless chatter filled the room with a not unpleasant high-pitched hum, different to a man who lived in silence.

"—and when the baron could finally not tolerate a moment more of her southern belle stupidity, he said, 'My dear child, you have the wit of Oliver Cromwell, the vision of the Romanoffs, and the sensitivity of Marie Antoinette.' The entire table fell silent. All that could be heard for what seemed a minute was the nervous clatter of silver on china. She looked up at him wide-eyed and said, 'Why, baron, y'all shouldn't say such nahce things.'" Gertie laughed uproariously. "Funny. No?"

Silence.

She stopped suddenly.

"Why aren't you laughing? These are my best stories."

Willie pulled on his nose and shrugged his shoulders.

"Do you understand a word I'm saying?"

"No, but I don't mind."

"Well, I mind, you ox," she sniffed indignantly, "You haven't said a word since you came in."

Gertie came toward him.

"What's your secret, Willie? What will loosen that tongue of yours?"

She moved to the piano. It was the hugest, blackest piano he had ever seen. With the bonnet propped up like the hood of a car and the belly gaping like an open mouth, the instrument looked to be a monster ready to devour the small woman as no more than a snatch of cheese. Once she was seated, an airy lightness, like the first inch of powder snow, dusted her and gently snuffed the fear of Willie's vision. She commanded the rig.

The first chords were huge and somber, a wall of black cloud. His ears could scarcely catch it all. Willie took a quick slug from his glass. Here was a depth beyond his small life. Like deft scalpels, Gertie's fingers dissected the chords into more manageable sounds that trickled and waxed, waned, and moved.

He closed his eyes. In the blackness, Willie could see a mountain stream, swollen with spring rain, violent, roaring downhill, crashing from dizzying heights onto rocks below and spreading into bell-shaped pools, quiet and ambiguous in their mood.

The fingers. They haunted his vision. Willie could not fathom such long, fine-boned stalks, running like spiders, so certain of which of the eighty-eight keys to touch. He felt a passion swelling for the fingers and shuddered as they feathered a melody on his legs and stomach, across his back. Goose bumps sprouted as the fingers tapped up his back and fluttered a trill on his neck.

Not once did Gertie look over. Willie knew he was no more important to her than the crumpled Hershey Bar wrapper in the magazine rack. When she finished, Gertie bowed respectfully, taken with her craft. Without frivolity, she was no more than a broken-winged bird. Spent and humbled.

"Quite a man, huh?" Gertie said, rapping her knuckles on a thick hand-carved leg of the piano. "This buck has been to places you've never dreamed of."

Willie nodded.

"I've slept under him and on top of him. One of these days, I am going to crawl right inside the damn thing," she said, brushing back a strand of hair freed by the playing. "Come, let's explore."

Gertie took his hand and pulled him to the stairwell of the house. They began climbing. At each level, the light grew brighter. The second floor was like a smoky, late dawn. The landing between the second and third was the luminescence of a newly risen sun. The third floor was a single tower room, like the bridge of a ship, and brilliant, uncontested sunshine boomed through the windows.

She left him for the vanity and pulled open the top drawer. Gertie lifted out a large, leather-bound book and held it front of her.

"Do you speak French, Herr Stockhausen?"

Willie shook his head. Herr Stockhausen. The name brought memories of blood sausage and cold winters. As a boy, he heard people call for his father that way.

"I think you do but don't know it. Look!" she said, smiling.

Gertie opened the book, and the lobes of Willie's ears tingled with blood. Pictures. Men and women. He couldn't tell whose arms and legs began where, but always visible in the pictures—extraordinary because he had never seen such a display before—were organs, graphic and fascinating.

"Oh, dear," Gertie said shutting the book. "I thought that was my scrapbook." Where is that thing?"

She left the book in his hands and rummaged through the drawer. When Willie figured she was occupied, he opened the book and peeked at the pictures.

He glanced up.

Gertie was staring at him with a coy grin like she had won at hopscotch over a dreaded foe.

"Oh, you New Englanders!" She shook her head, "I bet you smoked cigarettes behind the woodshed too."

Willie closed the book.

"Are you sure this ain't your scrapbook, Gertie?"

At dusk, she nipped his teat.

"Get! Get! A lady needs her rest."

He was happy at the dismissal. There wasn't much to say. As he hitched his trousers, she walked over to him, naked and lithe for a woman her age. She planted a lush, full kiss on his lips and said,

"Willie, you're the kind who doesn't talk, and it's not because you're stupid. Only a parrot who chatters as much as me could be so sure. I like that. It won't reach the wrong ears that you bounced around with ol' Dirty Gertie."

Willie could not think of a single reason to tell anyone, but to tease her, he said, "I wouldn't be so sure."

"I know your game," she said, pulling up his fly. "Besides, the man who boasts about his shadow is a lonely man at night."

"I'll finish the walk tomorrow."

★   ★   ★

The old man unhooked the padlock to his shed. It hadn't been locked. It never was. Knowing every person in the Village, Willie figured it would be an insult.

126

Anyway, a locked door hinted there was something worthwhile behind it. There really wasn't.

He grabbed a hammer and dropped it in the cloth loop in the leg of his pants. He tucked a few nails in his pocket and reminded himself to be careful if he sat down. The folding ruler might be useful, so he slipped it and some pipe wrenches into the other leg pocket and left the shed.

The Village was peaceful in the morning. Only the young and old were up and about. Little Kristin Townes was picking at an anthill on the roadside and Willie decided not to disturb such important business with a hello. Maddie Krause was sweeping her second story porch and lifted the broom in silent salute to him. She always was a touch dramatic. And the dogs. Willie wasn't partial to the local hounds, but he nodded to the ones he knew because, like him, they had an early start on the day.

The city papers didn't arrive at Louise's stationery until nine, so most of the fathers on vacation didn't arise until then. Their sons were even later. Sullen with morning daze, they stepped on to the porches in tennis shorts, T-shirts, and begged the sports section from their fathers reading there. Willie always heard the New York boys complaining their paper was an early edition and never carried the night game box scores.

"Aww, Dad, why don't we get the *Journal?* It has everything."

"There's more to life than Mickey Mantle, son."

Walking up the flagstone path to Gertie's house, Willie didn't pause to reflect it was his work. He did not stop to relive his first ascension of the porch steps at the command of the owner. He wiped his soles on the edge of the top step, pitted the key, and walked in. It was only on the inside that Gertie's absence, her death, inched close to real.

The shades were up and the windows were opened to half for ventilation. Gertie would have withered in the light and blown away like a milkweed in the draft. Willie started to shut the windows and then pulled the shades. The smell of cinnamon tea and musty velvet was gone. Dust, agitated by currents from the doorway, sparkled in sunlight from the windows still open. Those frames made cross-haired squares of yellow on the Oriental rug.

Willie went to the kitchen and looked under the sink. A depleted fifth of gin with a capful barely big enough to cover the glass hump at the bottom of the bottle was all that remained. He unscrewed the cap, threw his head back, and let the few drops splash on his outstretched tongue. He put the top back on and put the empty bottle in the cabinet.

Stroking his two day stubble, Willie planned the work. First, there were the seaside window covers. He'd have to lug them from the dirt floor cellar and pull the ladder to put them in place. Then the water. Turn off the house main and bleed the pipes. Tricky with two different systems. He'd have to wriggle around in the sand floor of the basement like a beetle turned turtle for those damn spigots. Drain the hot water heater, pull the fuses, winterize the toilets, sanitize the refrigerator, close upstairs shutters, lock windows, and go home. A one-day job.

But by noon, only two of the window covers were tacked in place. Willie had poked his elbow on a nail jutting from a basement beam and needed mercurochrome and a Band-Aid from his shed. The nails in his back pocket kept jabbing him as he bent for the window boards. He took them out only to realize moments later he needed them while on the ladder. He was an old man who could not estimate his working speed anymore.

Sitting on the porch steps, taking a breather, Willie rubbed his back. The soreness that plagued him since he wrenched it moving stones in the Kimball's rock garden squeezed like a noose tightening around his spine. It was a close, breathless August day. The sun was stoking its baking midday fires. His eyes twitched with the sting of perspiration.

Come in here, you damn fool!

Willie went inside.

⋆ ⋆ ⋆

The day after his sweet tussle with Gertie was overcast, the air filled with a Cape, cloying mist. Willie finished the trench and laying the stones, backfilling, leveling each as he went, his movements were self-conscious. Every time he stood up, he made sure to stretch to his full height, hopeful the woman was watching and hungering for touch as much as he was. He puttered around his wheelbarrow, taking too much time to pick up his tools and arrange them in the well. He walked over each stone, tamping them down, knowing full well they were solid. Fifteen stones. By the time Willie reached the last, he realized Gertie was not performing that day.

A few days later, Gertie, in a rare appearance on her new walk, called to him as he passed.

"Herr Stockhausen, you do nice work. What is your fee?"

She said it playfully, eyes shielded from the sun by her forearm.

"Bill's in the mail, ma'am. You'll get it."

"If you can remember, we can go inside and settle up right now," she coaxed.

"No, ma'am, I'm a mite busy today."

"Not even for an Irish?" she replied, moistening her lips with her tongue.

"No, thanks."

"You proud pauper, you! Willie, you're a scream."

He could tell she was pleased. Tossing fitfully in his bed that night, his daytime pride succumbed to the swelling in his groin, but Willie was a surfcaster, too. He knew creels to be empty one day, and, the next, you had more than you could ever use.

Dunes were built and blown away. Louise finally got a beat-up old freezer for the stationery to keep ice cream in. A rash of new family docks were built on the lake. It was all a social class gambit with Gertie, as usual, making a travesty of it. She commissioned Willie to build a dock with a sunroof, on which she never set foot. The Inn had a facelift. Part of the cranberry bog, gone to seed after the long-gone '38 hurricane, was filled to make a bigger parking lot for the rustic Tabernacle.

Willie lost a key here or there, some from death, some from financial reverses. The war years—WWII, Korea, Vietnam—were lean. Several families, in mourning or out of gas, never arrived during those summers.

The Villagers paid scant attention to the man-jack and wrinkled belle. Only with hilarity, in the most bourbon-soaked jokes tossed about at parties, did anyone suggest a bond between them. Yet, the two were like the few smallmouth bass left in the lake that rendezvoused secretly amid water lilies in the far cove. They were far too smart to get caught. They could ignore each other for weeks, flitting within a few feet of each other, without an eye blink to betray the intimacy between them. When the call came over the years, they sped a straight course to the tower room spawning grounds to nuzzle and bump, to fulfill a desire neither gave pause to understand.

They grew old together, not with or without each other.

"Willie, you feel like a beanbag, like everything is loose and rattling," she said one year.

He could have told her that her breasts felt like the loose skin of a popped blister but didn't. It wasn't kindness. Gertie knew.

Motorboats were outlawed on the lake after David Land, one of a rash of post-war babies, nearly ran down a wading fisherman. Louise's store got a few "scandal" movie mags, the kind the late Vicar Parsons had piously banned.

Even aristocracy was slipping. Architects, college, insurance people began moving their families to the less baronial houses at the Village end.

Gertie's Christmas cards arrived every winter, and every September Willie closed her house. The last few years, Willie frequently stopped in at Gertie's on the way home from work. They could talk on the porch now without much fear of stirring a storm of gossip. The most vindictive of the "old guard" were dead or relocated. To their sons and daughters, a pair of old people talking together in the waning sunlight was quaint. Even when Willie stepped inside, the neighbors scarcely dipped their martinis. Two such relics could hardly be jazzing anymore.

The stairs were taken more slowly, but, after playing the piano for a while, Gertie still took his hand and pulled him toward the stairwell. Willie gave her a boost on the behind whenever she needed it. The third story bedroom was cheerful, untouched in arrangement over the years.

As they undressed, they sometimes laughed until tears came at each other's jokes about their wizened, stooped bodies. They slipped between the covers to paw and tussle. Things were less acrobatic, but the familiarity of so many years made up for it. Afterwards, Gertie talked or tapped out the Emperor's Concerto on his back while Willie dozed or softly pinched her skinny thighs.

"Gertie, I ain't ever seen you with a dab of color, but your skin got it now," Willie observed.

"Returning to the bloom of my youth?" she asked.

"It's kind o' yellow," he replied doubtfully.

"I can't get my feet warm anymore either. Do you think I'm dying, Willie?"

"What's the difference? It's a day-to-day thing now'days anyway."

"Are you afraid to touch me?"

"Naah!" he said. He wasn't. He did.

Gertie died that summer.

He went back inside to cool off. The old man scanned the sitting room. The perspiration from his morning efforts dried to salt tracks on his cheeks. The piano was still there. He approached the keyboard. Willie had never made a sound on the instrument. The keys were yellowing with age. They felt soft as cushions under his fingers. A dissonant chord growled from the piano and faded to the corners before he released the keys. He attacked a few notes singly and grew bored.

A drink.

That was what he needed.

Maybe Gertie kept a stash upstairs. Willie had never been up there alone. From habit, he crowded to one side of the staircase, allowing for her presence as he climbed.

He raked the drawers and closets, even picked the latch on her old cedar chest with a nail. Nothing. Gertie was sly as an Arab in a bazaar with her booze. She wasn't wasteful. It would have been just like her to have lined up all the bottles the day she was slipping away and downed them one by one.

He backed his way to the bed and sat down gingerly. A fiery pain was slinking bump-by-bump up his rickety back. Willie slipped his arms behind him to massage the soreness. Something crackled. An envelope partially tucked under the throw pillow. A letter inside.

Herr Stockhausen,

Creep, creep, creeping. Here comes Willie. I knew you would be here sooner or later. No one else. Sooner than later and not from nostalgia either. Probably snooping around for spirits (not mine) or jewelry—I take that back; you're not romantic enough for souvenirs. Maybe it's for those secrets you love so much.

We all have kicks for making ourselves feel important in this village. Yours is the most devious. Having something on everyone. You're a bastard that way, Willie. Just listening. Just watching. Letting everyone jabber until you know all and their throats are parched. I commend you. Few people can pull it off. In one mad moment or another, we all sell a secret to a listening ear, tell a story in hope of laughter, or drop a name to make ourselves a smidgen bigger than we really are. But you, as far as I can tell, were always the ears. You come and go like the tide, each no more memorable than the last.

So. In the spirit of manipulation, I took the liberty of doing something for you—or to you, should I say. There is currently one person in the Village who knows we were long-time lovers. Exciting? Ha, gotcha! I can see your pointy-jawed, poker face as you read this. Think! Speculate! Worry a little! For the rest of your days, you will enter the Village staring at people, searching for the telltale sign that will give the one away. With a hex book and broomstick could I have cursed you more? Someone has one on old Willie Stockhausen. You can live with the uncertainty of your gilt-edge privacy being shattered by an indiscreet slip of the tongue.

Oh, Willie, I quiver at the fun. Like a spy running from the S.S. who has to depend on the old farmer without being able to speak the language. He dashes in from the rainstorm and is pointed to the cellar. A knock comes at the door. Nein, we have seen no one Herr Kapitan. What are those tracks? Silence. Our hound Rolaf in from his run. Danke. Guten Nacht. A sigh of relief. But for how long? And you know the Village. The story would spread like a nor'east wave rolling up the beach, right down to the size of your "privates investigator."

Why have I done this?

Drama is so alive. If only you could have seen The Thin Man with Bill Powell and Myrna Loy. The suspense was so delicious. But it was more too. I had no peace seeing you win the game you play so well every time. I had outlived all my secrets except one. You. Gertie plays Dirty.

You are proud s.o.b., so proud you never once pulled ME up the stairs. I played Shostakovich and Rachmaninoff with the passion of a tsarina, yet you were never overcome enough to have me on the piano bench or bring me caviar or even a smelly cod filet. You never asked for anything—not a bubble bath or a Japanese massage or a buttered rum. You never took anything you didn't work for (save for the swigs) or stole money from me to buy me presents.

You were a lover, Willie—Tiffany's, twenty-four carat with a pile-driving ass. You were an ox, too, with muddy shoes and dirty underwear. You were agonizingly predictable. Your strength. My weakness. Never a man walked the streets who was less imaginative and more stable.

In this letter, I want you to feel how sinister love—yes, stupid, I loved you—is.

Forty-two years. You and I were the only solid thing in this town.

I know a lot of people in New York—writers, directors—who, if they saw you would say, "The man has character. He wears it like a robe." Willie, we both know you don't have a morsel of character in that luscious old *body. Just peeping eyes, paralyzed vocal chords, lusty hands, a scheming mind, and six inches of hot steel. I loved it all.*

I could have left you the house, I suppose, but you don't want it. You never stole the silver, so you sure as hell don't need a place to put it in. No, to you I leave nothing, and that's a compliment. To everyone else I was either owing or owed. Those I owe will grab it fast enough, and those who owed me, well, champagne and boysenberry sherbet would make a nice celebration tonight.

You and I were always equal while we sparked. We still are. The secret that could have tipped the scales is, thanks to me, still a two-edged sword.

Love, Gertie

Willie had an eye for beached objects when he walked the shoreline. They sometimes washed in on the tide and snared themselves in piles of seaweed at the water's edge. A woman's high-heeled shoe. A hat. A child's toy. Things that didn't belong to the sea. He would stand over the curio, toeing it, speculating on how it came to be lost. There was never an answer, only stories. A lick of certainty, like counting the money in your wallet twice, crept over him. It was the same feeling as when he heard the final click of the last lock being bolted in the Village that fall, or when he opened the door to his room knowing there would be darkness and silence. It was this. Aside from your job, your life, all you could depend on was not knowing for sure. Reading the letter, the new uncertainty was familiar to him.

A bass-clef laugh rumbled across the bedroom. If ever a woman lived who he could stay with, it was Gertie. Someone to hold for a while. Someone to ignore if he wanted to. Same for her. Gertie had foxed him, taken him for a ride in the woods, and died thinking everything she knew was neatly packaged. There was no guessing who she told. It could be most anyone, maybe no one. A child too young to care. A matron too embarrassed to repeat it. Or a snipe too willing to torture him mercilessly.

He laughed because he knew Gertie wouldn't be mad at the one, still-loose end. Somehow he had hidden the eighty-ninth key from her groping fingers.

When he got home that afternoon, the old man would pull the letter from his back pocket, smooth the edges, remove the tie string to the pile of Christmas cards—all forty-two—he had saved since the first summer tryst, and gently add it.

You gave the ocean respect but not foolish sentiment. Every secret was safety for yourself, and silence was the biggest secret of all.

1972–LOVE

On tiny waves in the roadside puddles, the late morning sun sparkled like a shattered mirror. Natalie and Steve were surprised. Only last night they had sat on the veranda under an explosion of stars. Gathering in the night, the storm passed its water and left in stealth. The sandy soil gulped its share, but the slick streets and droplets hanging from the wrought iron lawn furniture told of a plentiful rainfall.

"Think the courts will be wet?" Steve asked as they walked down the club road.

He bounced a tennis ball on the head of his racket, concentrating on keeping the ball dead center on the nylon strings.

"Probably," Natalie answered.

"Wouldn't that be a deus ex machina? Our match of the century upstaged by the big Mother?"

"The center court is pitched a little higher than the others. It will be all right."

"If it weren't, you'd hold a fan on it," Steve smiled.

"No…but I'd brush off the puddles," she said.

"Suppose—"

The ball hit the top of his wood press frame and skittered off to the right. Steve broke after it; the chase scampered toward a deep puddle. The ball kangarooed merrily as if delighted at the prospect of a dunking. He almost won. The stiff ends of his outstretched fingers knocked the ball into the puddle. It was deep enough for the ball to float freely. He squatted, toes of his sneakers in the puddle, and fished the dripping ball from the water.

"If you weren't always fidgeting!" she said sharply.

"I wasn't," he protested. "I was involved in a game of skill and dexterity."

"You were fidgeting," Natalie declared in a final word tone. "Like touching your mouth when you meet new people."

"Suppose someone is on the court? Should we wait?"

"We'll see," she said, then added, "You're not trying to get out of this are you, Steven?"

"Not on your life," he snorted. "I've come to collect."

"The courts will be fine," Natalie laughed. "We can use your hot air to dry them."

They walked in silence. Steve's racket swung at his side like a tight, arcing pendulum. Natalie, slightly splay-footed as she walked, set the short, crisp pleats of her tennis whites flouncing with a sensual gait.

*   *   *

Steve checked the mailbox twice before turning up the circular, cobble-stone driveway. Perched proudly at the top of a small rise was a three-story, gabled Victorian house. He knew Natalie was rich, probably loaded, but the casual opulence of the house, gardens, and half-acre of manicured lawn declining to the salt marsh below drove home the point.

At school, Natalie never mentioned a detail of her personal finance. Still, he could tell. It wasn't the elegant lithographs when most dorm rooms were adorned with rock posters, the high thread-count, printed sheets, the imported cosmetics, or the designer labels in the closet. The wealth showed in the way she treated such things. They weren't worth drawing attention to, she seemed to say, but were meant to be enjoyed in a private way with knowledge of what they did and did not represent. Old, confident money.

It was early evening. Judging by the coolness of the sun, Steve guessed he was in time for cocktails. The four hour trip in his ailing VW bug left him feeling gamey. The parched bite of too many cigarettes clung to his palate. He cupped his hands over his mouth and exhaled to see if the gum had done its job.

Steve wasn't a smoker, usually. He bought the pack at a turnpike rest area for diversion. And nerves. Natalie had been travelling Europe all summer, a rich kid's right of passage. He hadn't seen her for two months. Postcards from art museum collections and cathedral shops were their only contact. The last card from London had cheered him somewhat. *I saw Cleopatra's Needle today. The obelisk reminded me of something. You! See you next week. Love, Natalie.*

The drive had been a mixed bag of longing and uncertainty. While driving, he could not shake the memory of how she nestled her lovely rear—a perfect, inverted heart—in the seat next to him on weekend drives up the New England coast to nowhere. Sucking on the thought like a tasty bone, he was amused to see his speed had increased ten mph. Natalie was the coolest of road buddies. Curious and fun. She was always up for every side road adventure or gnarly dive. He shifted from lane to lane like a mobile rook on gambit. Had the past weeks eroded their intimacy?

Mr. and Mrs. Hugh Adams. Hugh and Prill. Daddy and Mum. As the miles passed, Steve thought of them. He had met them once before at the university. They arrived in Boston unexpectedly one Sunday morning. Had they not placed a call from a few miles outside the city well…Steve could see Mr. Adams frozen in horror at the door to Natalie's room, repeating in a loop, his catch-all word for shock: "Blazes!"

Between the call and arrival, Steve and Natalie put on clothes and bumped hurriedly around the room, shoving all signs of Steve's cohabitation into a mahogany chest. When the knock came, they were innocently engaged. Steve was on the bed, fiddling with the Globe Sunday crossword. Natalie was pertly at her desk, working on a paper. Steve said especially loudly, "Five letters. An East Coast Bay."

"Penobscot!" was the first word Hugh ever said to him.

"What? Oh! No, five letters," Steve said.

"Hmmm. Scudder? Six, seven. No!"

"Hi, I'm Steve," he said extending his hand.

"Casco? Hugh," Mr. Adams said, shaking it.

"Nope. Needs an 'n' in the middle," Steve laughed.

"Well, why didn't you say so, lad? Fundy. Fundy. You can't fool an old sailor."

"Or shut him up either, I guess," Natalie rolled her eyes.

"We were on our way back from the Cape and decided to check on you, Natalie," Mr. Adams said, winking at Steve.

"How were the Tremonts?"

"They wanted to know how you were."

"What did you tell them?"

"That Boston was undoing twenty years of Republican education in just two."

He winked again at Steve with conspiratorial grin Steve figured he should return it.

"God, Daddy."

"Meredith is in India. Isn't that fascinating?" Prill offered.

"Do you know what part?" Steve asked, in an attempt at engaging.

"The villages, I think," Hugh butted in. "Aid work or something. It's all 'sahib' to me. Natalie, how are your classes?"

Prill receded. Except for a hello nod, there had been no introduction. Steve felt a strange affinity for her. Hugh was an "offensive" man. He doled out conversation to people and took it away. He was a central switchboard through which all connections with people in the room were made. His hand gestures were firm and directive. With his gray temples, mid-winter tan, white teeth, and Caribbean blue eyes, Mr. Hugh Adams looked airbrushed, like a presidential post card.

Steve knew not to be presumptuous about Prill. His middle class lineage didn't create much of that direction anyway. She was probably content on the gravy train. He saw her as one of the many wealthy, coasting housewives comfortable in receding because their husbands had to be urbane and gallant, witty, mixing drinks and opining. She probably did charity work.

Steve caught her slowly, and with focus, eyeing the room. He watched the targets of her scan—the Matisse print, the bulletin board loaded with stickies and syllabi. Her gaze caught Steve's can of deodorant on the dresser. His puzzlement was momentary, and he almost slapped his forehead. Natalie chided Steve frequently that her skin would break out in a violent rash if she used anything so harsh. Prill's expression was not shocked or disapproving. Steve figured she now knew their score but would say nothing.

How would the Adams be? When they left that Sunday, he felt he had bumbled and stumbled his way through the gathering, speaking trivia with misunderstood humor. He had talked too much, trying to appear confident. Hugh had caught a cold that day and swore it was "the boy." Natalie said he laughed about it. Steve wasn't as sure.

He saw a light flick on in the house.

⋆　⋆　⋆

Approaching the courts, they both heard the distinct *wok!* of a racket stroking a tennis ball. The tall pines surrounding the enclosure and the vine tendrils lacing through the fencing made it impossible to see which courts were open until Steve pulled the creaking fence door open for Natalie. He saw her eyes widen and her nostrils quiver. Game face.

"Look!" Natalie pointed and laughed. Steve joined in.

The only person on the courts was a small boy with sandy hair in bangs that fell over his eyes. He wielded a racket held mid-way up on the handle. Though choking the racket, the boy struggled for control over it. Dancing around the puddles on the far court, he slapped a worn tennis ball against the practice wall mounted on the fence and chased each rebound. The boy spent more time running after his misses than setting for his stroke. Occasionally, he dealt a full-face blow to the ball that resonated around the courts. He paused to look at them then returned to the wall.

The courts were damp but playable. The warmth of the high, curving sun radiated the promise that all but the most persevering puddles would shortly be gone.

"Beautiful courts," Steve said.

"These are the courts I learned on," Natalie smiled.

"Are they usually so empty?"

"Usually. Private, you know," she replied, harrumphing her voice with exaggerated pomposity.

"You should try the local high school courts sometime," he said.

"I wouldn't have the patience," she said, slipping the cover off her racket head.

Steve shook his head ruefully. "It's obscene having empty courts so close."

"Yes, even if you don't use them, it's nice to know you could if you wanted to."

Natalie walked to the near side of the center court as Steve retied his laces. He grabbed three balls from the box of Tretorns and left the still-wet fourth one on the bench. Turning to the court, he saw Natalie back toward him, lightly touching her toes. The elastic of the panties beneath the skirt rode higher as she bent over. Steve eyed the tan mark made by her bikini bottoms on her soft cheeks with every downward snap she made. He imagined her sun bathing on a beach on the Adriatic, legs slightly spread, eyes closed. He exhaled. *Later, my boy, later.*

"Hey! I thought the better player was supposed to take the near court."

"She's right here. You have yet to beat me."

"Oh, you hadn't heard," Steve lowered his voice sympathetically. "The USTA rankings changed while you were gone. I am now 4020. You are 4022. I played all summer."

"With me in absentia?" Natalie scolded. "You'll have to do me with an arrow in the heart, not a bullet in the back. Now get over there so I can shut your mouth."

He walked over to the far side, bouncing a ball off the court with his racket. He dropped a ball and swung with a forehand. The ball struck an unpleasant mixture of wood and string, bounced first on his side before hopping over to Natalie.

"This isn't ping-pong, sweetheart," she cooed as she swung gracefully and whacked a backhand at him.

Steve had no riposte. All his effort went into returning the ball off the short hop. They exchanged forehands, and Natalie hit a lazy slice to mid-court that failed to stay down. Steve closed and lashed a hard forehand with a topspin follow. The ball rocketed deep to her backcourt and the quick, sailing bounce left her swinging at air. She looked over the net with a bemused smile.

"If I see two of them, I'll believe you meant it," she said.

The warm-up was long and competitive. Steve disliked playing with people who, after a few half-hearted pops, approached the net saying, "Ready?" He was self-conscious with some of his strokes. The free-flowing perspiration in a long warm-up diluted the mental snags. Natalie enjoyed the warm-up to increase the stakes and tension. She started slowly, gradually lengthening her backswing, doubling the pace of her ball.

"Last one?" she asked, holding up a ball.

"Sure. Game on after this one."

The match had begun. They both wanted the last warm-up point.

Natalie lofted the ball to the baseline. It bounced to a teasing height. It was a dangerous ball—a "tweener"—requiring a deft return. Steve waited for the ball to drop into his hitting zone. His return was not well-controlled but gave Natalie a similar moon ball opportunity. She chose a high backhand slice. It was not hit hard and floated, angling to his right. He volleyed the ball from midcourt to her backhand. Natalie broke for the ball with nimble quickness and anticipation but had trouble reaching it. Her attempted arc lob to push him off the net did not go deep enough. Rather than risking an overhead, Steve allowed the ball to bounce and ascend blithely into a blistering topspin forehand that was to the corner baseline and into the fencing before Natalie responded.

"That's two," Steve said amiably.

"Up," she called as he spun his racket for first service.

*   *   *

Standing before the porch, Steve hoped Natalie would open the front door and step—no, leap—toward him. He needed a few minutes alone with her before the amenities and questions inside began. He walked back to his car as if he had forgotten something and slammed the door, re-announcing his arrival. He doubted the tinny pop even penetrated the polished oak door. He felt his middle class, we're-all-about-the-same confidence fleeing him. He looked from the house to the car, then down his chest. The VW with its door dent and worn bumper stickers from the previous owner looked pathetic. His cotton knit shirt with a shield instead of the alligator seemed fake. He disliked himself for wanting what lay in front of him.

"Steven, you needn't bow," Mrs. Adams laughed. "I thought I heard your car. Come in!"

Steve felt foolish. He was about to press the bell when he noticed a typed strip inserted above the buzzer. MR. AND MRS. E. HUGH ADAMS. He speculated on Hugh's neglected first initial. Edward? Eugene? When Prill opened the door, he was bent over the button, checking he hadn't misread the insert.

"Hello, Mrs. Adams," he said reaching for her hand and leaning forward to peck the cheek she offered so graciously.

"Natalie! Natalie! Steve's here," she called cheerily.

On well-timed cue, Mrs. Adams backed off with an excuse about dinner as Natalie descended the carpeted staircase. It wasn't necessary, he thought. They hardly were going to feel each other up in the foyer. They might not even touch.

"Hi, Steve," she said.

"Hello."

"Is that all?"

"You tell me," he said, extending his arms, pulling her in.

Her arms went around his waist, and she pulled hard. His torso would have arched back with the love tug were his arms not encircling her shoulders. In a tight, self-contained ball of pressure, they pulled toward each other. It felt very nice. Natalie reached down playfully and pinched his crotch.

"Hey!" Steve protested. "It's not a horn, you know."

"It's not an orchid either. Whose been pulling it besides you?"

"Dirty girl. Mmm. Let's see. Gwen, then Beth took her pleasure, and—"

"Sure. And Queen Elizabeth," she laughed.

He pulled his head away and looked at her face. Salt in her hair. Traces of a peeling nose. The powdered pink of a slight pimple. She always had one, only one, somewhere on her smooth complexion. The slightest split on the tip of her nose. She was quite pretty, sometimes handsome. Her eyes were too gray for her face to light up, but they held power. Her voice was the magic—soft, clear, soothing. She was laughing, nipping, clutching now. She planted a kiss that sent hard, swift blood running to his loins.

"Drink anyone?" a voice boomed from the veranda.

"Coming, Daddy."

Natalie didn't release Steve immediately.

"I'm glad you are here, Steve."

He nodded his assent.

"Let's not say anything," she said, "...about the summer, that is."

"It's okay," he said. "It'll all come out."

⋆   ⋆   ⋆

Steve met Natalie on the fringe of a campus anti-war rally. The well-groomed girl next to him was watching a ponytailed professor exhorting the crowd with a waving fist. She had a fly-on-the-ceiling aloofness that signaled she was probably writing a sociology paper on the gathering.

"You know," she said, turning to him out of the blue as if they were on a date, "what he is saying doesn't add up. And—I thought this was about the war. What's this? Unequal distribution of wealth is symptomatic, surely, but it is not of itself causative. Case not made. He's a weak-minded excuse-maker."

It was the third rally of the week, and Steve was fed up too—even agreed with her.

"I've heard that leveled in a few barrooms, perhaps minus the eloquence," he replied.

"Is that a knock?" she asked coldly.

"Are you serious, my dear? In this..." he waved his arm over the quad, "... the marketplace of ideas?"

The depth of her laugh warmed him.

"I think you should shoulder your way up to the mic and harangue those making excuses for life's dismals."

"Not my style. I'm more subversive. I just vote and write my congressman."

"Tsk, tsk," Steve clucked. "I won't tell and ruin your creds."

"It's all right," she said lightly. "I don't get along too well here anyway."

*   *   *

Fall passed to winter, and Steve moved in with her. She had a roomy single with a double bed, a signal of luxury beyond the norm. Sometimes it seemed they carried on the relationship on the borders of their personalities—contiguous, bonded, but not enmeshed. Alone, he pondered what the force was that kept them clinging, yet they did with feeling.

Disdain. Aristocratic disdain. Steve was mesmerized by it. He had been surrounded his first three years by hordes of people, each with a rap to peddle. His background had preached the sacredness of each person's opinion. His ears were slave to anyone with the nerve and words to collar him. But there were lies—if not lies, self-serving distortions. Facts, figures were selectively quoted to win, not enlighten. He knew that much. He was very bright, discerning, and bored with the polemics. Natalie was different too. She selected what she cared to absorb and dismissed, as with an errant servant, that which seemed foolish. Her disdain was sure, unremorseful, and very sexy. It was a scalpel, liberally wielded, to protect and isolate her from the vortex of indecision.

And sex. It was athletic, frequent, creative, and torrid. Under her direction, they acted out their passions: stranger and innocent, knight and tarty queen, street whore and john, casting couch—combinations and permutations of situations, fulfilled with panting, well-rendered Oscar performances. They lay in bed, sometimes for hours, Steve making funny faces, Natalie giggling. Natalie tickling, pinching, mimicking no one in particular with zany voices—she did a marvelous Betty Boop. When the sweat in their navels had dried, the pace sometimes changed with excruciating abruptness.

"Steve, do you care I can only cum if we do these crazy things?"

"What crazy things?" he replied, patronizingly naïve.

"Jesus, you know. The talk. The roles. You have to admit, I am a dirty little girl."

"What is not to like about a gorgeous, patrician, dirty little girl. It is served up on a platter by God, I would think."

Love? They didn't bandy that word about. Only once had the faith been exchanged.

"I don't get any points for living here, Natalie," Steve spat in an all-to-frequent, volatile exchange. "When I stay, we argue. When I suggest moving out, we argue. 'Go ahead. I'm not stopping you.' Steve screwed up his face like hers.

"That's just the way you look when you say it too."

"I'm not stopping you."

"Like hell. You won't come out with me, but when I get back from the campus pub seeing friends, I have Miss Iceberg to deal with. Might as well stab me, but you don't."

"You must feel guilty about something to think that. I don't treat you any differently," Natalie said.

"That wan little smile of yours could chill a snowman, Adams."

"So go."

"I want you to come out with me. Circulate a little!"

"No, I meant leave. Period."

"Do you want me to?"

"You're not getting any points," she said bitterly.

"You are crazy, nuts, I swear," Steve exploded. "The Doomsday Kid. Every disagreement that comes up, you pull out the biggest club—'so leave.' No subtlety, no alternatives. Some people call that intimidation. If that's the way it's going to be, yes, I will, thank you."

Steve grabbed his coat.

"Wait."

Natalie stood and blocked his way. She wore a strange smile of satisfaction.

"This is no way to end it," she said softly.

"Why not?" he snorted.

"Because," she paused, "I love you very much."

Steve reached out and grabbed her. Pulling her close, he felt himself holding a gem of hard, cold beauty.

"I do love you too," he whispered. "I do you too."

*　*　*

"Up it is," Steve called, scooping up the ball in front of him and batting it across the net to Natalie.

"Taking two!" she yelled from the service line.

Steve studied her serve. He thought her The Windmill. Her service indicated lessons by an experienced pro. Still, something was awry, as if the lessons ended a month too soon. It was not a flowing motion. Each part, the backswing, the toss, the whip had been broken down and practiced individually. There were slight breaks between each like a windmill in intermittent wind. Any awkwardness disappeared at the moment of impact. She hit a hard, flat serve, controlled, but not sissy, with placement in mind. She slackened little on second serve.

Both practice serves bounced deep in the box. Steve swiped them casually across the net. Natalie looked up after each return.

Her first serve was long. The second bounded to his forehand. Steve went cross-court with his return and slid to the middle baseline. They exchanged crisp forehands. It was good tennis, low to the net, each of them pressing for advantage. Natalie pinned Steve to a deep backhand. He overran the ball and was off-balance. He swung awkwardly close to his body. The stroke lacked power, and Natalie loomed netward to put it away. She volleyed. SMACK! The ball hit the net cable and dribbled back to her feet. Steve spun his racket in relief.

He attempted a drop shot on her next serve. Natalie had looked slow coming off the service line. He chopped, but gave the ball too much loft. Natalie charged and reached the net in time to choose her corner. With a satisfied grunt, she rocketed the ball to his right. Legs pumping, limbs outstretched, he managed to get a racket on it. He jammed his legs hard into the court to halt himself and broke the other way, trying to salvage some open court. Natalie hit behind him. He looked over his shoulder as it passed him.

"You bastard," he laughed.

Natalie curtsied politely.

The next three points went quickly—a passing shot, a muff, a lob. Steve was ahead for the first time since they started playing the previous spring.

"Exchange courts?" he asked.

"I don't care," Natalie said, "I don't think there's an advantage. Do you?"

"No, the sun's equally distracting where it is. I just didn't want to hear any excuses."

"Enjoy it while you can," she said, planting her feet and crouching for his service.

* * *

Steve rattled the ice in his glass thoughtfully. Drink number two and a half. He hadn't eaten since breakfast and had a pleasant, mild buzz going. Keep it easy. The view was a classic marsh scape. The house overlooked a timeless, inland estuary lined by salt grass—mostly salt water, but spring-fed at its end. The lightly swelling surface was gentle and seductive. A threesome of heron waded and bobbed downward spearing inlet prey. The sunset westward was a Degas of salmon-pink clouds offering benevolence to all below.

Cocktail hour was going well. Steve had forsaken timidity early. He had taken the role of summer visitor, the entertaining stranger bringing anecdotes laced with chatty humor and word from beyond. He settled deeper into the white wicker chair, feeling very much a part the grandness.

"Steven, Natalie tells me this isn't a very fashionable question these days," Mr. Adams chuckled, "but what are you going to do after this year?"

Steve was thankful for the remaining year in school. He had eight months to answer whatever he wished.

"Apply to graduate schools. Law and psychology. I'll probably take a few job interviews in February too. See what's being offered. If all else fails," he shrugged, "there's always Tibet."

Laughter.

"How about this summer? What have you been doing?"

"Digging swimming pools."

There was little he could do to make it sound exciting.

"I thought it was something like that," Prill said. "You look very hard." She clenched her fist. "And tan."

"Thanks. The work is tough, but it's a welcome change from school. The people I worked with were pretty thick, but I got an education in blue humor."

"Like what," Natalie giggled.

"Unmentionable, I'm afraid. But funny."

"Oh, go ahead, Steve, if it isn't too bad."

He glanced around. No frowns. Everyone waited expectantly.

"I disclaim all responsibility for the easily offended," he laughed. "The thoughts expressed here are not necessarily those of the innocent."

"Come on."

"Above and beyond all else, sex is the number one topic of discussion on construction jobs. No detail is too intimate, no story too gross, no exaggeration too unbelievable. This one guy, Jim—wiry, small, always unshaven—was bemoaning the fact his wife had been sick and they weren't consummating—not exactly his word choice—lately."

Steve stopped for twitters.

"One of the other laborers in the pit with us stops, leans on his shovel, and asks, 'Well, ya been gettin' any on the side?' Jim, actually a natural comic, slaps his thigh, stares wide-eyed to heaven and says, 'On the side? I haven't been at it in so long, I didn't know they moved it.'"

"Marvelous, Steve."

"Precious."

He took a long gulp from his drink. Hell, it didn't take much to hold your own around here. The bourbon was cold and sweet. He emptied the glass.

"So what's on the agenda for you two tomorrow?" Mr. Adams asked.

Steve shrugged.

"You could race the boat. Jim O'Brien called from the club. He was trying to scrape together a regatta."

"Or you could go to the Indian dig in Carver. Natalie says you know anthropology, don't you, Steve?" Prill asked.

"We could play tennis," Natalie said.

"I thought you'd never ask," Steve said with cheek.

Natalie had drubbed him badly when they last played. The sets they played were not defeats. That would imply some level of competition. It was evident from game one she was the better player, and it was a practice session for her. She carried him through each game, toying with her shots, experimenting with new strategies. Steve ran, sweated, and chased. Each serve was a starting bell for him to run laps sideline to sideline and forecourt to backcourt. He didn't control a single minute of the exchanges.

They saw tennis as the one sphere of meaningful interaction in a relationship that often lacked measuring sticks of comparison. Their grades were comparable, but their majors vastly different. Their social styles were dissimilar. Their tastes and means were cut of far different cloth. The one thing never spoken was that each wanted superiority where outcomes were clear.

Steve fondled his trump card. All summer he had practiced with purpose, panting at the board through the twilight hours after work, stroking through the weekends. He had honed his game with cold precision. He used the practice wall to sharpen his reflexes. He challenged players better than himself until he could beat them. He played the town tournament and made it to the final sixteen. Love of the game toward summer's end was supplanted by the thought of whipping Natalie.

"Of course, I can see you might not want to play," she said slyly.

"You didn't fare so well, Steve?" Mr. Adams asked.

"No, but I have a few surprises."

"I'll play with a blindfold," she teased.

"Things aren't the same," Steve smiled thinly.

"I'll play lefty—"

The Adams watched the escalation with amusement.

"I've put in time."

"—or with my foot."

Steve knew he was being led to a declaration. He made it.

"I guess I'll just have to beat you, Natalie."

"Make sure it's not the booze talking, lover," she said happily.

"Tomorrow morning."

⋆   ⋆   ⋆

"Five–two!" Steve called.

She nodded once and prepared to receive.

The score was closer numerically than psychologically. He had dominated with a big serve. Serve, return, volley; the three-step pressure wilted Natalie's resistance. She was frustrated. In several games she had rallied when she was two or three points down, pulled teasingly close, playing well only to have a thunderbolt rifled at her with which she could do little.

Natalie knew her tennis. She had changed the pace of the game, trying to throw Steve off his stride, retrieving balls quickly and taking less time between serves or tying her shoelaces and toweling off slowly. She took pace off the ball and threw junk at him. She employed knowledgeable tricks but couldn't alter the edge Steve held.

With game at deuce, Steve lobbed. Backpedaling, Natalie caught her heel and fell unceremoniously on her rump. She got up slowly.

"You okay?" he laughed.

She waved him off.

"Set point."

He zinged his serve to her, and she blocked a return low and hard. Steve's cross-court had been humming all day. He smacked the ball off the low bounce with maximum leverage. The ball, on the rise, slammed the cable and spun like

148

a gyroscope, creeping almost six inches along the net's top before falling on Natalie's side.

He tossed his racket in the air and caught it. He won the set.

Natalie looked tired. Her bangs were wetted with sweat to her forehead. She had a scrape on the back of her thigh from the fall. It had the makings of a raspberry burn. Should he suggest quitting? No, if she wanted "out," she would have to ask for it. Natalie had set the stakes, now she would pay.

She stared silently at him. He met her stare. A second passed. She walked to the net, gathering balls for her serve. Steve was elated she could not choke out a submission. The sun was warm; the day was cloudless. His racket felt light, a natural extension of his arm. Beads of sweat dribbled from his chin. The combination of sun and flush from exertion turned the tan on his arms to hot bronze. A dip in the pool. A sleek sailboat passing off a tight, bubbly wake. Lobster dinner tonight. He was having fun.

The set was dismal. Natalie was out of condition from Europe. She hadn't played since spring. With the games at 5–2, he toyed with the idea of throwing her a game. She was dragging now. The loss was probably eating her badly. He dismissed the idea. Fair was fair. He would be gallant and gentle in a few short minutes.

Her last shot fluttered weakly into the net. She stood watching the ball and looked up at Steve approaching the net. Her smile—big, white in the sunlight—stopped him. He had charming compliments on the tip of his tongue, but she spoke first.

"You really put it to me," she said, extending her hand, shaking his.

"I've been playing a terribly lot," he said warily.

"It shows. Completely different player."

As they gathered the balls, Steve heard the pines rustle in empty silence. He couldn't select a feeling. The match was over and meant very little. He cared only for her aches and tiredness. She looked beautiful, not in defeat, but with the grace of a games woman. He didn't feel sorry for her. He couldn't; she obviously was not disturbed. She could take it. Steve lowered his head. He could not have. He had played with pride and anger, not his heart. Not even in the end. The Doomsday Kid did it again. She raised the ante, made the choice inevitable, left no alternative, and lived the outcome.

"You tired?" he asked.

"A little."

"Maybe we shouldn't have played the second set."

"There was no sense leaving any doubt about it was there, Steve?"

She had him on a new hook but didn't exploit it.

"Shall we sail this afternoon?" he asked.

"You go with Daddy. I think I'll rest up for tonight."

Steve pulled the gear together mildly untethered. He had won fair and square in a matter between them but felt now he lost—something. He drew up and shrugged to Natalie. Way it is.

The floppy-haired boy skipped his way past on his way to the fence door. He was at an age where a tooth was a rarity in his smile.

"What was the thcore?" he lisped.

"Two–love," Natalie answered.

"Oh," he said and continued to the door.

The boy stopped in second thought.

"Love?" he asked, scrunching his nose.

"Yes. It's a polite way of saying you have nothing."

1984–The Beast

Royce and Danny were lying on their backs on the grass at the far end of the Village green. It was 1:30 A.M. on a humid, early August night. They were stoned silly and thought themselves philosophically acute, particularly about the summer moths butting the quaint, pseudo-gas, actually electric, street lamp above their heads. Neither paid attention to the fact CeCe had wandered into the shadows to do a mind-clearing tai chi thing. The mostly empty Cuervo fifth lying between them after a night of hitting the waterfront bar decks in town had not done a lot for their fervency and less for their lucidity.

"I really try to understand those poor bastards. I do," Danny slurred, looking upward. "They are so goddam insistent. To what end? For Chrissake, it's a light that ain't gonna do shit for them. They only have so much energy, and butting their bodies against a light gotta be killing them."

"Probably wrong, doofus. Maybe it's like a bar with a neon Corona sign to them. Cold beer and possible pussy if you are cool," said Royce, his highly re-fined, preppy put-down voice somewhat enfeebled. "They're at a light show. Who knows?"

CeCe came in from the shadows and wanted to know where the reefer was.

"Wasted and wanting as usual," she sighed. "Talking moths. Okay. Is there a roach left for a hit?"

"I believe there may be."

"That's the horror with you, Royce. 'I believe there may be!' How about an answer to a simple question? Like yes or no? Do I have to go on faith?"

"Yes, CeCe. You do. Because you have so little."

"Do you have a clue how far you are from anything important to say?"

"Yes, bitch queen of open legs, I unfortunately do." Royce said absently. "You are doomed to vapid conversation with no psychotropic relief unless I rummage about here."

Amidst the pot and tequila vapors, the anxiety of their pending, senior college year and life beyond roiled. By any measure, the buddies were both stunning and flawed. They flaunted envious health, model good looks, and marginal—really no—accomplishments. Spoiled brats. There was not a damn thing to distinguish their tanned, athletic, genetically honored bodies from oblivion. None had a job at the moment. They had little a sense of soul. They were wasted biomass of high quality in the moment. They seemed destined to be lawyers, bankers, or social workers with appropriate accomplishment given their birthright and looks. They had nothing really bad in them except being feckless and wondering.

"For Chrissake," CeCe repeated, "where is the reefer, Royce?"

The trio, they preferred "troika" for literary value, had been together since toddlers in the Village and on the conjoining beach.

It was a summer place. In the simplest of descriptions, the Village was a 240 acre plot of old-timey, marginally productive farmland. It was bordered by the ocean to the south and overseen there by a gentle bluff with a grand view of an arcing curve beach below. The ancient marsh river to the west ebbed and flowed tides, guarding the sunset flank. Two ponds to the east stifled entrance save for a narrow traffic causeway.

Cut off. The Village was a dot on an already small peninsula that jutted into the Atlantic. It was, though land based, its own kind of geographical peninsula. No description applied with accuracy. It had a history, not exclusively, of a non-denominational, Christian, natural worship but was losing it to social changes. Most current inhabitants of the 150 cottage homes—some homes more grandiose with historically accurate and chic upgrades, others favoring "authenticity"—knew it was a sacred place. It was quaint, subtle, and timeless. It had quiet, natural beauty, native American bones, colonial settler roots, and a history of holy-roller evangelists whose forbearers created a revival campground a hundred years prior there with subsequent cottages popping like mushrooms around it.

Anyone, resident or visitor, spiritual or atheist, who walked the Village knew it was a quiet kind of special.

The threesome members were privileged but in no way equal, as far as backgrounds. They were of early twenty ages, and there had been many generations of the sort in the Village before them. The issue, and it is hard to describe, is that they were sort of "flat"—without "juice," so to speak. They had made no contribution to the Village vibe of "doing for others," loved and hated their parents in equal measure like most do at the age (CeCe excepted because her history was a fog), and had, so far, no test of their resolve to be anything. The lust was for "cool." They all had cool—Danny and Royce with shekels in their wallets, keys to sharp cars, and CeCe, mixed blood, exotic beauty—and all with what passed for witty conversation in the nearby larger town bar scene. Just like so many others.

Danny showed up in the Village by birth. His family cottage was already owned before his appearance. His parents, Joe and Jo, heard about "this place" through a mildly inebriated, yet prescient odd fellow, a really old man – ninety at least. It was Willie Stockhausen, who they met at the Compass Bar on a weekend lark from Boston. He owned his stool and the bartenders made sure no one took it at Happy Hour. Willie told them, "Don't miss this place."

They drove through the Village and were sold on its otherworldly charm. Lovely cottages abounded with a green quaintly posting Village "rules." They heard it was an evolving Boston-Irish summer enclave. They bought a darling cottage early enough when it was affordable. Stockhausen dealt them a total solid in his strange way.

Joe was department administrator at Logan in Boston. Jo was an executive secretary for a honcho in health care insurance. They had solid middle-class scratch. They mortgaged a tad to buy in, but it was not a big stretch. They used good credit for a nicely situated cottage with a peek-view of the salt marsh—not prime, but sigh-worthy. They stretched a little further and built an admirable rear deck to catch a piece of view.

Danny, an only child, was not silver spoon, just coddled. He was going senior at Roger Williams College in Rhode Island. It was a party school on the 'Gannset Bay. He was, maybe, high 500s SAT when the scores mattered and a more than fair small college athlete—baseball team and intramurals mostly. He lived large with great *joie de vivre* on the back of Joe and Jo. He was a good kid with "never a word said against" him" but few words to extoll him. Now he was up and at it in the Village, drunk, stoned, talking about moths.

Danny had the "Irish." He could drink, and he could be crazy, loving, charming, witty, and worthless all at the same time. If you have no clue about what the "Irish" means, then you wouldn't get it. This isn't profiling, it's a compliment. It just is. The Germans don't have it at all.

Royce Jr. showed up in the Village by birth too. His origins were quite different. His parents, Royce Sr. and Cassie, had an Episcopalian, gene-perfect, no thread of hair misplaced, even in a nor'easter, presence. Their roots, at least Cassie's anyway, went back to the Mayflower. She had the bona fides of historical largesse and entitlement to be a bigger, huger figure for comparison to anyone in the Village who had history coming through Ellis Island or ship-jumping along the coast. It would not play in Idaho, but in the New England front it rocked. Royce Sr. came from New England industrialists in machine tools. The line knew what they were doing. Starting later in the Bay Colony, it was they who built fabulous wealth and coveted it in trusts. The wealth held. He was a man of great opinions and sonorous gravity, born to opulence with no opposition to his bunk because money talks and people will always suffer listening at the grand parties, if invited, to a bombastic host.

Royce Jr. had an unflappable, continuously aimless adoration for his parents. He had little sensibility for himself. He existed in their strange bounty. He, too, was an only child who was raised by nannies, music teachers, doting sycophants, but rarely by his parents. Royce Jr. knew something was wrong and strange in that he did not see himself beyond the privileges of his life. He had nary a conviction, yet he knew with a sonorous voice like Dad's, he could sound convincing of what he knew not. He sometimes thought it could make him president or a shyster.

Royce went to Taft and, as often happened, it did him little good except for the sense of pedigree. He went in, went out with no passion of a life path. Still, the school network was a semaphore of possibility. He rowed crew but was kicked off the team for his inability to take advice from anyone including the coxswain on stroke counts. Family money then put him at Yale and the right colleges therein. He was a whist wizard and gained minor renown entering his senior year, his grades mediocre. He was not destined to the Skull and Bones Society like his forbearers. Little to show. A tequila bottle between his legs on the Village green suggested little good was happening here. Still, it was an early, experimenting life and, perhaps, too soon to judge.

CeCe was a girl to be loved and hated all at the same time. She was a townie. She was native to the Cape and was, ever since birth, a sprite-limbed child. She had insinuated herself into Village life with ease and no standing. She was of no known origin or history because her roots had no means of being analyzed in the Village. No one even knew where she lived, but enough clues dropped to suggest it was with grandma.

She was drop-dead beautiful. CeCe had a bit of the Wampanoag, Azores/Portugeuse thing going, maybe with a Nordic fling in her genetic tree. Her mocha skin was so pure, it could create poems or a coffee commercial. Her facial features were remarkably refined and interracially delicate. It was only fate that some fashion magazine had not taken notice, yet she was of a kind of flashy, trashy. She could not help it. No history, no advocates, no nothing.

CeCe was clever. She attached herself to Village doings—the volleyball games, the band concerts, the teen parties—and simply became seen and accepted as one of them. Her origins were not debated. She entered the beach for all her years with no one asking her of her membership status. It was a compassionate free pass. CeCe strolling the beach shore in a bikini was worth something. The laughing face and tight body elevated the testosterone of the male populace.

She could be a kind, spiritual beacon with total belief and a questionable slut in equal measure. She took more than a few boys down and left them bereft. No one, even geniuses, could figure it out. She loved them and left without regret. No one trusted her, but the lucky few who enjoyed her body remembered it fondly as they knew she rarely deigned to offer. They knew there was no capture. She could not connect.

The troika was not heavenly, memorable or composed, especially in this moment. As always, it was self-centered need by each.

Their drunk driven dialogue begat an ill-conceived plan. It was stupid.

"You know what we gotta do?" Royce Jr. slurred.

"No," Danny and CeCe answered in almost perfect unison.

Royce was foggy in his phase of need. The need burned large. He wanted to be known as somebody in this Village on his own account beyond his parents where the committed citizens kept alive a rare dream. He knew his moral fiber was currently deficient for greatness of their sort but felt his outrageousness may be capable of grandiosity. He wanted legend in a bad way.

"Listen," he said. It came out more as *lithen,* given the hour and libations, pot, and weariness. "We are going to capture the monster of Red Lilly Pond. It is a beast known to all who know."

"Must we? The monster outlives the Village. Why?" Danny asked.

"Because we will live forever," Royce answered. "We will be the ones of legend."

"I don't get it," CeCe said. "It's just a fucking snapping turtle."

A moment did strike to register CeCe's thoughts. She was prescient.

"That is why you fail, CeCe," Royce intoned. "It is the mega-monster of pond snappers. There are stories of geezers in this Village who stalked it thirty years ago with axe in hand in rowboats. The Beast was invincible—ever elusive. We will live forever in Village lore in its capture. This Beast most likely heard the sermons and hymns of the Village's founding a century ago."

All this—not all, of course—was untrue, but when Royce waxed large with mythic hyperboles, he became stupidly interesting. Yes, true, some now, grown-old geezers in the Village had hunted for the Beast with no skills learned from their experience and little courage to find it. It was entirely overblown. If anyone were correct, it was CeCe. *It's just a fucking snapping turtle.* Not to Royce. The craziness of the myths and Beast descriptions captured him with the portent of greatness

To be fair, snappers, *Chelydra serpentina,* are not the beasts they may seem if ignored. Their unfortunate lot in life was to have evolved into something really ugly like a military tank as opposed to the softer curves and slow-motion in-nocence of, say, their box turtle cousins. Box turtles are quaint and sleepy. Snappers look hardcore Nazi. They have never been likely to launch aggressive attacks on the populace. They were not likely to steal into cottages and rape the Village virgins. Their species was more a "hide-and-thrive" sort. The troika did no research, but this big sucker could drop to a one heartbeat a minute in the ooze and raise a neck for his nostrils to pull hours of life within. It was why a hundred years was possible.

Also, to be fair, this pond snapper was actually a terrifying monster. Records were vaguely kept in the Commonwealth, but it was an imprecise science. A slew of citizens in the Village with a pond view had watched mallard mommies leading a brood of imprinted chicks on the pond and seen turtle murder, the turtle dragging tasty chicks into its maw. That was documented. Others had seen a snapper big as a tire crossing the causeway to the adjacent pond. The Beast seemed to favor a pond-side cupola behind the Inn.

If you ever saw his clawed fins drive to the surface—it was definitely a "he" by size—you would be brought to prehistoric anxiety. He was huge and scary. The Beast had to be a hundred pounds of primitive bite, which might set records. He was big, ugly, and smelly. His sulfurous odor arose from the muck before him and long-lived in clinging scent. No one ever brought him down for maybe a hundred years. Actually, the leviathan may have pre-dated the Village. His fin span was six inches with claws on each appendage as told. When he pushed pond biota away on a trip to the surface, it was something beyond mortal sensibility. Those who saw it reeled back in awe.

Royce, CeCe, and Danny were fuzzy on the details. They agreed it was a "thing" of interest. Royce, in his vainglory, was resolute on establishing the Village lore to be gained by conquering the unconquerable. He had no accurate plans, but he thought it fetching and knew, no matter how distant it seemed, the Village populace would be intrigued as hell. Danny was also a follower with no bigger plans. Why not? His every sense told him following Royce on this one was ill-conceived, but he was drunk. CeCe, the townie, shook her head in supplicant agreement. Stupid, but why not? No one had come close to challenging the monster.

They had heard stories talked on the Green for years about teens seeking adventure, dragging bait, and waiting. It never hit. For the most part, the privileged kids wanted to tout their hunting as a badge of bravery, but they really did not want shit to do with the Beast. It was tomfoolery.

Tequila gone, pot exhausted, they repaired to their respective dwellings, CeCe's unknown. Their heads were foggy, their resolve ambiguous as it usually was. It was another brain fart that required something more than their currently deconstructed conscious allowed.

It was Danny who awoke with a plan. He was not feeling too good, but the power of youthful excess burned the overindulgence of last night straight away.

Baiting! It was about baiting. Cunning baiting. Nasty baiting. Joe and Jo had some Louisiana origins—actually it was only Jo. She claimed she was no part of it, but her people baited 'gators. She talked of it, often confessed the shame of being low class, and rebounded to the joy of being away from it and now acceptable, but Jo had some Cajun blood. She was real about it and could spin a story descriptively cool. Danny now realized she had seen the whole "gator deal." She knew baiting.

The next day, the troika met at the beach.

"Of course, we are to go on the hunt?" Royce asked with somewhat bleary eyes.

Royce Jr. had that stupid, imperiousness language that led colonial England to disaster. Still, it carried a sort of command.

"If so, what is the plan, m'lord?" Danny asked.

"Take the small dinghy and dredge with capture weapons."

"Stupid, methinks," said, Danny. "People have been doing this a long time and failed. You bait and capture. Your lack of tactics appalls the troops."

"Well said. I submit to superior knowledge. I await you for a plan."

"Jesus Christ," said CeCe, "I live with crazies. A fucking snapping turtle? Why are you talking like colonial freaks? So many gnarly choices? What is the point, you guys?"

That is when the string that briefly connected them broke on the issue in ways not reconcilable.

The young men ignored her.

CeCe wanted no part. She didn't love the snapper but knew it was a pond creature who lived as it did. She wanted it dearly to be left alone and thought it more important to maybe figure what her life might be. She was at the four C's trying to conjure up an associate's degree. These two, Royce and Danny, were on a different plane in good colleges. They seemed to want something they could not get because, if they ever got it, they would never know what it was. Why was a big, old turtle in their equation?

"This is how you do it," Danny said, the newly christened New England bayou trapper. "Get a quarter raw chicken from Shaw's, seventy-pound line and a shark hook from SportsPort. Bend a counter-levered bank sapling with chicken on the hook into the pond. Done! Game over!"

"You amaze me, friend," said Royce. "It is so far beyond your questionable upbringing. What is this counter-levering?"

"Fuck off, prep ass-wipe. I doubt you could find dead north on a compass. You have your head so far up your ass, you believe to see the light at the end of the tunnel as you speak."

"Actually, Danny," Royce said, "that is poetry."

"Screw, Royce. You are delusional. I will handle it."

The troika partook of a minor Village deck party that evening. It was replete with soggy shrimp—Jesus, why didn't people press the water out—cream-cheesy, spread hors d'oeuvres, decent Chablis, and ample Tanqueray and tonic. CeCe, in her daring summer shift and espadrilles, was ever the focus of wildly aroused, middle-aged guys full of themselves. Nothing really was happening there. No one was going anywhere except a masturbatory experience. Danny hung back with drink in hand and not much enthusiasm.

Royce Jr., slightly, not abundantly lubed, was fishing for approbation.

"Has anyone set forth to capture the Leviathan in our ponds?" he asked, twirling a stirrer in a gin and tonic.

His question attracted mild attention.

"Leviathan?" someone voiced.

"Yes, the legendary Beast of all our childhoods," Royce Jr. sonorously voiced.

"Why?" was the response of a few who heard.

"Because it is bigger and longer lived than all of us. It heard the Village revival songs." Royce Jr. said evenly.

"It's just a fucking snapping turtle," someone muttered.

The approbation he wished for the mission did not flow. To put a finer point on it, no one expressed care. The turtle Leviathan drew no interest.

*   *   *

Around ten that evening, the troika commandeered Davis's snub-nosed, plywood dinghy. He had not rowed in it for twenty years but kept it at a rotting pond dock each summer just in case. They rowed to the causeway and portaged the boat to the pond of the Beast. In her Celtics T-shirt and green, satin basketball shorts, CeCe held the hunting goods and sat aft. Danny pulled the oars. Royce, ever Columbus, more James Cook, sat fore and directed them to a tree-lined bank near the cupola.

None of the three were all that handy, but the task was not really that complex. Danny and Royce had baited drop-fishing hooks in the sound but not with a quarter chicken on a shark hook. Still, it did not require a license or college degree. The real issue was finding a strong, bendable sapling that would droop the bait to the water and hold when the hook was taken.

The hunting gods rewarded them. Maple saplings abounded everywhere––thin, whippy, and strong. Danny drove the prow to the bank. They jumped ashore, carefully knowing they were in the domain of the Beast. Royce Jr. pulled over a two-inch thick maple sapling.

The art, which they sort of knew, was to securely tie-off the line on the sapling for serious vexation of a hooked beast. They got that point, having taken physics in reputable schools. They baited the hook and used a big stone they brought to counterweight the maple and tied it at bending point of the thin trunk so the line hovered just below the water line with now-rotting chicken. The spare linage gave a two-and-a-half-foot clearance above the water line. They were fools on a mission, but not stupid. It was Louisiana clever. Neatly done. They rowed away with different thoughts. None were practical.

Royce Jr., using military-class binoculars the next morning, given to him by Dad in hopes he might find peace in bird-watching, knew something big had pulled on the maple sapling—something very big. He knew in his soul this was the "big one." It quickly dawned on him he knew he had no clue as to what to do. There was no plan. Nothing. It wasn't "gator baiting" in the bayous where you shot the brute in the head, hauled it aboard dead, then motored to the game station for bounty. He fretted.

He summoned Danny and CeCe by phone to the beach snack bar. They were as yet unaware what was happening. True, they had been there, planned the attack, and set bait but figured it was probably bullshit. It was not. Reality was upon them, big time.

"We probably have a record-sized snapper on a line, and what do we do?" Royce Jr. said separately to each when they answered their phones. "Snack bar at twelve."

Fucking panic. No planning. Why? What?

"Okay, Royce," CeCe asked, snagging ketchup-laden fries from a snack bar cardboard tray, "what is your plan, given we may have snagged a centurion turtle."

"I would imagine there would be much biological interest," Royce said.

"Oh, yeah," said Danny. "Just another pond snapper."

"But egregiously large and ancient," Royce responded, defending territory as if he knew something about it. "As we prepare for capture, the path will reveal itself."

Danny and CeCe rolled their eyes at each other.

"We gotta get the poor thing off the line," CeCe said with a finality that made total sense.

That night, past twelve and in the dark, they purloined Davis's never-used dinghy again, did the portage to the smaller pond, and approached the twitching maple sapling with massive fear. They had the sense to arm themselves with a pair of tough, chain-mail gloves and a twenty-foot nylon rope length from Bradford's, a pair of neoprene sleeves for elbow injuries for arm protection from CVS, a scabbard-held buck knife, a flashlight, and a first aid kit.

Danny insisted Royce Jr. pay for the incidental purchases from his ample allowance.

"So what is the plan, Oh, Captain?" Danny asked as he rowed.

"I am vision and not tactics," Royce Jr. answered.

CeCe and Danny groaned in unison.

"In other words, you haven't a clue," Danny hissed. "Nary a one. We have put the Beast at jeopardy and, as we heard, no one in the Village will love your royal, stinking privilege if harm comes to it. It is 'jafsp' in CeCe's words, and its own legend is bigger than us."

"A plan will emerge to define our glory and show our humanity," Royce mumbled, sounding scared as a boy scout at camp in a north woods Maine outdoor latrine.

Danny was practical. He may have been a bit coddled, but he worked construction in a few high school and college years. A person learns a lot there. He loved can-do-it guys who figured shit out. This, now, was a problem demanding solution, and he had a thought to end the insanity that may work. Screw Royce who was proving a ridiculous sinkhole of need. Danny's respect for him was evaporating like desert dew under a hot, rising sun.

As the prow of the dinghy approached the bent sapling, Danny halted rowing and reached for the of coil rope he had stowed under the aft seat.

"This is what we are not going to do and, then, what we gotta do," Danny said, with an even calm.

"Carry on, mate," intoned Royce Jr., sounding like an unhinged Ahab.

"Shut up, Royce, and do what I say. First, we are not putting the snapper in the boat. There's barely room for us in this dinghy, let alone a tire-sized, angry turtle. Second—and this will be tricky—were going to cut the seventy pound test line from the sapling, hoping the turtle doesn't go crazy, and I am going to tie a sheet bend knot, joining this nylon rope to the line. Then, we are going to row to the causeway, dragging the load behind us."

"Why not just cut him loose?" CeCe asked.

"You must be daft," Royce spat out. "And abort the mission?"

Danny was preparing the nylon rope end to tie a quick knot to the line he remembered from Outward Bound camp a few years earlier. He looked at the two of them. First, the one aft—clueless, then the one fore—daft.

He dispassionately said, "There is no mission. The turtle has a hook somewhere nasty, and we have to get it out, or it may die."

The dinghy bumped into the peat bank next to the sapling. Adrenaline was flowing in the troika's veins in wild surges. They had hunted frogs like all the kids and drop-fished, after rowing to the beach rafts in the evening, for porgies, sea robins, and the occasional sand shark. They were not hunters in any real manner. It was dead dark. The night offered only a bare sliver of moon sliding in and out of clouds, and the pond was silent and opaque. Nearby bullfrogs throated mating calls among clusters of lily pads that reflected silver with ambient moonlight. There was nothing welcoming about it. Danny and Royce stepped on to bank. Maneuvering side-by-side in the prow of the tippy dinghy would be impossible.

"Put on the gloves, Royce, and take this knife," Danny commanded. "Then grab the fishing line about a foot down from where it's tied to the sapling tip, and twist a loop around your glove. You have to cut the line, leaving me with a good foot of slack. I will tie the knot to the slack. You might have to hold on like hell. I don't know."

"Are you nuts, my friend?" Royce choked out. "My hand will barely be a foot above the water. What if the Beast rises for revenge?"

"It's what the glove is for."

Sitting aft in the dinghy and having just lit a joint, Cece started laughing.

"Just envision yourself as a harpooner on the prow of a whaling longboat, Royce, ready to strike for fame and glory. It comes with the territory."

"You are really easy to hate, CeCe," Royce said, knowing everything manly about him was in question.

Royce did grab and twist the line gaining purchase on it and cut it and Danny, working with an expertise he had hardly practiced, joined the lines. Royce was jabbering, whimpering really, about the weight and movement he felt.

"Clear," Danny shouted, and Royce let his grasp of the line loose.

It was moment of triumph with the whole mess far from concluded—very far—but Danny and Royce high-fived at their teamwork, and CeCe gave a squeal of admiration. Whatever was on the line was now on a long lead rope that opened possibilities, but still the situation raised more questions than answers.

"What now, mate?" Royce asked with much confidence restored.

"Will you stop with the 'mate' shit, Royce?"

"Yeah, Royce. Stop with the mate shit," CeCe giggled.

She had, with the help of THC and a predisposition to disconnect, come to see herself as an observer to a documentary. She had little clue as to how to contribute figuring her major contribution had been the "jafst" line that seemed to have traction in the Village.

"We row to the causeway, pull the sucker on shore and figure how to get the hook out," Danny directed. "It ain't gonna be like pulling hooks from a porgy. If we are lucky, there won't be any traffic at this hour."

"And how do we document our legendary triumph?" Royce asked, ever consumed with legacy.

"I have a Kodak in my purse," CeCe answered, emerging momentarily from a psychotropic haze.

"Well done, wench." said Royce, "Useful for something at last."

"Fuck off, Royce," she said. "I was waiting to smell the shit in your pants. If Danny didn't take charge, you would still be using binoculars."

They started the row with Danny at the oars. The first strokes swished water with no progress. They had a big anchor. Something was digging in. Then, there was audible slurp of muck—a sucking sound—and the dinghy inched forward. The distance to the causeway was not more than sixty yards, but whatever they were pulling, bound by lily pad tendrils and muck, was not cooperating. Danny and Royce took turns rowing, slow and hard. They each looked with concern at the oarlocks on the dinghy which were frizzy with age. Were one to bust, they could not make it by paddling alone. Ten yards off the causeway, Danny and Royce jumped off into what they knew was sand, figuring the turtle, if there, was a good twenty yards behind. Grunting and puffing, they pulled the boat to shore. CeCe had the grace to disembark in knee-high water to wade to shore in her act of teamwork.

"Okay," said Danny, "Let's see what we have."

They grabbed the lead rope and pulled hand over hand. The sheet bend knot was holding. A car passed with some oldie couple who paid no attention to young people doing stupid things. Having a good time?

Slowly, incredibly, the hugest turtle witnessed by the troika—maybe anywhere—was hauled, not willingly, onto the causeway, sand bank shore. The reason was a Sportsport shark hook showing at the top of its beak and below the nostrils. It was like a bull in Spain led by a nose ring with a tender hook tearing its nostrils. How the biology withstood the pull across the pond was painfully considered. Torture. The turtle seemed unperturbed on the sand. It was lizard brain. No thoughts.

The fins were indeed a good six inches across with claws. The carapace was at least compact car tire diameter. The beak was four inches of nasty. If it were not a record, and Massachusetts had some records, it was damn close. It was indeed a snapping turtle leviathan.

Royce Jr. pulled a flashlight from the tool bag. He flashed it on. It was intensely more horrible than shining a light under the chin and making scary faces at sleep-over parties. The Beast had presence. It was stoic and looked pissed. Snappers always looked pissed. They had no business with this thing.

The moment hit the entire troika at the same time. Get this Beast back to the pond healthy. He was too prehistoric, too magnificent, and he did probably hear the hymns and sermons of the early Village. He had to be a hundred. He was more memorable than they. They would document the capture and release it and live minor legend in the Village. The problem was the bull had a nasty hook in a sorry place that portended no good for its survival.

"Could we come close for a Kodak for glory?" Royce Jr. asked in an uncharacteristically subdued way.

"No, not yet," Danny ordered. "We have to get the hook out."

"Any ideas, ma—no, Captain?" Royce said.

"The only thing I can figure is bull snips. Long handles, and if the damn thing will hold still, we can cut the barbs on the shark hook, and it will fall out eventually."

"And where is this tool?" Royce asked, ever befuddled by practicality.

"In the Inn shed. They never lock it. I used it doing some summer work."

Danny took the short walk to the shed and rummaged with the flashlight. The Inn had trusty maintenance men with tools in order. He grabbed the bull snips and went back to the causeway beach.

No one had a clue as to how the Village Beast would react to bull snips in its face aggravating its terror bite. There was little to do but try and snip quickly. Strangely, the monster turtle never flinched with bull snips in its face. With CeCe holding the flashlight and, perhaps, the turtle never having seen such light, he never moved. Danny cut the shark hook barb. It would slide out. It always did with fish and would with this brute.

The crazy bullshit seemed over. It could have ended then, every good thing accomplished. However, the troika was now outrageously full of themselves and realized both legend and humanity were in their grasp. They needed a picture of triumph. Besotted with the concept of being remembered for something—not civil duty or Village sustenance; not humanitarian acts—they wanted documentation of fearless, Village hunters.

There was a flaw. All three, having accomplished something very interesting, had never researched snapping turtle evolution. Snapping turtles have a neck that can extend almost fully behind them like a telescoping horror and in all directions. Royce, Danny, and CeCe stood a foot off the snapper for a shot. CeCe snapped and, with the flash, the snapper neck shot out like a viper. It crunched Royce's right pinky toe straight off.

"Jesus, God in Heaven," he screamed. "He bit me. I'm bleeding like a stuck pig."

And he was doing just that. CeCe in a nurturing moment of clarity ran to the dinghy and grabbed the first aid kit. She lovingly doused a major gauze pad with Neosporin and staunched the bleeding stub with big pressure. They scanned the sand for the toe. The toe was never found and probably swallowed. The snapper backed away into the dark water. Royce Jr.'s pinky toe was the sacrifice.

The troika motored to the nearby hospital ER. The bleeding had mostly stopped with CeCe's pressure. Surprisingly few questions were asked, and the direct statement, "It was bit off by a snapping turtle of monstrous dimension," was not required. They cleaned it, snipped a bit, and flapped skin to cover the missing digit and sewed it up."

Luckily, the photograph was just before the strike and the concept of legend assured. If anything, it made the story greater.

It was true, the troika adventure was told, and retold, in Village stories of stone-cold, crazy people of the age. Fantastic and stupid if that is the way you want to be remembered. Still, really, it was brave stuff and well done.

*   *   *

Royce Jr. endured, thrived with family money as a hedge fund guy, but he was ever to be, behind his back, thought of as a fool for messing with "jafsp." His golf handicap was never quite right with the need for the balance of the pinky toe. Danny went on to great success at Logan—ran the place—with Joe's connections. He remembered the incident with fear, pride, and a knowledge of stupidity. He went to AA and never looked at booze again. CeCe disappeared and was seen on a magazine cover shot for a boating magazine, not a personal on her, just beautiful bikini flesh in an Ibiza harbor. She never came back. The Beast was spotted for another decade, then no more. Its spawn, if they were that, were brutes too. It was all better than nothing. It was all lore, but it was not a meaningful legacy.

2014–THE REAPER

Careful of my steps.

I remind myself of that every time I set out for a walk in the Village. Being ninety-three and it being late and dark when I choose to walk, I hate the caution, but I acknowledge my stupid, undeniable frailty. I don't give a damn that I am simply old—like it's a surprise? I am ticked at the mocking weaknesses that are the cruel and unfathomable curse of being old. My gait is slow and cautious on this dry summer pavement devoid of wet, ice, or obstacles.

I watched my shadow walking one day in the sunlight and marveled how stooped and hunched I was. It was sad. Call it fear of falling from a man who scaled Kilimanjaro, skied the back trails of the Bugaboos, and ran Pamplona with the bulls. Glad for all that—thankful— but, Jesus, old is tough, and there ain't no good happening here. Ugh.

The Village is a friend. Can't say a bad thing about it. Timeless, but not really. It only came to being in the late 1800s by a bunch of holy rollers buying land and a strip of God's best beach on the Sound, setting up a nature, Christian revival spot. I never got the religion thing, but they had an eye for sure. Most beautiful, tiny, modest spot in the universe. If you have never seen it, you would not know—always had a vibe.

It doesn't take much to know the current denizens—old-timers, spawn of old-timers, newcomers—like to see me half-stepping down the lanes, though

I am more a night-walker now. Indomitable, they think. Grabbing life, they project. Inspirational, they swoon. Jesus, I hate all that. Wake up. It's nothing but old. The only dignity it implies is what I give it, not you, and it's not much. Still, grudgingly and not wishing to be a jerk-of-a-know-it-all curmudgeon, I say thank you, folks. I guess.

It is an obsession with me to summarize, maybe an unconscious attempt at an obituary I might wish to, but won't, write. It is all rearview mirror, and I don't much care anymore. I know now what my dear mother was talking about when she said the scariest thing about getting old is you don't care so much. You really don't. I have outlived all but a scant few. I am 93. Think about that one. Like tethers on a dirigible—as if but a few know that concept now— breaking loose until the big balloon breaks away. My balloon, I am the captain with no crew.

A decade hence, my ashes long ago spread and gone, there will only be the faintest of a footprint of me in the minds of relations I don't know well, if that. There will be those to whom genealogy is a hobby. My name will be a line on a family tree no bigger or lesser than any other that nobody knows. "It" is over.

My summary?

Born to reasonable privilege. Did a noticeable bit. Fought in the war. Adventured. Got a cushy job. Married a good and loving partner but failed in later life execution. Had a kid, brilliant and loving but geographically impossible. I screwed up, triumphed a fair bit. Did kind things. It isn't documentary quality. No different from most others when all the froufrou gets sorted out. Interesting, even novel in places, but not compelling. The depth and the texture is lost forever—no journals to be donated to the Library of Congress here, mostly toss-out.

So, anyway, I'm hobbling along, a paragon of gritty survivorship, ugh.

*   *   *

I cannot ever look over the lake I am passing on my stumbles to a view of Turtle's Paradise without remembering my first, love-sodden kiss. Damn, I could forfeit a whole life to experience that one once again.

I am a lad never having, at twelve, the experience of tongues and lips. I am rowing in a small prow with the innocent object of my feminine divine to a private, lush grotto. We land and tie to a tree. It is moonlit but shaded with pathways and nature-like gazebos created from limbs of trees. We sit, my arm around her shoulders, in this most secluded of places and—she screams! It was her joke. It unrattles me, having been born with a notable startle reaction.

I scream louder than her in shock. Nuts. She calms me, and we find a way to kiss beautifully—lips, tongues, gentle biting. So beautiful. I hold her dear as much for the joke in the dark as the kiss—the kiss in passion, the scream of "gotcha." I remember it as dearly as my first real sex. Not with her, alas. Back that night, I would have asked for marriage, declared my candidacy for president twenty-three years hence for her to be First Lady and built a log cabin by my own hand for us to kiss within forever.

So I hobble past the Turtles Paradise memory. The place doesn't exist any-more, gone to condos. That exquisite beauty with timeless allure is dead. It is why a stumbling ramble is not always a picnic. I want those kisses again—in-nocent and full of every promise of man and woman, if only pre-teens. Hell, I look in the mirror at my face now and wonder why people don't run in horror. Old, ugh.

The Village is its own thing. Not easy to encapsulate. My parents were into it—the Grand Experiment in Natural Christianity. Nature. To commune with the incredible natural surrounds of an environment to be, paradoxically, sinfully coveted. It worked for decades, still does. The sensibility and beauty of those Christians, Protestant Christians at that—no apologies to other beliefs—was realized and based upon the forward-thinking sense of acceptance of "all God's chillun." It was pretty true, though there was never a person of color who ever settled here.

All of that stuff never hit with me, but I was profligate anyway. Sincere, nice enough, but a party guy. No role model to point a kid toward. Yet I am now some kind of icon, simply by longevity, here among people who think I have something to say. It is a laughable irony that descends upon me for simply being old and sentient.

The kind, sometimes off-putting, Villagers want to know, "What was it like then?" I answer, evenly as I can with glass of wine in my hand on someone's deck, overlooking God's own sea marsh—a glass of wine that knocks me on my ass when a score of martinis could not do it back then. "No different from what this all is for you now." That passes as wisdom—laugh. Yet, it is taken as from an Oracle. When you're ancient, any rubbish out of your mouth sounds good. I would guess people like it with the hope they might get as old and still be talking coherently without drooling. Damn, I wish I could handle a martini.

* * *

I ramble past the homestead of my best kid friend, a cocky, cheeky, neer-do-well killed in the war. It is almost incomprehensible to be irresolute as a teen. Kyle was all of that. He was alcoholic before reaching a legal age to drink and always was—not that I saw him in the winter months growing up a few states away—but I heard.

Let me say this. He was, beyond debate, the best and worst influence on my life. He was also a remarkable athlete—All-New England prep school diving champion, near-Olympic gymnast—and a sympathetic—to me anyway, others not so much—scoundrel. I was blind, sadly, to his torture of people who loved him through his deconstruction. I missed that angle.

His best was teaching me "authority" was a bogus sham. Kyle's belief was no authority really knows what it's doing, but it has society, laws, and cultural sensibilities—none of its making—to rule you. As God is my witness, he thumbed his nose at all of it with irascible humor—as a kid! His insouciance regarding "appropriate" was a comedic play. It made me bolder for a lifetime. It was not always a great way to live, but it was clever and often effective.

His worst, he said it, was he wanted to die before forty and did, but not the way you may think. Not exactly intentional, but inspirational. He died a hero in Belgium with high medals. Truth was, he had to enlist or go to jail.

If I was profligate, it was a minor "p." I was chicken-shit in comparison. True, we boosted a car or two for fun and cruised, nothing malicious. We left them safe, sound, and with a full tank. He was major "P" in the off-season and was behind the wheel when a bad buddy decided to rob a bank. He swore—I believed him—he had no idea what was happening. He thought the mook was cashing a check and heard him yell upon exiting, "Get the fuck outta here." Busted. Enlist.

The rhetoric surrounding his selfless heroics at medal ceremonies at his memorial was a joke only I knew. He took out a tank in France while his buddies escaped. Dove under it with amazing athleticism and shoved a grenade in the tracks. He wanted to die, I knew that, and it was then and there or to the bottle thereafter. Hey, my friend, crazy bastard, you did good.

I think about the war—or try not to. The more you try not, you do. It was a crazy, quixotic, and stupid time. Nationalism is a dangerous elixir, but sometimes the quaff is the only answer—God hope it is seldom used. The Japs bombed Pearl Harbor, and Europe was aflame. All options for a young man like me evaporated like the dew in a desert. Enlist or live as a coward forever. It was time to save the world, I guess.

I was no rah-rah patriot, but I was pissed at Tojo and Hitler and signed up. I angled for something safe in a non-combatant role, but, by Army snafu, wound up in infantry. Nothing I could do. My luck in two landings was I was third wave in both. It was still very bad. I live with the thought of comrades I did not know bobbing dead in the surf, many mangled, bumping off me. It was the choppy kind of surf I loved as a kid on the Village beach. I thought, *You poor bastards.* It haunts me still, but I kept running and diving and dodging—always forward, forward as trained with a will to not be a poor bastard. All luck, frankly. If you were not there, no description suffices. Fear, killing, horrific noise, and hell. A busted body smells like a butcher shop.

I follow the travails of recent wars and totally get this PTSD thing. We didn't have a label other than "shell-shocked" or "war weary" after our stint. The only thing I can say as to why my comrades in arms and I were not more screwed up—and many of us were—is a two part theory: 1) we were more primitive in nature than today—less sensitive from living a harsher life, and 2) we were fighting to save the world. Those in wars to follow were fodder to ill-defined purpose—the moral compass lost. It was the purpose that saved us—and, yes, I did kill many. All the rest of my life and dreams carried the burden of what I saw and did.

I reach the bluff. In the moonlight, it is a panoramic view of the marsh to the west and the beach to the south. I see the lighted steeple of one of the first Congregational churches from the 1600s across the marsh a half-mile away. Feisty New Englanders. God isn't in Rome or in some regional synod. It is in the congregation right here, now. That was the basis of them. I loved that view and agreed but didn't practice.

The bluff is not the gasping beauty of panoramas around the world at higher elevations, mountain to sea, with breath-holding seascapes below. It is of human and beautiful scale—inviting, not awesome, but gentle and ancient. The Wampanoags held sway right there on the marsh river before the Pilgrims came. I know that for a fact, and I swear you can hear drums and chanting when it is late and quiet. I sit for a moment on a bench in the gazebo that is entryway to forty stairs—with landings—to the beach. The drumming and chants have never been more distinct. I never heard them in my glory years, but I do deeply now. It is not Christian here—it is pagan and soothing. It calls.

So I amble on, every house occupied, sprite with flowers in the pale moon-light and cleverly decorated in New England cottage ways and colors that say, "We have our shit together." They are occupied too by the ghosts the current residents do not know who have come back to enjoy the summer. I see the ghosts and nod. I ignore certain reveries—too many, too little time, and I have already been relived them countless times.

I do laugh, or chuckle and cough up phlegm, on these sojourns. See, it is almost macabre but very cool that "the oldest in the Village" is kind of a com-petition. I so wish Ladbrokes of London took on betting odds. It would make this end game much more fun and enterprising. Bet on death. Only the con-testants could laugh. My competition is two people I have known forever. Bill and April.

We have all been "Mayors of the Village" in the charming Fourth of July parade and flag ceremony on the Green. I won't waste time describing it, but it is a total throwback to small Village celebrations. The "mayor," one each year, rides in a convertible car for a half mile route with a Dixie band in a pick-up truck behind, surrounded by the youngsters on bikes decked out in all forms of Americana, pedaling alongside with waves all around from the Villagers. For years, I laughed at the doings. It was never close to me. When my turn came by age, not merit, it moved me to tears I hid in shedding. Foolish, yet dearly real. My Village.

Anyway, I say to my competitors, "The way I feel most days, I hope you win. Why don't they just put us on the beach straight-away on a 97 degree day and say, 'Go'. See who drops." And we laugh. We know. Still, I'm in the game. Not feeling well, though. I am not gonna win.

I pass the tennis courts and every good thing races through my body. Health. Competition. Gentlemanliness. Laughs. Banter. The courts were life in the lazy summer days. Kyle and I took on the Palmer boys pre-war. We were all brats, but they were Princeton brats, a despicable lot. Not really, but moti-vation was needed. We battled them and lost more than we won, but, Jesus, did they hate losing. The joy of our wins far outweighed their petulance at losing even as they won more.

Later on we had our geezer group. No one slept all that well, and we were on the courts playing doubles at seven. A lot of lobs, no blistering forehands. There were a few guys—I never got it—who had to win and cheated like crazy. They got more brazen with age. They called shots out knowing good eyesight was in diminishing supply and protests were unmanly. It pissed me off, but I wouldn't let it ruin a morning in the sunshine. If I had the chance, I would try and hit the bastards in the balls with a net volley. It worked occasionally.

I played well into my mid-seventies, even waxed some of the young-un's full of themselves, them not knowing I had seen far worse than them. Hey, lads, keep the focus. I did not blink in circumstances that you would have shit your pants.

I reach the Village green, a modest but spiritual oblong lined with trees and benches and a sand-based volleyball court. The energy of that patch prickles and hisses in my ears always. It was here the holy-rollers, coming by train, barge, and cart to an unused piece of farm devoid of much housing—maybe an inn or two to service the comers—pitched a big tent in the 1870s. They invited some of best of the preaching circuit of the time to orate. It was no small thing, I figure, and the ozone of spiritual revival lingers in the pine-scented breeze.

I shuffle to the south end and sit on a bench under a towering pine with scimitar-arcing lower branches, big dippers. The tree was a sapling to be sure at the time "Amens" were joyously shouted from the tent. The coast is clear. I pull my ju-ju bag from my windbreaker and take out a rolled joint, flip the top of my army Zippo, light it up. The sweet aroma of lighter fluid wafts, and I take a puffy toke.

It is too funny, I think. The ancient mariner, yes, I did sail well and far— across oceans— now in the Village smoking dope on the green. Well, let me tell you, you smugs. You did not invent sex. You sure as hell didn't discover booze or pot. People caroused and cavorted long before your blinking eyes took in first light. A party is and always has been a party, and if you were lucky enough to find it, life was a joy. I knew juke joints with kick-ass jazz up and down the eastern seaboard. Sexy women, manly men, and a sense we would never die. In truth, you folks seem a bit tame, like rough edges are seen as a bad thing. A lot was rougher before your time, but we kind of hung together, especially in the Depression and the war years.

Surprised? Stupefied? Offended? Babies!

Where does an old man get reefer, you ask? Like, oh? To an old time party boy, pot was always there. It would boggle the mind of the sensitive citizenry here that a doddering dude like me scores pot. Look, I'm old, not dead.

I still get a haircut in town with an old, black barber. Say, one time, we see kids he knows out the window lighting up on a corner.

I say, "Jesus, they're bold."

He says, "Crazy mothers."

I say, "You gotta problem with it?"

He says, "Naah, never did."

I say, "Got any?"

He laughs his ass off and goes into his scissor drawer. Life is not that complicated if you ask the right questions.

But, Jesus, I have to be a bit careful. The concept of an Oracle of the Village, a bit grandiose given Bill and April, doing anything but ambling and cycling memories on a ramble would be shocking. The idea of this guy smoking weed on the green might set the Village back to the Tent. The fact he has an eye for beautiful wives, lithe and tan in sundresses, may put a few into therapy. Actually, it may be refreshing for some. It's refreshing for me to know however much age ravages and deforms my youthful beauty, my mind is as young as it wishes it to be. Quite beautiful, really. But, shit, I am ugly. That is a physical fact.

I only take two hits, rich and full. I get the feeling, and it is peaceful. Time for the slow journey back to my beloved cottage in a Village I adore.

"Hey, good evening, sir. Got any more of that?"

Oh shit, I think, *busted*—not by cops, but some citizen, a Brit by accent, sounds like a trench buddy I knew in the war. Maybe it was him.

Play the old man, confused ruse. Hell, you are one. Use it.

"Sorry, I didn't mean to startle you," he says.

"Well...you did. I don't sleep well and go on an old man's walk at night. Going home now."

"And smoke pot on the amble?" he laughed in a way that almost made me laugh too.

I always had a soft spot for Brits. With their accents, everything sounded intelligent, even if they were dumb as bricks. He was clearly, to my still-good eyes, a well-put–together person in the dark shade of the tree with a touch of ambient moonlight. A stranger whose face I could not see.

Pheww, I thought, *I am not outed.*

"Cheeky lad, eh?" I said in my best Brit accent.

"Often said, mate."

"Well, I got a bit for you as a fellow in the night."

I took out my ju-ju bag and dug out a joint.

He sat on the bench, and I gave him a light.

"Old-timey lighter," he said. "War?"

"Yeah, and no picnic finding lighter fluid. Best to you. Enjoy. Past my bedtime."

"Could you sit a minute, mate?"

It was the "mate" that got me. Reminded me of the war. We don't have a like term—maybe "friend," maybe "bro" as I hear the younger kids say, sometimes. The damn term "mate" is so meaningless but endearing. When someone calls you a mate, if you are a sucker to it, you'll listen.

I sat. He toked. I never mind the silence. I was getting tired. For me, this was a very big night. I am amply age-spotted, a little shaky, have to clear my throat of phlegm constantly—not my best. Old and feeling older by the minute.

"Look," I say, "I gotta go. We aren't going to find new things here. Enjoy the weed. Best to you."

"No, please wait—a second. I want to ask you something."

Here we go, I think. *The secrets of life.*

"Okay," I sigh.

"Where can I get laid?"

I burst out laughing until I was coughing, worrying it was too much for my heart.

"Not here, son," I said after composing myself and wiping my mouth with a handkerchief. "This ain't the Combat Zone in Boston—that's gone too. You'd have to go into town, but I never heard anything good about it, and I think it slim. Why are you asking here?"

"Checking you out, mate. Seeing what you know."

He was leaning too forward and offensive. I didn't need him.

"Well, I suggest as best I know you go play with yourself. Gotta go."

"How about this?"

"What?"

"Would you like to be young and vital again?"

Stupid comment out of left field. I wanted to be away from this guy with his featureless face in the shadows.

"The pot wasn't that good. You are nuts on your own accord. Not your business. Bye."

"No, would you?"

I turned away slowly on the bench to think and ignored the man. He did not take offense or say anything. He sat smoking the joint.

When you get really old, the sensibility of time changes. I sat wrestling with the idea as to whether there was much more I should have understood or seen but could not feel it. Life was less a teaser now, less the crossword puzzle beyond my solving. Closer and less elusive. Age was a throttle toward understanding.

In my dreams lately, random people of little moment I barely knew have come. They appear in their youth and beauty as it was then, though all are ancient or gone now. My dreams are as real as my reality. Understanding comes faster and faster in ways over which I have zero control. As a boy, a year was century. Now it is a minute.

It dawned on me. It is in the repetitive learnings about people and situations I know, have seen and relived over and over again. The real way it is. There is nothing new. Little left to learn in my tiny corner. A full sponge beyond absorption. Tonight, I feel how much I loved and cared and hated all I lived. It is a flash of integration that reveals my life in seconds, and it is upon me.

"I know you, 'mate,'" I said with sarcasm. "The Reaper—right?"

"The Reaper? Is that not a bit dramatic, old man? Seeing the empty monk gown with hood and the scythe? I am simply here."

"Don't patronize me. My short answer on your offer of young and vital—no."

"Don't be hasty."

"Go blow. I have seen you before. I am stoned. I have no idea who I am talking to and find you weird and unsettling, but you are not a surprise. Get this. I faced death in all its faces. Try combat. Try broken love and passing of beloveds. Try ugly aging."

"Would you not want the machine of your young body, sweating and powerful, or the sensuality of your first kiss in Turtles Paradise, or the power of your first big business deal that propelled you to riches, or the birth of your daughter again?

I thought deeply on that. It may have been a second, a minute, or an hour. No, I would not. I won and lost in life, but the game was fair.

"No. Been there, done that."

"You are sure?"

I knew the old game, having played it with gusto. It lived within me, all of us, I guess. What would I do with another go-round? It was all too confusing nowadays with no passion in me for what it is now.

"Yes, sure," I said, "but now my turn."

"Have at it."

"You collect souls. Are you the only one, or is it a franchise? "

"There is no Reaper—collector of souls."

"You disappoint," I say.

"Frankly, there is no Reaper. I am a product of your imagination. The deep Thanatos of the collective conscious in your brain, just like all others. You knew death by being born. Every moment you knew the clock was ticking. Too deep? Your 'ughs' and resignation called me forth. Few are sentient to have the luxury."

"So I want to die?"

"Probably. The universe embodies life and death. Galaxies, stars, planets, black holes, quasars created and destroyed for eons in an incalculable, devastating vastness. All built, every atom and molecule, of the same stuff as you. Living and dying. All back to one. Your juice is running low. You know it. It is a natural imperative."

"Wow, a philosopher and medic all at the same time. And…?"

"Seems most default to some God for answers. I never met that countenance and know no more about the construct than you. I frankly do not know my job, just a part of humanity. Spirits leave by countless numbers every day— stillborn, dead of starvation, disease, or deadly strife all over, domestic violence, murder, old age, by accident—all of them spirits. I do not see them all. I have no clue why some are lucky, if lucky is to live out a life.

"So you, the collector, have no clue?"

"Some clue, mate, if I can use that term. I bring you back. Make it easier. I am older than you, primal to ancient wisdom. You will die. I think the Creator was gone long ago as far as I can tell. No message or instructions to me is embedded in you. He or she or it left the palette of human existence for whatever it is in you. You embody the divinity and grace of life, the horror and the road to perdition, and the choice always. Quite clever. You picked your way. Smoke some weed."

"You are a sad element, but I get it. You have no control over anything. Suggestion of a renewed life a lie?"

"Kee'rect, mate. No, no renewal. Do you want to live? I am not supposed to tell you this, but I will. I have a view of what it's like when you go. Even if I am in your imagination, I am the collective among humans, ancient as it gets, and maybe right."

"Okay," I cringed, "deal it."

"Your sense of self, ego—isn't that what anyone holds on to like a spar in a raging sea?—holds for a few moments beyond passing and—boom!—gone. You are not 'you.' Impossible to grasp, but easy too. Do you really want 'you' going forward? Might that be limiting? Dear, dead souls seem to gather in the moment. They reunite for only that moment to welcome you to the universe, and they fly away back to elements. I think they are really only a residual within you recombined. A moment, that's all."

He paused for a toke, and the spirit continued.

"Forget heaven—too weird and strange as described—but a better thing is out there. There is no ego and self beyond death. Your own energy is revealed back to the universe in ways I am not privileged to know. Your spirit energy, but there is no 'you,' is returned to be gratefully part of the universe from which you came. The Divine Perfection. It is so huge and accommodating it works. You were only renting space here anyway."

"Do I have choice? Tonight?"

"Yeah, the pot was a crazy twist. I don't reap souls. I am you. You have a bit of juice and are feisty. The only point I would make, mate, is no day is likely to get better than the last. That is the way it is at your age. Your call."

"Thanks, I guess. Bill and April will have to duke it out. My money is on April."

They found him on the bench. Slumped as if in sleep. There was no ju-ju bag. He was the Oracle of the Village, knower of old histories, now gone and privileged to have made it his own call.

2097–THE WATER

Caleb Farker was laboring hard and resentful at the moment. He was wearing the "Cadillac" (the term for "top-of-the-line" survived in lingo only) waders of his trade. They were flexible, tough, almost weightless, and amazingly waterproof. Gear was the game. The waders were light and designer form-fitting.

They were constructed with a nano-fiber, technology that excelled in total performance. The waders could not be punctured and had the strength to withstand glancing blows of flotsam with a "slip-slide" deflecting texture. They were flexible and agile as comfortable jeans.

Caleb's purchase of them was simple. He provided metrics online by imaging his legs, torso, and reach. A lab store did an on-demand design assessment. They placed it for bid around the country to licensed shops who did "u-form" manufacturing for twenty-four-hour delivery to home by drones. Manufacturing and logistics were that good. Right now, he was grateful for the pair.

He was a hydrological engineer trained in water management with a specialty in coastal water sea rise. He was pissed, distressed at the need for his job. How did it all go so wrong?

He really did not need a lesson. Idiots of former generations, with a seemingly total inconsideration for anything but themselves, damned the planet's climate in a frenzy of self-pleasure and gluttons' joy. They couldn't get enough from the materialistic pig trough. More and more they wanted while less and less was necessary. He knew, though, he must forgive as the spirit of this time demanded. Anger was no longer the way. It did not help. Those people did what they knew and it proved ungenerous going forward.

Modern social theory held everything moved too quickly for the human species from the Industrial Revolution with its promise of all for everyone. Human consciousness could not adapt quickly enough to foresee possible outcomes clearly. For every amazing step forward there was a regression to extremely short-sighted decisions. The concept that abundance and opulence were the specie's destiny lived on too long as a model. The planet was so much smaller than people thought. The scale of all technologies shrank the orb to a neighborhood. Now, almost everyone understood that fact across the globe, there were almost no "deniers." Caleb was living the new model of deconstruction. Many felt it too late; many knew it probably occurred decades before.

Caleb was thirty-two and MIT-educated. He actually learned most of his craft in Holland right after college. He worked in a government-sponsored exchange to encourage "best practice" sea rise solutions. The Dutch had been successfully fighting back the North Sea assault on their lowlands for centuries. They were masters of the craft with innovation and a survival passion.

The sea rise and water management textbooks he studied always included a chapter on the "failure" scenario where the U.S. Army Corp of Engineers paid no heed to Dutch offers for design help. New Orleans suffered mightily in the famed, early century Katrina hurricane disaster and for decades more. It was pure, nationalistic hubris. "We know better," except the fools didn't, ignoring a small nation who knew and conquered ocean ravages.

Caleb was project manager of a mid-sized mitigation and remediation effort, not a cure, for the rising sea level surrounding the Village. The project was in final phase. The "horse was out of the barn," but short-term manageable. Nearly a fifth of Village residents were, starting to be, or would, live semi-aquatic on raised structures or sell out to those who chose to. The future was only a calculated bet, not a certainty. The Village, much of it, was a credited National Historic Site and received rescue grant funds.

It was all water management now, and the larger peninsula on which the Village was situated had been a frustrated bystander. The peninsula, though historic and popular, was too small in population and politically unimportant. The land was ignored for bigger, savior grants going elsewhere in the U.S. to New York City, Miami, and southern coast low country that were drowning.

Caleb knew the Village well. His ancestry of 460 years ago placed a known forbearer—a Plymouth wanderer—on this very ground. He felt a deep kinship and a resolve to protect this piece of turf because he was Wampanoag, "People of the First Light," too, in heritage. He was both. Colonist and Indian. He was angry but knew in the mantra of the day he had to relax. Think stuff through. Figure it out. Pause before acting. The margin of error for the Earth to absorb bad thinking anywhere on its grid was razor thin.

His knowledge of ancestry was not scholarship. In the early 2000s, the genome was revealed and the composition of anyone's DNA was known. Coincidentally, ancestry websites arose taking public records and digitizing them. It was a fortuitous marriage. It was an industry to "understand your past, create your future." It only became more massive and more impressive beyond expectation.

"Big data" kicked in with small firm entrepreneurs digitizing all manner of minutia from both obscure public records and private sources. Nerds researched everything—town records, church records, school records, hospital records, business records, court records—all over the world, digitizing them and analyzing them with AI tools and sold the results to "ancestry farms." It was a glut of information on the past, often in torturous truth.

By 2090, if your ancestors lived with a record of immigration, jobs, taxes, town registration, church records, deed, family birth or death, crime or even deviated with hidden transgressions, the entire "known" history was available in remarkable detail. For $3,250, a pittance in 2090, one could get a digital rendition of your family history in America—and far before in other countries for an extra fee, It was complete with holograms created by an AI-driven composition engine that ingested old-time photos and recreated ancestors to show like a movie.

The AI engine took photos provided by family or other sources, projected back in time, and recreated an ancestor's persona, including voice patterns from later ancestors' videos and recordings. Whether lurid and shameful, mundane and placid, or heroic and hopeful, probably all three in some combination, the details of your lineage, often with tagged photos from public record and those you provided, were an open book.

Caleb knew the trading records of Caleb-the-Elder, the Plymouth Walking Man, from the Aptucxet trading post of the 1600s. He knew how many treated pelts, carry bags, leggings, and coats his ancestor—a furrier and leatherman out of Brighton in 1635—sold. He created the goods with the Wampanoag tribe, delivered and profited in service to his chosen Mashpee tribe with whom he made his life. He had married Wetamu and had spawn.

Caleb, like many who dove into their ancestry, was beyond flustered at the phantasmagorical energy and productivity of that age. Every factor of the peoples' existence came from their own hands. They were relentless and clever. They created every day. They secured their future through a desperate need to survive and celebrated every great happening with spiritual joy. He sometimes cried tears for his ancestors—so brave, so human, so focused.

It was accepted fact the human race had grown less intelligence since then. Anthropologists, sociologists and psychologists wrote learned articles that human intelligence was a fraction of that of the crafty people who made life from nature in any setting. Few argued the point, given the state of the world. The people back then were industrious, purposeful and immensely active. How to keep sheltered, clothed and fed absorbed the mind. Cyber-intelligence was a meager substitute. Studies opined that important parts of the human brain were nearly inactive. The motivation of survival necessity—the basics—had become dormant in developed countries and had short-changed the ability of undeveloped nations rooted in poverty.

Most people now did not know how to do much except what they re-searched and were told. Going whale-killing as the Elder did with absolutely no experience was inconceivable. Who did that? To Caleb, even the most basic execution of day-to-day, self-survival skills were rare. The arts were lost to spe-cialist services. Specialists ruled everywhere to soothe lost life skills. The Ren-aissance man was a long ago fantasy from decades ago.

He knew Habbamock, the Mashpee *sachem,* who befriended the Walker, and thus Caleb considered him his Godfather. He knew Wetamu, Caleb's bride, as the first legally married "Native" in the region. She was, in his mind, his grandmother. He knew the Farker/Wetamu clan to be solid New Eng-landers—yes, with a few waywards—who fought for their country in many wars over centuries. They got married, divorced, remarried, built and lost com-panies, rebounded, and lived distinguished or quiet lives. Caleb was damn proud of them all, even the waywards.

He could never remove from his thoughts Caleb-the-Elder, his grandfather of old. The man was as perfect a human being as could be, he thought. Yeah, he ran off on a bad family, stealing ill-gotten gold. Every moment of his life afterwards was living true to himself. He made the world different in his time.

The Elder was an impossibly strange hero. He prayed to him in joy and wanting. Please, give me your strength and purpose.

And this was the sentiment of the time: Understand your origins. Know your strengths. Know the greatness and sins of your family. Be honest! Work together! We must! The world needs us! We are but one in a lifeboat. Together, we will survive.

It was the way of the world everywhere. Wistful hope and determination abounded, but there was a fear the "pooch of planet Earth had been screwed." No one was fighting anymore except in highly distressed areas. Nationalism was dead. Building a planet tribe was the future. Hope was harder, fear of the future greater, and, thankfully, a sense of working together across the globe was ruling and soothing. The outcome was in question. The resolve was survival. The facts of planet deterioration were everywhere. Parts would live and parts "thrive", but the chaos was erupting.

Planet media, now insuppressible even with technological blocking from rogue nations, railed at the failure of spirit of the 2000s. A famous documentary called it out around 2050. *Century 2000: Failing the Planet to Move Forward*. It played everywhere and in every language. It was epic as any tale may ever have been. Everyone, all over the world, now knew. Take sea rise and oceanographic warming with land ice the size of small countries falling into the sea driving the poor in low-lying countries to who-knows-what. Take failing habitats, the Amazon rain forest "lungs of the world" abused reducing the cleansing. Take clean, potable water as a failed privilege around the world. Take the encroaching of desert due to deforestation that is the only fuel. It went on.

Accurate, reasonable, even conservative, sages all over called out the failure to move to "one world" as a passion. They seethed at the stupidity of idiotic, talking heads in the early century to not see the limits of nationalism on a single planet. Now, they all howled at the early century derision of climate change. They mourned still-born confusion about the loss of purpose for the "green, blue, and white marble." Oh, yeah.

It was particularly bad because everyone across the Earth knew—some more by intellect, some by environmental incursion—a "tipping point" may have toppled planet survival. Still, the bastards reigned, in power and denying as deep in evil.

The Tower of Babel had been scaled. Translation programs into any known language on the planet existed with exquisite nuance and accuracy. It took a few decades, but now most bought into communicating in worldwide honesty. From every corner of the earth:

"What do you see?" (Erdu to English)

"Are you okay?" (English to Yemeni Arabic)

"We gotta fight all this!" (Spanish to Russian)

"No more bullshit!" (Thai to Brazil)

The world was aflame as one in anger, but trying to forgive. Anger was adrenaline and peaceful thoughts were essential. Many could not find forgiveness, but it was needed.

Particularly, all howled at the hubris, folly, and cowardice of the last few generations going back to 2000. It was clear as a bright, cloudless day that governments were gutless ostriches with heads-in-sand, looking to find a way to keep their maw at the trough of plenty without taking climate change seriously. In particular, it was the giants—the U.S. and China. Really? All were complicit. All had to show up, but they did not do enough. There was simply no passionate, "politically suicidal consideration" for "paying it forward" to anyone, even their own spawn. Brazen, fearful cowards.

It was amazing the geezers could have done wondrous, impossible things regarding climate change. Instead, they ignored every sign and signal that required insight beyond their own sorry lives and chose greed. All the scientific evidence was present in perverse abundance, but capitalist nay-sayers pooh-poohed it, awaiting the next Ice Age to reverse the tide while holding dear to earth-deadly technology to extract deadly profit. It was now a disaster in bloom. The physical planet was a fighter, panting heavily, having taken too many body shots.

The current T-shirt trade thrived everywhere on one theme in three parts. The first, most popular T-shirt, copied in all the world-wide languages, with all creativity of fonts said, "WTF Were They Thinking?" Everybody knew what it meant. The world was seriously compromised as a sustainable organism in the nanosecond humans had their shot at it. The follow-on T-shirts, two lines, gave a choice in similar manner: "WTF Were They Thinking? Not About Us" or "WTF Were They Thinking? About Themselves." Take your pick.

It was sorrowful to Caleb Farker. He was in a little way like his ancestor of the 1630s or even the blowhards of nearly just a century ago who ignored the environment.

What were they thinking in the 1600s? What was their reality as new tides pressed a relentless expansion on the continent and a murderous agenda on the indigenous people, seeing it as righteous? Was he in any way the same as them now? Could he ever connect on common purpose? Would he be alien to them? Could he even talk?

Yes, he believed the Walker, Wetamu, Habbamock would love and accept him. He felt that. It was hope with uncertainty. Yes, it was the same species, but so much wild good and wild bad had happened. Maybe a different species? Maybe they would not?

He did think of history nearly two centuries ago. The 1900s intrigued him, though each century always did. What really did a 1999 being of the century have in common with a 1900 being given the craziness of that span?

⋆　⋆　⋆

It was a radical century in the 1900s—electrification, automobile introduction, massive, quick-growing industrialization, radio, two world wars with a few lesser over time, Depression, telephone, television, moon-landings, media-covered social disruption, computers, internet, scientific genius in medicine. It was ridiculous! No evolution of the poor human mind can absorb all that. All of it had surely started rewiring the human brain in important, maybe not best, evolutionary ways. And what of the 2000s? The first half was a tragedy of destructive self-interest and obscene greed. The latter half was, hopefully, the nascent emergence of the human spirit.

Caleb was a solid man, engineered in sciences of his century. He always went back to the same question. A century is a long time. Caleb had studied every single one of the centuries relating to America, and he wondered big questions. He wondered, how are we all connected?

He gave up on the reveries. The Block-Lock machine was being hauled into position, and he was trained. This stuff he knew. He was a pro.

The planet was suffering huge migrations from coastal habitation around the world, particularly in southern Asia and the Indian Ocean, with little infrastructure to accommodate it. The people were poor and oceans were a cruel mistress. There was migration of the rich to salvage what they could and the migration of the poor, desperately larger in number, to survive. The build-up to stress had been initially slow and conveniently ignored. The result of a vengeful sea rise acceleration far beyond predictions rendered it to chaos.

Its disruptive character preyed upon contested borders, arable land, livable land, wetland sustenance, migration, economic loss, and generated a foul-smelling fear of war for an enfeebled planet. It was beyond depressing. It was bad and going nowhere good except a newfound spirit of humanity had arisen.

Now it was up to hydrology engineering. Maybe decades too late.

He had to get at it. Caleb remembered in his soul the words spoken by a Dutch engineer:

"The world is 75% ocean. The ocean will win. Find what is possible to delay the disruption. That is your goal. Figure it out!"

It was a difficult situation depending on one's elevation in the Village. Sea level rise on the marsh was not good. On the bluff, it was exhilarating with ill-begotten, interesting, and beautiful changes to scenery but obviously corrosive.

Caleb's project was to secure the National Historic Register site for the Village from sea rise. He understood it was doable for now and, maybe, for a hundred years, probably not longer. The goal was to protect the Village Green, the historic site of natural, Christian revival in the late 1880–1900s, and, more importantly, distressed cottages lower to sea level around the green that provided character. Once upon a time, they were old family tents, now wood-built homes of refitted, even opulent comfort.

It had been predicted as early as 2015 what ocean rise would do to the peninsula. That study, considered a landmark to the day, was a powerful road-map but underestimated the sea rise in its "worst case" assessment. The peninsula itself was not disappearing but growing fat and thin in places different from the "crooked finger." The peninsula was body-morphing to something not defined. A four foot sea rise had changed some places forever.

One place was the Village. It's isolation by bluff, marsh, and ponds made it a peaceful fortress for a long time. Now the sea had overtaken and crushed the marsh flows. Consequently, it stifled pond outflow and impeded circulation. Nowhere to go. The raised waterlines were breaching property lines, disrupting lawful septic systems, and changing the passion of a young man.

Caleb was not the Plymouth Caleb who walked free, built an amazingly brave life, and died a "good death" with beloved around him eighteen generations ago. He was a divorced guy with financial support issues. The divorce agreement was, as ever, messy and unpleasant but resolved. Caleb carried three things: hope, humility, and pride. He could carry the child support with visitation rights and deliver water rise mitigation success to the Village for a while. He would do that. Still, he was of foul mood this morning because he had little tolerance for stupidity.

The Village ponds were heavily saline now and, for the century and beyond ago, had been invaded by non-indigenous flora species that fed on bad septic leakage. They were swamp-like. The good news was much of the flora did not like salt and died; still, enough of species remained to fill the voids.

It was no longer two ponds. They were now a single entity due to water rise with a little bridge over the causeway between the two former depressions. To call them ponds was a stretch. Wetlands was probably better—open water was down to 15%.

The battle was interesting. The ponds were spring-fed, and the aquifer was intact. The springs were pumping good water into the non-hospitable salt. Who wins? Caleb knew it was the ocean, but he would do what he knew and fight the bastard.

The project was actually simple. Sea rise change was predictable with incredible accuracy. Monitors had been strategically placed on and within every melting ice cap worldwide measuring flow as good as an old-timey gas pump. Ocean volume expansion due to rising water temperature was known science taking into consideration surface and deep water convection and currents. Many good things were happening environmentally in a world of common purpose. It was brilliant, shared knowledge.

Carbon emissions were 10% of their worst in the century—a huge victory. Land-based methane release was 40% from its worst due to innovations of capture-purify-release from farm life and swamp technology, but, unfortunately, no one could stop the gas release of the deep-water, rotting biota under the shriveled polar ice caps. The northern and southern heat sinks of black water now with no glare-repellent ice protection—darkness—had sent the former submerged rain forests at the poles to formidable, rotting degradation. There was nothing to do. A primeval, ancient force killing the world.

The Block-Lock system was an engineering marvel and a "savior" technology. Caleb knew it well. He helped invent it while in Holland—the "stone" printing part. The technology built inclined, rock-solid berms.

It was mega-jigsaw puzzle builder on-the-fly. The prep along the west bank of the "second pond" where the work was needed was done. Huge pumps had sucked the pond bottom and spewed sand, lily pads, and muck to a height of ten feet along the shore—an unstable berm. It truly stank for a few months as it settled and dried. It had to.

By environmental protection mandate, he had watched the marine fauna scurry to safer surrounds through a water-scope as the pumps worked their fury. Maintain, do not destroy the environment. He saw a snapping turtle so large it left him breathless swimming and lumbering to safe haven. Caleb had to laugh at what was Village lore of a crazy troika of kids a century ago, trying to capture a beast of similar proportion. One got his toe bit off. It could be the same turtle.

The Block-Lock was a platform combining tractor treads for the shallows and flotation capability for deeper waters. The system used a highly precise, 3D camera to assess a form-fit "stone" for every portion of the irregular berm. The data was passed to a huge, on-board 3D printer that used an environmentally safe mix of components to print a "stone" with interlocking features for its companions. It was a kid's puzzle. With technology of the day, a one ton stone took twenty-five minutes. The printer shell then opened, and a crane plucked it and placed it on the berm to micrometers of precision. The Block-Lot could could build one thousand square feet of accurate, puzzle-pieces in a day.

Caleb was disgruntled and in his waders because parts of the raw berm had not settled sufficiently. It was mushy. Stones were sinking into the mush. Always a rush job. The berm had not completely cured, so it was back to crane pick-up, shovel and backfill manually. Detail work often occurred and was always in the muck. It was a sunny day with the cloud people lollygagging in the sky. He sensed the ancient around him and muttered a prayer asking for forgiveness for his petulance and all of past humanity that caused this unnecessary calamity.

⋆   ⋆   ⋆

Caleb had gratitude for an incredible transformation that began some fifteen years before his birth. Something divine occurred for a world sickened by the disappointment of foul leadership and corruption.

A survival movement called the "Era of Truth" arose around 2050 and captured the sensibility of individuals, institutions, and, reluctantly, governments all over the world. The Era of Truth was a soul-cleansing time, engulfing the entire planet, and changed the cognizant world to common purpose. The world was that sad and needed something that big.

The paradigm of action for every nation of any means or power—some small potatoes, others goliaths—in the early 2000s was to be out for themselves. Nationalism on a small planet was rampant and it had created an evil toxicity. The deconstruction of sensibility had led to tactical military action for national interest led by the "have" nations, though in total fairness, not alone, and it scared the holy hell out of any sentient being. It required no genius, whether "have or have-not," to quiver in fear. By 2050, all foresaw nuclear dust with cockroaches dominating the earth's landscape or a collapse of ecosystems.

Then, a leader of humble origin arose. It was finally a prayed-for leader, and he wasn't much at first. It was ridiculous as only the distracted pessimism of the time might allow, a new pet.

Noah Whitehall, a man of decent breeding but no following whatsoever, was caught on news camera at a mass shooting in North Carolina. The media interviewed him briefly by accident—a bystander. He was saddened, looked calmly at the camera and said, "Our history is a myth. Do not buy in. Myth is everywhere. It will kill us all."

What?

Praise to heaven for a journalist who caught the whiff of something.

"What are you saying?"

Noah went on to say humbly but with laser precision:

"I am a nobody, but I have examined a lot. This is an atrocity. The tragedy here is but a symptom, very unfortunate, but small potatoes. Why the mayhem? What created it? We live in myth. The reality is victors always write history and create heroic stories that create myths that glorify more atrocities. It creates a culture of falsehood and bad intention. It is bullshit. Myth kills. Examine it! Do not buy in and give up your soul. You are better. Do not buy into myth. Try reality. If we want salvation, it will only come through understanding what was and is real, not myth. Do you want to know evenhanded real? Join those who do."

It was simple, but a stunning viral transmission in an aching world.

Who knows why, but the stream went viral across social media. One ineffectual man who caught a vibe. Given circumstances, people knew they had been lied to forever since history became a game. They wanted more. They wanted honesty as best as it can be said. They were scared. Things were falling apart. Everywhere, across every nation, worldwide. What are the myths? What am I not seeing? Truth. I want truth.

As it turned out, Noah was a gentle soul of the century, maybe like Ghandi, King, the Dalai Lama, all with their human peccadilloes, perhaps placed by a higher power, but up to the task with wisdom and lack of ego. No doubt he was wise, and people had now given up on corrupt, self-seeking leaders in abundance across the globe, with so many seeking a true leader. He was of slight, ascetic build, wore wire-frame glasses, a little Ghandi-like but cooler, in an era where glasses were not needed. He, anyone could tell, was consumed with the survival of the human species. His humanity oozed from him. He was a man "in grace" wanting absolutely nothing.

Most of all, he spoke truth so pure it was breathtaking to a world in decline. People inhaled it like newfound oxygen. His twist? Forgiveness. As a single planet, we cannot live with self-interest and resentment. First, understand and forgive everyone. Give it up Black and White. Give it up Hindu and Muslim. Give it up Jew and Arab. Give it up Chinese and Asians. Reach out in brotherhood. Give it up, however hard, to live in a brother/sisterhood of planet. Forgive. The forbearers were always, for the most part, people who lived with what they were taught, tried, however imperfectly, to make it and failed as we all have. Accept and do not resent them. They did the best they could. You can be better. Forgive and move on. To do less is wasted energy.

He and a newfound army of followers gently tore up country after country for their bilious myth-making that shaded their atrocities. His biggest themes were encapsulated in worldwide interviews:

"Our remarkable, blue-green-white planet in space was formed four billion years ago. So tiny and inconsequential. So beautiful. Who knows what is in a universe that is a hundred billion times bigger with galaxies. True. It is phantasmagorical. It is not just puny solar systems such as ours, it is so much bigger. We, us, now sentient homo sapiens, did not even have traction until, who knows, a half million years ago being generous about sentient thinking. We have in .000125 time from the planet inception trashed it to insensibility. Think about it. In an eye blink, frankly shorter, we have put the planet in mortal jeopardy. Our mother is only so big and sustainable, barely capable any longer. We have melted immense glaciers, poisoned great rivers, denuded immense forests, and fouled the air and aquifers—all in an eyeblink."

"We have always dehumanized the indigenous or enslaved people of any land who stand in the way of dominance and progress. We asserted cannibalism, savagery, and wanton lusts against them to degrade or to kill and annihilate them if we were more powerful. We take land and subjugate the survivors to servitude or death. We have embraced that logic for the rape and pillage of the less fortunate and then extoll our heroism as brave. Do not wallow in it but embrace the shame of slaughter. It has been the bad way. We humans slaughter land and people. Don't do it. Do not live in greedy shame."

A cry arose from many quarters: *Tell us, tell us more. How do we survive?*

Noah's piece on the United States came in an internet stream. It was powerful word. The nation was still the world leader in its thinking.

"Myth Number One: The U.S. was not founded in Plymouth or anywhere near it. There was ample, violent subjugation of indigenous people a century before in the south in Florida by Spaniards and, later, in Jamestown. It was always the same. Guns, germs, and steel. Kill with disease, terrify with European armor, and use technology of the time to subjugate. The conquerors were manifesting their destiny without regard to anyone but themselves. It was all they knew. Forgive them. It was born of investment capital and a need for return on investment in a pure land. It made total sense to them. It was not pretty. Forgive.

"Myth Number Two: Our nation was founded by religious people looking to do good. It doesn't play. Not true, by record. It was capitalism. The North was little better than the South but cotton proved the evil. The settlers over time proved quite nasty. Four hundred thousand slaves were brought primarily to the South to build a southern economy free of labor cost. Get it? Free production of cotton at near minimal labor cost. Labor is always a factor of production. Keep it free, except for the minor cost of brutally enslaving the people. It was horrible. That slavery mentality lived far beyond Emancipation and into Jim Crow with cruel, prejudicial laws and five thousand public lynchings of blacks with no justice for a hundred years after the Civil War. Slave families, if they had one, were cut, sliced and diced, and separated by trade all through the process. Any sense of family, respect, culture, or self-esteem was obliterated. If they ran, they were hunted within law and hanged, whipped, and beaten to crowds of white, smiling bystanders with no justice ever. The South lives in shame with no admission. Forgive.

"Myth Number Three: Our westward-bound citizens were sorely beset by savage Indian tribes. It doesn't play. Not true by any record. We, our government, was heinous. We slaughtered them to oblivion. The U.S. settlers abetted by the U.S. army and paramilitary groups wiped out indigenous tribes in a lust for the tribes' rightful lands, often by defaulted treaty by our government. Journalists of the time, nowhere near the action, wrote stories of military heroism against the bloody savages. The U.S. abrogated treaties, falsified agreements, and used deadly force everywhere. The mistreatment from any supposed 'democracy' was bloody slaughter. The Indians, in many cases, were weakened already, and their defense against European onslaught was hopeless. It was genocide, pure and simple. We subjugated the indigenous to a horrorful existence.

"Myth Number Four: The Founding Fathers are almost immune to criticism for their productivity, insight, and passion. They changed the world. In fact, they were slave owners often taking liberty with nubile female slaves. The point? 'All people are created equal' was not even in their mind. They were fundamentally racist. They, from Franklin to Washington and Jefferson, were 'holding' slave owners with Jefferson being the biggest phony in American history. Jefferson with the greatest statement of human rights regarding government, not even thinking of including people of color at all, should, while defiling his slaves, be regarded as a narcissist damned to hell. Wondrous ideas and bravery, but racist – all of them.

"Myth Number Five: Robert E. Lee was a great general and a moral cleansing soul. He was far less. He was puffed up by the South for myth in a revisionist "the South was noble" history. He personally whipped slaves. He never wanted a Union. He was a separatist general of poor tactics who led an inferior army to decimation. He was no hero and a myth built to say the Civil War was not about slavery."."

Whitehall's point was we are not often who we think we are. Just understand the time of the people and forgive. We may have done our best. In the U.S., we were takers and predators, very often heroically good agents. No spin erases any of that—ever. The U.S. must acknowledge and live with all its good deeds but our bad legacy, too, in kindness and with sensibility.

The reaction by the Whitehall army—never organized, just myth busters—analyses country-by-country was mesmerizing. Pretenders tried to spin things but were quickly called out by superior intelligence. No one listened to defense. It was not needed. Someone was saying the best they knew and not blaming. It caught the world. They wanted honesty.

The "myth busters" incisively called out the bullshit of failed myth everywhere. They were hard, fair, and incorruptible. History told itself. It was beyond belief people had the scope to sully countries—India and China, in particular—for their overblown, myth-based rhetoric and subsequent horrific abuses. The citizens of the world, better educated than ever before and fearful, knew and truly felt the weight of historical, mythical falsehood was never to be believed again.

The "Era of Truth" began almost everywhere. Established governments hated it, fought it with derision, but then it dawned on them as a flash in a darkened night. People everywhere were looking with jaded eyes and hatred at mealy-mouthed government drivel. It might be a survival tactic to be honest. Fess up. Get out in front. Share your shame.

It began a truth-fest that changed the world. It was time to admit shame—everywhere—with forgiveness. Come together in hope and shame. A feeling emerged that world citizens wanted to try and live together however difficult it seemed. If Noah Whitehall accomplished one thing, it was to reveal the insanity of nationalistic belief for a small planet. He was assassinated in 2080. It was a killer in an open forum where he was speaking who took a gun upon him. Whitehall, while dying, simply said, "Okay. Time."

He had been deemed "the future of myth-free humanity." He was called a guru. He hated that. He predicted he would be killed and said simply, "It won't matter. The truth set free is a new universe."

Caleb was a Whitehall believer. He was not born when the movement began but lived when the man died. The man brought the world to a new understanding and forgiveness that was his key.

Whitehall's death seventeen years before was iconic and dreadful. Caleb knew the man spoke only the truth without regard to consequence. Whitehall was the only sense that made sense. He was the greatest entity of the century: no more myth, only reality and to forgive those who did the best they knew however wrong and, now, figure it out.

Caleb was directing the Block-Lock machine, and it was going well. The initial "mushy" section of the berm was an anomaly. The rest of the berm was cured. The "stones" popped out with relentless monotony, each configuring with sensual interlock to the next around it. This "pond" would not breach the Village habitat for a hundred years. The machine meandered northward, laying printed stones to protect houses. Mission accomplished.

Caleb shed his waders and walked to the bluff. It was the very bluff Caleb the Elder came upon, emerging from the forest and saw the Wampanoag camp. He sniffed the air, and it was good. It was the very place Habbamock had his burial. It was where the Elder cried his tears and moved on. It was a place for which he would fight.

The 2000 century had its miraculous successes and failures. Human health was a precise, gene-based science, personalized to every idiosyncrasy in one's body. CRISPR technology had eradicated devastating auto-immune diseases. It was getting hard to die except from old age. Personalized psychotropic drugs attuned to brainwaves kept people acute and hopeful. Nuclear fusion, the long-awaited savior for endless, non-polluting power, was coming on-stream. Artificial Intelligence had been revealed as a blessing and curse, and people knew the difference. It took a long while. One could hope.

In an act as old as mankind, Caleb prayed on the bluff like the Wampanoag he felt in his bones. He was on his knees and mindful.

"Dear brave Godfather. Might we find the beauty you knew in nature. Might we find understanding for our selflings around the world. Might we be beautiful in spirit again."

He bent, then bowed. He kissed the marker and left.